M000240425

DO NOT
FORSAKE ME
ANDRE DRAPP

DO NOT
FORSAKE ME
ANDRE DRAPP

A Novel

JOHN W. AUSTIN

SUNSTONE
PRESS

SANTA FE

© 2013 by John W. Austin
All Rights Reserved.

No part of this book may be reproduced in any form or by any electronic or
mechanical means including information storage and retrieval systems
without permission in writing from the publisher, except by a reviewer
who may quote brief passages in a review.

Sunstone books may be purchased for educational, business, or sales promotional use.
For information please write: Special Markets Department, Sunstone Press,
P.O. Box 2321, Santa Fe, New Mexico 87504-2321.

Cover painting by Mildred S. Austin
Book design › Vicki Ahl
Body typeface › Minion Pro
Printed on acid-free paper
∞

———————————————————————————————

Library of Congress Cataloging-in-Publication Data

Austin, John W., 1939-
Do Not Forsake Me Andre Drapp : A Novel / by John W. Austin.
   pages cm
ISBN 978-0-86534-962-9 (softcover : alk. paper)
I. Title.
PS3601.U8625D66 2013
813'.6--dc23
                              2013023601

———————————————————————————————

WWW.SUNSTONEPRESS.COM
SUNSTONE PRESS / POST OFFICE BOX 2321 / SANTA FE, NM 87504-2321 /USA
(505) 988-4418 / ORDERS ONLY (800) 243-5644 / FAX (505) 988-1025

FOR

Luke, Ali, Lily, and Cole…

…This is what I would say to you

And if I could I'd tell you now
There are no roads that do not bend
And the days like flowers bloom and fade
And they do not come again.
And we only have these times we're living in
Yes we only have these times we're living in.

—Kate Wolf

1

 They sat alone on the porch, waiting for the last October sky to fade. They talked of how their lives were almost gone, but not with sadness. They wondered at all the happiness they had been blessed to enjoy and how they were still able to think and talk about the way their lives had played out.

He said it was still amazing to think that he was even here. How he had just thought about talking to their oldest grandson about how he shouldn't have been here at all and how that would have changed everything, not just for him, obviously, but for all of them. He never dwelt on it but it was always there in the back of his mind, just how close he had come to not being in this life he had enjoyed so much. She didn't like to talk about it. She never liked to think about how much change that would have brought. It was almost as if she would go away when he would bring it up.

So she changed the subject and talked instead about the way the last light of the fall always brought her sadness, sadness in knowing that another year had flown by, and sadness in knowing that another long winter was approaching. They had tried to beat the winters, first by looking for a place further south where the sun wasn't so far gone in the winter, and then by slipping away from it for a month or two and staying in their campground on the lower Colorado.

They never felt that they could leave the northwest because they knew that would mean even less time with the children and grandchildren, and that was something neither of them could stand to think about. Still, they liked to think and talk about how it would be nice to have a place back down in New Mexico, maybe an old adobe a little farther south than the one they had loved in Taos in the early days. Those had been days that were forever etched in their minds as memories of almost mystical proportions. Of course they also knew that the more time passed between those days and the present, the more likely they were to remember more and more of the good times and less and less of the not so good.

But the boys had been so little and so alive and they had played so hard and long with the Hispanic neighbor boys; they still talked about their friends Ernie and Frankie even though they had never seen them again after the move away from Taos. The oldest had started to school there and had fit right in, even with his Southern/Spanish accent and lighter skin. The youngest went to kindergarten for half a day and waited for his brother to come home later so they could start some kind of game in the fields around the old adobe.

Even after they moved from Taos to Albuquerque they still enjoyed life even more because the little girl came along and enriched all their souls. And they had moved into a brand new home in a brand new subdivision, with neighbors who all had similar interests in kids, schools, little league, and making a living.

The house was such a joy, their first house they actually owned, and even though Albuquerque was a big city they were never more than an hour from the hills or mountains, with most weekends from early summer to late fall occupying them with camping, fishing, hunting, and sometimes just exploring.

Finally though, the time came when they had to make a decision about moving again. His job almost required that he move somewhere to stay viable in the agency he worked for, plus the kids were getting up into junior high school and the schools were larger and tougher than they liked.

So they had moved to the northwest to raise the kids in a smaller town, and they had been very happy with that decision. But it had led directly to the situation they now faced, which was that the very reason they had moved was the reason they were tied to the place now.

The kids had grown up in this area and had chosen to stay there, which was nice because at least they were all fairly close, but now they couldn't turn around and move away from them. So they did the best they could to survive the hard winters, spent as much time as possible running back and forth to visit the kids and grandkids, and saved enough time to enjoy each other in between.

And one of the things they enjoyed was sitting together in the fading day, thinking and talking about their lives and all the times that had made them so happy. He tried not to think too much about how he probably shouldn't have even made it to this point in life.

One thing he was sure of: Life had been all that he could imagine it to be so far.

2

 As she stood beside the freshly covered grave, one of the girls came over and put her arm around her. The girl was crying but she was not, so it was the girl who really needed the most comforting, and she was always there to provide comfort to all of them.

She looked over at the boy and the other girl to make sure they were okay, and they were standing together some distance away from the grave, looking at the sunset and the mountain that seemed so close to the little cemetery.

James had always wanted to be buried here close to the place where he had been born, even though he had grown up in another part of the country. There was just something about the peaceful land around this area that had always made him happy when they returned for a visit.

Some of his folks still lived around close by, although his parents had long since passed away and were buried elsewhere. The two of them had agreed that this would be their final resting place, and now she was there to carry out his wishes. She just wished it hadn't come so soon.

Everyone else had left after the service, and they had also left for a while, but they had come back for one last visit before they had to leave for their homes. The main service for him had been held back in their home town where all their friends and co-workers lived and the rest of the family had attended there. She and the children had traveled back here to carry out his burial.

Most of the people they had seen that day were folks none of the children knew, and some she barely knew. But they had come because they were friends of his parents and other relatives who had stayed behind, and because that was what people in these hills liked to do. She and the children all lived back east and she knew they were anxious to get back home to their lives and their children's lives. She was not quite ready to go herself, for she knew that once they were gone she would be leaving a big part of herself here in these hills.

They all had planes to catch out of Little Rock the next morning and would drive the rental car up there to spend a night in an airport motel. Before she left the cemetery she had one more thing she wanted to do, but it was best done alone.

She asked the girl to join her brother and sister for a few minutes, and when she was alone again, she walked down to the lower corner of the cemetery to look at a small gravestone. She took one small rose with her to the little marker which almost seemed to be there by itself, with no other stones next to it.

As she stood there looking down at this grave, she saw that the boy and two girls were watching her carefully. She knew they were wondering why she had come down to this spot. She also knew this was neither the time nor the place to try to explain, but she promised that she would tell them someday. Some other day.

Jimmy saw that his mother was standing by herself down in the corner of the cemetery. She seemed completely alone in her thoughts and he wondered what was going on. He had seen her like this a few times in the past, when she seemed to disappear into a distance that was beyond even what he could imagine. Where was she now?

The boy walked down across the short-clipped grass, trying to walk around the obvious gravesites as much as possible, and as he came up to her, she glanced toward him and seemed to come back to the present.

What is it, mother? he quietly asked, not meaning to break into her silence, but wondering.

When he asked her the question, she simply turned her head toward the little mountain top that lay to the northwest a few miles, smiled slightly, and said all she thought she could say at the moment.

Nothing. Maybe I'll tell you what I was thinking about some day. But not right now.

They walked back up to meet the girls who were standing by the rental car that was parked by the little white church building where the funeral service had been held earlier in the day. The oak and hickory trees surrounding the little building were silently guarding the place as they had done for close to a hundred years now.

They would hold that silence when all the people were gone, waiting for the next day when the music and prayers would be lifted for another son or daughter of these hills.

Evening was coming on as they drove slowly out of the cemetery and onto the little paved country road that led back to the highway. Nothing made death seem more certain than a last look back at the top of the mountain.

They drove out to the highway and turned left to travel through the country setting that was now almost foreign to her, although she had grown up in it and had felt it in the back of her heart all the years she had been gone. The children talked of their father as they drove across the Caddo River and on toward Hot Springs.

She thought of James, how they had met in college and were married soon after graduation. The two girls had come along first, only a little over a year apart, and they had been inseparable buddies from the start. They were both married now and had children of their own, living close enough to her to visit regularly.

Claire was the oldest and was married to a dentist who adored her. She was pretty sure that Claire loved him too, but she could never be so sure of that because Claire was not one to give her heart to anyone. Just like her Mom, she thought, smiling. It is okay to make a commitment, but it's not okay to lose your heart in the process.

She remembered how James could never quite understand that concept, never realizing that it had absolutely nothing to do with him. But over the years he finally came to accept that she loved him as much as she could ever love anyone and it was just her nature to hold a small piece of herself inside.

She was deep in thoughts of her past along these roads when she was roused by a question from the other girl, Tilly.

What were you looking at back at the cemetery, Mom?

The question came from nowhere and she almost blurted out a quick answer that she knew she would have regretted. But she didn't. She took her time, looking out the window at the horse ranch along the road coming into town before casually answering.

Oh, it was nothing much. I just needed to get away for a few minutes.

They didn't speak for some time, and she knew they doubted what she was saying. But they had no clues to go on so she wasn't worried. And she knew there would come a better time, maybe in the near future, to explain.

3

 I will admit to not being able to remember the first house we lived in after I was born. After all, I was only a year old when we left it, a little one-and-a-half room shack over in Punkin Center, Arkansas where my Dad, Marvin "Pete" Austin was beginning his teaching career.

Dad was following in the footsteps of his father, William Lafayette "Fate" Austin, who had taught school in various locations around Pike County from the early part of the century until his untimely death in 1922.

Grandpa Fate had gone back to Tennessee, where the original Austin clan had moved from in the 1880s, to attend college at B. A. Tucker University to get his teaching credentials before coming back home to teach at several "academies," as they were then called.

Dad had not been able to secure his own credentials but had lucked into the teaching job at Punkin Center when the "headmaster" there had been sent packing just before the next school year was set to begin.

After they were married, Dad and Mama (Mildred Brinkley) lived in the home place with Grandma Austin, Uncle George Davasher, and Dad's sister Aunt Jewel. Uncle George drove a school bus on the west route out of Langley and Dad rode part of the way on the bus and then walked from there to his teaching job every day of the week, a distance of "only" five or six miles round-trip through the back trails.

All went well with that first teaching job, which consisted of a one-room school and a total of four students ranging through the entire grade structure of such schools. At least things were going well with the teaching part of the job; not as much could be said about the income part of the job because the agreement was that Dad's monthly salary of forty dollars would be withheld until he could find the time to make a trip to the county seat in Murfreesboro, about forty miles away, to pass his teaching examination.

This was going to be tricky at best because the only time available for the exam was during the week, which is also when Dad had to be teaching. It wasn't as if he could call on one of the substitute teachers for a day or two while he hitched a ride to Murfreesboro and back.

But as the story was handed down to the family by my Dad many years later, it all worked out just fine. As the days grew closer to time for me to arrive, Mama decided she would be better served by staying with her parents down in Lodi while Dad was at school. The plan was for him to catch a ride down to Lodi on the weekends before heading back up to Langley for his daily hike to the schoolhouse. All this was working out as planned, until I decided that I wanted to arrive a little early and thereby screw up everyone's Christmas holiday.

In order to obtain a teaching license you had to go to the Murfreesboro to take an examination that was given by the State Board in June and December. Dad had to be hired on a temporary basis, until he could take the next exam, which was scheduled for December. He planned to take the test during a brief Christmas vacation.

He was staying with George and Jewel during the week while Mama stayed at Lodi with her parents, where he usually joined them during weekends. The doctors that were available then in the area had no knowledge of when a birth was to occur so all they knew for sure was that Mama was pregnant and Dad was not getting a paycheck yet.

The time finally arrived for him to take the examination, which happened to be scheduled on December 21, so Uncle George was giving him a ride to Salem where he could catch a bus to Murfreesboro. When they stopped in Lodi to check on Mama they discovered that the baby AND the doctor were on their way, so he said that John, Pete, and the doctor all arrived at almost the same time, which put him in quite a predicament. He had already been "sponging off" George and Jewel until he felt like dead weight and now he was worried that he was going to have to wait another six months.

After the delivery went smoothly, the doctor assured him that Mama and John would be fine, so he told Dad to hop in and he would give him a ride back to Murfreesboro! They arrived about noon so half the first day of test time was already spent. Foye Cagle, who would become a lifelong friend of Dad's, realized his problem and quickly got in touch with another friend, Boyd Reese. They went to the courthouse together and the three of them finished the test in half a day, a test that normally took two full days.

Dad caught a late bus back to Salem and when he got to Lodi he found everything in good shape with mother and baby, and he said the only thing he remembered about that Christmas was taking turns sitting up and rocking the newborn. He also said he didn't know how long it was after Christmas when he got the call that the test results were favorable and he could come back down and sign a contract and get a warrant for payment of his last five months of teaching.

He said one thing that always stuck in his memory was that he wished someone could have been there with a hidden camera to get the expression on his face when the cashier began to lay twenty dollar bills on the pay window, and every time she laid one out Dad said his eyes got bigger. He said he drew a lot of paychecks after that day, all of them considerably larger, but he never got one that meant more to him than that one.

Dad continued to teach at Punkin Center for the rest of this year and the next, but Mama and I joined him in a little shack that was close to the school. From what I understand, once the school day was done, Dad spent the rest of the daylight hours trying to cut enough firewood to keep us from freezing to death in the old slab-sided building.

The next year we moved to a newer and bigger one-room school down south of Murfreesboro. This was in Boto, and this is where my first memories come to me. I can very distinctly recall the house we lived in, and also playing on the school ground at Boto. Funny thing is, I can't remember the house we first lived in when we moved back to Langley.

After a year at Boto, Dad got the call to come back home to Langley. He was ready to begin a long career there that would span almost all the school years of my life. We moved temporarily into a little shack of a house over on the Black Springs road, which ran from Langley down to U.S. Highway 70 about halfway between Newhope and Daisy.

The Langley school at that time consisted of two buildings located on a small tract of land about half a mile east of the crossroads. The main school building housed all twelve grades, while a smaller office building stood nearby. A few hundred feet from the school grounds stood another building, a house of sorts that was called the "teacherage," and there we ended up living shortly after our move back. Although I don't recall anything about the short stay on the Black Springs road, I remember most of the time we spent in the teacherage.

The house we moved into consisted of a large front porch, which was probably more spacious than the house proper, behind which stood two rooms plus a small area that was partitioned off as a kitchen. Entering the house from the front porch took one directly into the living room, while the only bedroom lay off to the left, with the kitchen at the back of the living room area. There was a back door that led out of the house and down into the woods to the south or down a little pathway that went across a small draw to the school grounds.

A gravel road ran in front of the house, no more than twenty feet from the edge of the road to the house. This could have been bad, but luckily back in those days the traffic consisted of maybe three or four vehicles a day, including the mail car driven by Eb and Becky Welch.

Although the road and the front yard were in very close proximity and

I usually spent a lot of my time playing in the dirt of the front yard, I never felt any danger from passing cars. Not even when, a couple of years later, one of the neighbor boys who had been off fighting in World War II came home and began to show the locals how to drive a new car on gravel roads.

Hersel "Chick" York had been one of Dad's students in high school at Langley and when he came back from Europe with a Medal of Honor, Purple Heart, and a new coupe-mobile car, the dust rarely settled between his house and the Langley store or school.

Chick lived over east of us about two miles on Little Blocker Creek and I could hear him coming not long after he started the car at his house. By the time he came into view just east of our house he was flying low and his favorite thing to do when he went airborne over the little rise of a hill in front of our house was to tap out "Shave and a Haircut, Six-bits!" on his horn.

That is a sound that I always associated with that old house place and I assume that the echoes from that car horn are still bouncing around somewhere in those hills.

⁂

Soon after we moved into the house by the school grounds, Mama made another trip down to Lodi to stay with her parents for a while and when she came back, I had a baby sister, Judy. And although we were still right in the middle of the second big war, plus folks in north Pike County, Arkansas were still very much just beginning to think about creeping out of the long depression, we were better off than most. Dad had a good job teaching in the school that was only steps away from where Judy and I were growing up, and in addition to his teaching duties, he began to assume even more jobs.

I guess it was only natural that he took the bus driving duties on the Langley route since he could park the bus right at our house and not waste any gas going away from the school. Floyd Cowart was the other bus driver on the Lodi route, which ran east almost to Salem where it turned around at one of the last large families (Johnny Duggan) down that direction. Pete's route went west from Langley to the top of the hill past all the Golden and Thornton families.

There were two more short runs north and south of Langley to pick up kids that lived on the Black Springs road and up toward Albert Pike. Although these were both short runs, they certainly were not both short on kids. I believe Dad said once that when the bus turned around over at the Arivett's (pronounced "Avirett" by the local families) place, came back by Claude Parks', Earl Dowdy's, and Herbert and Millard Morphew's houses to dispatch the kids at school, there were something like two dozen kids that stepped off the bus.

Another thing that Dad said many years later was that when he and Mama moved back to the little house on the Black Springs road someone asked him where he lived and he laughed and told them he lived on "Pregnant Avenue."

So Dad drove the bus, an early Chevrolet pre-war model but a long bus, and also began coaching the boy's basketball team. Coaching was a natural job for him because he had played basketball at Langley when he was attending school there so when he became a teacher those duties fell to the most qualified person, which happened to be Pete.

This coaching job would give him much pleasure through the years, and would also be a source of many fun trips for me too as he hauled me along to games in distant places like Saratoga, Wickes, Cove, Vandervoort, and many other long-forgotten towns.

And his bus driving duty would serve me in another very important capacity a few years later in my life. But I'll get to that.

4

It was a dream wedding. They were married in a rainstorm in early June and headed west soon thereafter. He was still in college and they would come back from the honeymoon and head straight for Fayetteville where he was trying to finish his civil engineering degree.

Even though he had graduated from high school two years before she had, he had bounced around in and out of college before finally ending up where he wanted to be while she was going full bore ahead and getting her teaching degree in three years.

She had already worked a year as a teacher when they got married that summer and had been fortunate enough to secure a teaching job in Springdale, which was only ten miles north of Fayetteville. The plan was for her to work and he would try to finish up with his studies in a year if possible, which he would almost manage, having to take one last class in the summer to finish.

But first the honeymoon was an adventure to be lived and remembered for all of their days. Starting off with a routine stop in Hot Springs the night after the wedding, where a favorite cousin had a bottle of champagne waiting for them (their first taste of bubbly).

Then on to Oklahoma and along old Route 66 to Texas, New Mexico, Arizona and the Grand Canyon where they spent a night in one of the original rustic lodge rooms. Her sister brought a camera that they had forgotten to Mt. Ida where they met briefly, taking a few minutes to clean up the mess that had been made when the champagne bottle had gotten too warm and popped the cork in the back seat. They stopped for the night in El Reno, again in Gallup, then the Grand Canyon visit on the south rim was a sight they could only have imagined.

From there they were not nearly through with the journey but headed on north from Arizona to Salt Lake City where they spent two nights, visiting the Pioneer Chapel of the Mormons and going to a movie that they always remembered and watched whenever it came on later in life: "Lonely Are the Brave," with Kirk Douglas, Gena Rowland, and an early Walter Mathau.

They didn't know it at the time but the movie was filmed in and around Albuquerque, New Mexico, mostly in the Sandia Mountains, which would play a part in their future lives some day.

On up through Idaho, where they saw snowcapped mountains, a rare sight for someone who hadn't seen much snow even in winter, and into Oregon where they stopped for gas in a little town named Baker, Oregon, and then for the night at the North Powder Motel. From there it was across the Columbia and on up to Seattle for the World's Fair that was their major destination.

They spent a full day at the fair and almost didn't get to go up into the Space Needle, which was the main attraction, because the elevator line was full and the last trip up was about to happen. Someone in the line found out that they were on their honeymoon and offered their spot in the line, so they managed to have dinner in the rotating restaurant at the top of the needle. She said she had to close her eyes on the ride up in a glass elevator that went up the outside leg of the needle.

Heading toward home through northern Washington they made it to Missoula, Montana the first night. Next day they took in the wonders of Yellowstone and left the park just about dark that night, planning to stop somewhere east of there. But the road they took was fairly desolate and they were so wound up they decided to just drive all night, which took them all the way across Wyoming and down to Denver, where they thought about stopping for the night. They weren't sleepy so they ended up driving all the way to Kansas City.

They found a room in nearby Independence, Missouri, and managed to attend a baseball game between the Kansas City Athletics and the Chicago White Sox (baseball was one of his passions), before heading on south the next day, arriving at the state line of Arkansas in time for a quick picture and to pick a tick off her leg, which assured them that they were back home.

They had traveled in a new 1962 Oldsmobile Dynamic 88 and started out from home with a total of three hundred dollars. They originally planned to only take two hundred, but her dad had slipped them an extra hundred just before they left.

They paid cash for everything they bought along the way, including gas and motels, and when they drove back into Kirby they still had ten dollars to spare.

* * *

There wasn't much time for hanging out with the parents when they got back to Kirby after the honeymoon. School was waiting and he had to get enrolled in a serious way if he was going to graduate in one more year, which had been the promise when they decided to go ahead and get married.

They loaded the Olds with all their possessions (clothes) and all the groceries her parents could imagine they would need for the next couple of weeks (here's where marrying into the family with the biggest and only grocery store in town paid off) and headed up into the Ozarks for a rented apartment in the student housing section at the University.

He was starting his senior year that fall while she got ready for her new teaching job up the road at Springdale High School. When school started she began the every-day drive back and forth to work while he walked to school and did his best to finally commit his best efforts at studying hard. Seven years of practice must have helped some because the grades came in much better and the year went by fast.

Almost every Friday night after work and classes ended they jumped in the car and headed south to stock up on parental love, guidance, and groceries. Before too long they decided it would be better if they moved out of the student apartment and into a little rent house just outside Springdale. That way she would be closer to work and he could do the back and forth driving every day.

The school year rolled along and he had everything figured out so that he could finish almost all of his required classes by the end of the semester in May, but there were a couple of problems that would keep him from graduating with the upcoming class. First of all, he had to take one summer class, which would mean running over into mid-summer.

He was taking another class by correspondence, which was going well but that was also going to take a little more time. In fact, the final examination for the correspondence class was not going to be scheduled until later in the summer.

Try as he might, he could not make it in time for the current graduating class, but it was just a minor technicality because he could finish his schooling, go on to work at the job he had chosen, and still be counted with the December graduating class for the following school year. Not a problem as far as they could tell.

* * *

He had interviewed for several engineering jobs and had chosen one which would place him in a federal agency in Amarillo, Texas. They talked about that. Should they take the easy way out and find a job in-state so they could live closer to home? That's what the large majority of the folks were doing, and that was certainly what the parents would prefer. They decided to take the job in West Texas.

His summer class was due to finish up in mid-July and he had discussed starting dates with the agency folks out in Amarillo, telling them that he could come to work around the first of August. However, a "minor" problem had entered into the equation. She was pregnant. And the baby was due sometime around the first of August.

So he wrote a letter asking if it would be okay to wait a month or so until after the baby was born to start work, and they wrote a nice, official letter back stating that such an arrangement would be just fine.

That letter was the official line of the agency, but the unofficial note that accompanied the letter, handwritten by the chief accountant and personnel specialist, pointed out that IF he chose to come to work BEFORE the baby came, the health insurance maternity benefits would pay for the expenses.

Well, that was probably going to be upwards of three or four hundred dollars that they didn't have at the time, so it was an easy decision to make. It was easier making the decision than it was explaining it to her mother and father back in Kirby.

The Oldsmobile was a really nice car, but it did have one major drawback, as they quickly discovered as they drove across the Texas countryside on a late July day that saw temperatures topping out at a little over one hundred degrees. The car had no air conditioner.

She was very pregnant and it was no fun driving from mesquite shade to mesquite shade out through Wichita Falls, Quanah, all the C-towns, and finally into Amarillo. But they made it by the weekend, and he was scheduled to start the new job Monday morning.

Monday morning found him sitting in the agency office in his suit and tie while the Personnel Officer was calling the University to find out why there was still one class left to finish up before he had officially graduated. He had a good explanation but it wasn't going to solve his problem.

The correspondence class, which he had been doing so well in and in which his professor had assured him that there would be no problem taking the final exam on his first trip back to Arkansas, was now a deal breaker as far as starting to work. The agency had no flexibility. What to do?

He got on the phone and talked to the people at the University, explained his situation, which included a wife holed up in a Ramada Inn downtown and ready to go into labor any day now, and miraculously got an agreement that would allow him to come back over and take the test immediately upon arrival. That sounded like a good deal, except for the fact that (1) it was a day's drive back to Fayetteville, one way, and (2) his wife was still holed up in that motel.

One of the supervisors in the office heard his dilemma and to their everlasting gratitude offered somewhat of a solution to the latter problem. He and his wife were leaving on vacation and their house would be available for her to stay in until he got back from taking the exam. Not exactly what they had planned for, but much better than the Ramada Inn.

Now all he had to do was drive like crazy all through the night to get to Fayetteville by early the next morning, take an examination in Structural Dynamics, drive like crazy all the rest of the day to get back to a borrowed house in Amarillo, and just hope that she and the baby could be patient for a couple more days.

She was and it was, and somehow everything worked out. By the time he called the office the following morning, the professor had graded his paper and the school had qualified him to graduate. He started work the next day. And the baby came the next week.

5

 It was easy being born into the toughest times most of our parents ever would endure. I came along right at the early stages of the big war but never felt the effects of it, although I do recall discussion of ration stamps, and clearly recall the quiet celebrations when we were sure the war had ended. It seemed to me that there had been some kind of dark cloud hanging over everything and all of a sudden, it was summer and the sky was bright and clear. New things began to happen quickly.

My mother had a large family of sisters, most of them born in East Texas around Paris and raised in West Texas near Dunn. Aunt Nora was the oldest, deaf from an early age from whooping cough, and married to Uncle Tom Brooks, who was also deaf. They had a daughter, Alice, who was Judy's age and who had no hearing problems, although she did have a slightly crippled hand from a touch of rheumatic fever.

Next came Aunt Nina, the beauty of the bunch, who had married a roughneck, Jack Hopper and lived in Katy near Houston, Texas. Their oldest son, Jimmy, was the first grandchild and they had a second boy, Jerry, who was a little younger than I.

Aunt Lucille and Aunt Floy lived in West Texas, one at Rotan and one at Snyder, and they had married brothers; W. D. "Dub" and Doyle Eades. Aunt Lucille and Uncle Dub had lived around Langley for a while after they married, and in fact, had spent some time near Punkin Center on an old farm place before moving back to Texas. I don't know if it was because I had been around them more when I was young or if it was just because they were both wonderful, loving people, but they were always my favorites from the Brinkley side of the family. And of course both couples also had two children, which seemed to be the norm. Lucille had Mac and Barbara while Floy had Tennie (named after our grandmother, Alice Tennessee "Tennie" Jones Brinkley) and Herbert.

Papa and Granny had also had two other children who died young. Cobert, their only son, died of pneumonia in West Texas when he was eleven years old. Another sister, Lorene, died at an even younger age.

Most of the early Christmases I recall were spent at the old log house at Lodi when all of the families would come in from Texas for a few days and fill the house with laughter and games of every kind. That had been the only time I had seen most of them until the summer before I was about to start to school down across the draw from our house, when Mama decided to brave up and take a bus trip down to visit Nina and Jack in Katy. Judy was almost two years old so it was definitely a brave journey to undertake.

I don't remember too much about the visit; playing with Jimmy and Jerry around the little ranch house, getting my shins peeled from top to bottom when they boys let a trailer catch my legs in the wrong place, and watching the combines throwing wheat from the fields into the trucks, which Uncle Jack was driving at the time.

Somewhere on the bus ride home Mama must have called home to Langley because that's when we found out that there had been a semi-disaster occur while we were away. The school house had burned completely to the ground.

The way I remember Dad describing it was that he had been working down there during the day and had built a fire in one of the old wood stoves that heated the building, partly to warm it up but mostly to get rid of some papers that were always piled up.

He said he woke up in the middle of the night and could see the sky lit up outside the bedroom window almost like it was daylight. He knew immediately what it was and didn't even look for the door but jumped out the open bedroom window and ran down toward the flaming building. It was too late to do anything but watch the dry old wooden structure melt into the earth completely, leaving only part of the chimney stack standing the next morning when daylight came.

Now I don't know all of the details of what was going on back then, but I do know that there had been some discussions held over the need for a new school building, which of course Pete was strongly in favor of as he was always looking forward. I suspect there was a huge element of opposition to such a wasteful and silly fantasy, knowing the climate of bare survival that most of the folks around there had suffered through for a long time.

So it was only natural for the rumor mill to begin putting two and three together and coming to the conclusion that maybe the fire had not been totally accidental…maybe Ol' Pete had been a little extra careless with his warming fire that day. Maybe it was just an accident waiting to happen.

The subject was never discussed at our house, and I never had any clue as to the actual truth of the matter, but I always suspected that it wasn't something that Dad would have been able to muster the nerve to do even had he wanted to. After all, losing the school house could have been disastrous to him because of the possibility of losing his teaching job, at least for a good period of time while a new building was being built.

I have concluded that it was indeed an accident, a very fortunate accident as far as the community was concerned because the timing was right for that kind of change. All I knew for certain was that I was ready to start school soon and it would either be in a brand new school building or in someone's vacant barn.

⁂

We had no close neighbors with kids at the teacherage house location, but it was only a short walk down the hill from our house, across Little Blocker Creek, and back up to the Black Springs road to where we visited the Parks family regularly. The well-worn trail was usually a challenge for Judy and me because we had to dodge several obstacles that were more threatening to a toddler and a five year old than they were to the grown-ups.

Wading the creek could have been considered an obstacle, but we just considered it fun, especially in the middle of a hot summer Saturday. But there were plenty of those southern abominations, red chiggers, to hitch a ride and sneak up into places where they could only be found after a long night of discomfort.

Mama would go over us closely when we got home for the visible creatures, mostly ticks of every size from seed to dog, but there was just no way to find a chigger before the damage had been done and they had bored into a pore in the most irritatingly painful locations.

One other bother was a plant that grew alongside the trail and which our bare legs would quickly identify as stinging nettle with the first light touch. The stinging would go away after five or ten minutes and caused no long term effect, but there was also nothing that could be done in the short term to relieve the intense itching. Even a quick wade into the creek seemed to have very little effect on soothing the tender skin.

Once we arrived at the Parks' house we were entertained by a house full of females of all ages, from the oldest, Imogene, on down through Beatrice, Betty Sue, Maxine, and Phyllis. Phyllis was Judy's age and I was somewhere between Maxine and Betty Sue.

Imogene and Beatrice were older and either already in high school or soon would be, and they suffered from having names that could be readily mispronounced, a common occurrence as I recall. I suppose it was natural to pronounce the name as "I'm-agene," whether that was the original intent or not; and the same went for "Be-Atris," instead of possibly "Bea-tris."

Of course these minor fluctuations in names paled somewhat in comparison to what happened to Eloise Bashaw. Folks around Langley commonly headed north to Indiana for the tomato harvest as soon as school ended, or sometimes even before. The Bashaws were no exception and it became quite the talk of the next school term when we all discovered that one of our own had gone off to Indiana as "E-Lois" but had come back as "El-Louise."

Somehow, some way, the local people, including Pete, all came together and managed to build a new school building within a year after the old one had burned down. And not only was it new, it was a magnificent structure of beautiful native stone, hardwood floors, and six individual rooms that would each house two grades.

There was even a grand auditorium with a stage for the school plays that were always a major production every year, plus an occasional passing troubadour or, more commonly, a country singer like Webb Pierce, Ernest Tubb, or country and western bands like the Wilburn Brothers that happened to stop on the way through.

Two front entrances marked by tall stone arches led the lower six grades into one end, while the upper classes took the other end. A large walk-in basement around on the back side served as the lunch room, with a big kitchen and picnic-style tables rowed up for the hungry kids.

Out in front of the building stood a flagpole inside a decorative brick triangle, while the pathways leading out each entrance came together up near the top of the slope where they crossed over some steps to the bus loading area. The entire school ground was fenced and completely cleared of trees and shrubbery.

Steps out the back of the auditorium went down to the back side of the building and out to the smoothly graded basketball courts, where basketball games were played for several more years before a real gymnasium could be built.

That first summer as the school building was being completed Judy and I were given a grand tour by Mama and Marie Marsh (soon to be York). I felt like I was the luckiest schoolboy alive, getting set to start my first grade of school in this beautiful building and with "Miss Marsh" as my first grade teacher.

6

 Coming home from a month in the sun along the Colorado River in their RV, they stopped at Albertson's on the way into town to grab a few groceries, knowing that there wouldn't be anything fresh at home that evening. They stocked up enough to get by for the next few days and drove on toward the house.

It was early April and the trees were just beginning to sprout a few tiny green buds along West Campbell Street as they drove on through town and across the railroad tracks toward home.

Don't you think it's funny, he said, that when we are gone from here for a few weeks and come back, we don't see anyone who looks familiar in the grocery store?

She laughed and admitted that, yes, it did seem strange.

It's almost like we've never lived here, she said.

They had lived in Baker City for over thirty years now, had raised their three children here, and both had retired in this town. But the people they had seen in the store had seemed like total strangers. And this wasn't the first time they had noticed this phenomenon.

But as they turned the corner and saw the home place, everything seemed natural and normal. The grass desperately needed mowing and she looked hard to see if there were any blooms on the cherry or apricot trees.

We should have had one of the neighbor boys mow our yard, she said.

He laughed, knowing that she would always think that.

Oh, don't worry. I can do it tomorrow and it will look fine.

**

It gradually became a ritual for them even before they were both re-tired and through with early morning rising for work. The coffee pot was set to come on at seven o'clock on Saturday mornings every Saturday when they were home.

He usually woke up an hour or so earlier, even though they almost always stayed up late the night before. Five or six hours seemed to be enough sleep, especially when he was always ready to turn the music on.

They had listened to the music for most of the time they had lived in Oregon, but for a long time they didn't pay much attention to where it came from. Eventually they knew that it was coming from Idaho. Boise State Radio broadcast the music every Saturday. First came "The Laz Spectrum," with Linda Laz, starting at six a.m. Idaho time, followed at ten a.m. by "The Private Idaho Show."

For many years the latter was programmed by Victor Pocono but Victor died of Pancreatic Cancer and Carl Scheider stepped in. Carl still played some of Victor's favorite songs. And they both played songs that they loved.

When the coffee was ready one of them would fill the cups and they would sit up in bed and listen, waiting for the inevitable and familiar...Kate Wolf, Greg Brown, Eva Cassiday. Kate would sing about the golden rollin' hills of California or green eyes that don't miss a thing, and Eva would bring tears to their eyes when she sang of fields of gold or I know you by heart. Greg would sing about Kate's guitar. Eventually Bruce Cockburn would be pacing the cage.

Sometimes they would just listen. Sometimes he would listen and she would drift back into the sleep that she hadn't been able to get during the night. And they would talk about the music and all the other parts of their lives that seemed so close in these early morning hours.

Do you remember what "our song" was in our high school dating days? he asked one morning. She always knew that they had both thought The Platters "My Prayer" fit them best among all the possible fifties choices.

They had managed to see many of the singers they liked through the years but they always regretted not having seen this song done by the original group. But they felt lucky to have been in Fayetteville that magical night in the sixties when two smooth-voiced guitar players and a striking silken blonde with a voice as smooth as her hair had come to town. They both remembered special moments from that first Peter, Paul, and Mary performance.

He liked the time when Peter Yarrow came out alone and sat on the steps of the stage and sang about Gilgarry Mountain. She especially recalled the hushed crowd listening as Mary sang Motherless Child.

I was thinking, he said, about all the singers and players we've been lucky enough to see in person since that time.

I know, she answered. There aren't many that we wanted to see that we haven't, and we lucked out seeing some we didn't know much about at the time but we later learned to really like.

At the top of their list of the lucky times had to be the night they had sat in a dinky little coffee and do-nut place in La Grande with about thirty or forty other people while they listened to Townes van Zandt sing about Pancho and Lefty.

I always remember that song by Willie and Merle, she said, because when I was driving back and forth to La Grande for my fifth year work as a teacher, they played that song all the time and I never got tired of hearing it. But I never imagined I would get to hear the real version sung by the writer.

They had seen a small story tucked away in the corner of the newspaper a couple of years later telling about how Townes had been found dead on the road in one of those cold old hotel rooms. Maybe it was in Cleveland where Lefty had fled. He was fifty-two.

And they had been lucky enough to see Elvis in Albuquerque on his last big tour. Albuquerque had also brought them Roger Miller and Kris Kristofferson. They hadn't been concert junkies at all but only went to see those people they really liked and only when they had good chances to go without traveling all over.

Some of the singers were big names, some were just singers they had heard and liked. They were lucky enough to catch Don Williams, Neil Young,

Joan Baez, and one of his all-time favorites, Gordon Lightfoot singing about the Wreck of the Edmund Fitzgerald.

They had been thrilled to stumble onto one of their own one night in Jackpot, Nevada, as they listed to the Rhinestone Cowboy from down in Billstown, Arkansas, just a couple-dozen miles south of where they had grown up. And lo and behold, they were double-lucky enough to catch his final farewell tour over in Lewiston, Idaho many years later as he gave his fans a glimpse of courage with his determination to deal with Alzheimer's in his own way…singing all those Jimmy Webb songs and still playing many of those hot licks on his guitar.

When they talked to him briefly after the show, his eyes lit up and he gave them a hug when he found out they, too, were from Pike County, Arkansas. He handed her one of his guitar picks.

Some of the ones they went to see were not so well known. They saw Lacy J. Dalton, The Drifters singing "There Goes My Baby," Ian Tyson singing at the Pendleton roundup about four strong winds blowing up in Alberta, Robert Earl Keen singing about his Christmas with the fam-o-lee, and a couple of her favorites, Greg Brown and John Prine.

They went back to the coffee house in La Grande for a second helping of Texas soul when Guy Clark and his son came one night. And they were in Baker City for the Paint Your Wagon Silver Anniversary celebration and return of The Nitty Gritty Dirt Band.

One summer afternoon in Washington Park in Portland, Oregon, they had sat on the grass and listened to Mr. Bojangles his own self, Jerry Jeff Walker, talk and sing about the ramblin' man life in South Texas.

Recently they had gone back to see Michael Martin Murphey singing in his cowboy style and they had even talked to him after the show about their common love of a place he had also lived for a while, Taos. They found out that even though he had moved up to Wisconsin to live with a new wife on a ranch, he still had his cabin in Red River.

They felt lucky to have seen him in an earlier time when he was still singing in his balladeer style and gave his performance of "Wildfire" the full treatment. At that same concert in Boise, Idaho, a young girl named Patty Loveless had belted out a few tunes to open the show and they still laughed about how they had predicted that she would never make it.

Soon the Laz Spectrum would shift into The Private Idaho Show and they would get up to begin the day, turning the old solid-state short-wave Zenith radio off until the next Saturday morning.

7

 None of them were ready to sleep when they all finished checking in at the motel. Even though it had been a long day, they were not quite ready to leave the day behind. Their plane wouldn't leave Little Rock until mid-morning heading for Atlanta where they would catch their connecting flights; she and the boy on to Fayetteville while the girls would fly to their homes in Charlotte and Wilmington.

For now they gathered in her room wanting to talk about anything and everything that had been their lives. They knew their futures would be different from this day forward, but they wanted to hold the time in the present for now by looking at the past.

She listened with a smile as they all poured out their hearts about how much their father had meant to them, how much they appreciated the time they had spent with the two of them, and how they all would do the things that were necessary to hold on to the past. She knew part of their holding on would be for her sake as much as for their own, but that was okay too. She liked the thought and knew very well how lucky she was to have them by her side tonight.

She mostly listened, but added her thoughts as they reminisced about the times in their lives when family had been so important. When they had all talked themselves out, the room was silent for a long time. It seemed each of them had to regroup and see if they had left out anything of major importance. There would be few chances like this to speak from so deeply in ones' heart.

Claire thought it was okay to leave the past for now, so she spoke up.

Mother, what do you think you will do now that Dad is gone? Have you thought about it?

She knew they would all become the group worriers for her sake, trying to make up for all the years when she had done the same for them.

I don't know, she said finally, looking into some far away distance. I really haven't thought about it much.

She and James had done everything together for so long and she knew it would be hard to think about striking out on her own. But she also knew that she was strong and healthy and still felt young, so life was still there for her to enjoy. They would expect it, and she knew it would be okay to expect it for herself. She just wasn't quite ready to discuss anything definite.

There will be lots of things to take care of in the next few months, she reminded them. After that, who knows? They thought that might be all they would get from her for now, and it was enough. But she surprised them a little.

I think I might want to do some traveling, she said quietly. Nothing major. But I think I would like to see the West. I have always wanted to go out to New Mexico, maybe even up to the Northwest. I have heard that Oregon and Washington are nice. She hesitated for a moment.

And for some reason I have always wanted to see Taos.

8

 About the time Judy and I got used to having things our way, Mildred got pregnant again and soon I was escorted down to Lodi to stay with my grandfather, Papa Dock, while Sandra was being brought into the world. As grandfathers are supposed to do, Papa made this an adventure for me.

They lived there in the little log house where I had been born, on about twenty acres of hardscrabble farm land, and I had already spent about as much time there with them as I had at home. But now Granny was needed at Langley so Papa and I were on our own.

Breakfast was our first dilemma. Papa looked around and only found one lonely egg in the cupboard, so we proceeded to split it down the middle and share breakfast. But Papa's efforts to show me a good time and share everything with me failed him when we started out the back door and down the steps to perform some kind of little chore. He took one step down and his brogan shoe landed smack-dab dead center on a little kitten that had crawled out from under the porch and was lying on the steps in the sun.

I don't think it traumatized me nearly as much as it did Papa, but I can still see him trying vainly to coax some breath back into that little dead kitten, even pouring cold water on it until it was apparent that our next chore was going to involve a shovel and a secret burial that Granny would never know about.

Things were getting a little cramped in the little two room house by the old school grounds after Sandra showed up one cold January day. It was time to move the family into something a little roomier. Movement over on the old home place was working in our favor, as Uncle George and Aunt Jewel had decided to move out of the house that he had built when he had married Jewel.

They were moving up to Norman where he could be a little closer to the sawmilling work that he was doing. He had acquired a small "gypo," or portable sawmill while still in Langley and had moved it around all over the country, even as far away as Chama, New Mexico, cutting timber here and there and milling lumber out in the woods, which was one method common to the logging of that time.

His house had been built down at the bottom of the hill near the spring that provided the most reliable source of water on the one hundred twenty acre farm that grandfather Fate had left my grandmother when he died suddenly in 1922. She had been left with three young children, including my

Dad, who was the youngest at ten, Lowell, who was a couple of years older, and Jewel, the daughter who was about sixteen at the time.

They had scratched out a decent living there on the farm, thanks to a hardworking mother, Tamsen, and three kids who knew they had no choice but to pitch in and do their share. She was still living there on the original homestead in a house that was located up on the hill above the spring when I was born, along with Uncle Lowell, Aunt Jessie (McElyea) and their twins, Jack and Jill. But I never got to know my grandmother Tamsen, whom everyone called Tamsie. She had a stroke and died before I was a year old.

The original house that Grandfather Fate had built after acquiring the place was located down off the top of the hill to the East. Uncle Lowell had somehow saved up enough money to build a new house, so the original was torn down. Not long after it was built, the new house burned and the neighbors had pitched in and thrown up the current building, which was the house we were scheduled to move into.

Now that George and Jewel had moved out of their house, Lowell and Jessie were moving down the hill into it, leaving Dad, who was obviously at the bottom of the Austin farm pecking order, the house on the hill. We didn't hesitate to move our meager belongings the half mile or so back to the home farm.

The house on the hill was definitely roomier. But try as I might, I cannot for the life of me come up with another favorable comment to make about it. It was clearly thrown together hastily after fire had destroyed the house that Lowell had built, and from the rapidly shrinking and already warped sweet gum lumber side walls to the white clay and straw chimney, the current version was clearly not exactly a shining example of top notch carpentry work.

It had one large room in front, with a kitchen and eating area off to the side in a separate room, with two bedrooms toward the back. It was built in the "shotgun" style that was common in those days, with a door in front and one in back, mainly for keeping out larger creatures such as livestock and dogs. The cracks in the walls were certainly not going to keep out anything smaller than a full grown cat, and especially not the howling winter winds that found the top of the hill so inviting.

The three hundred and sixty degree view that we had from the hilltop soon became less and less inviting as we soon understood why grandfather's original house site had been down under the hill to the southeast where it was protected from the wind and had full exposure to the winter sun.

But winter came and went, and then it was spring. Suddenly I had a new world at my beck and call, with a hundred and twenty acres of farm land to explore. About half the farm had been cleared of timber over the fifty years or so since it was homesteaded. Most of the area around the houses was cleared for farm crops or large gardens. Almost everything that had been cleared was planted with some type of crop, from corn to watermelons to peanuts.

A large garden area was located out by the big barn that had been built to hold crops such as hay and peanuts, and to provide some shelter to a few milk cows or young calves. The corn crib stood off in the corner of a fenced area that kept unwanted livestock out of the yard at the bottom of the hill.

Also within that small fenced enclosure stood a good-sized chicken house, for eggs and Sunday dinners, and a tightly built but lightly used smokehouse where an occasional ham would be hung and smoked.

The farm had been passed along after grandmother died with forty acres going to each of the children. Jewel got the Southeast forty, Lowell the Northeast forty, and Dad got forty acres of mostly pasture and wooded land that was the Northwest forty. Before we had moved back onto the house on the hill, Dad had planted a portion of his in pine trees, which he carefully cultured for the next twenty or more years.

George had cleared off a portion of their acreage and it was always called "Uncle George's new ground," a term commonly applied where timberland was converted to farming. It was on a hilly section in the far southeast corner.

One of the major features of the place, especially to us kids, was the little stream that ran through the farm from north to south. It was always just called "The Branch" and as far as I know, never had a formal name. It came from a series of springs that usually flowed year-round from an area between the farm and the main road between Langley and Lodi. A second source of water for it came directly from the good spring that lay down by the lower house.

That spring supplied most of the drinking and domestic water for both the family living at the bottom as well as on top of the hill. A shallow well had been dug at the top of the hill and it did provide water part of the year but it always went dry in late spring, forcing us to carry our water from down below at the spring.

Now this branch that ran on down through our place and eventually into a larger stream that we always called "Rock Creek," played a big part in the lives of the three kids who were living on the farm and who were big enough to be turned loose to find their own entertainment.

Long before any of us were big enough to go on a real fishing trip, Jack, Jill, and I would spend hours standing on the banks of that little stream with a willow or small cane pole with a piece of thread attached to a "hair" hook with a tiny touch of worm on the end, trying to catch minnows. We may not have learned much about real fishing but we certainly learned the art of being patient. And so was born a lifelong love of fishing.

*＊＊

Actually I did walk to school some. Especially at first, when we lived over at the old teacherage house. When school started that first year I couldn't wait to go. The newness of it all made every day exciting. And I wasn't the only one excited.

It seemed that a new school building, coming on the immediate heels of the end of the big war, had lifted Langley up another notch. Miss Marsh came back to work at Langley just in time to greet me, I felt.

She had spent a year at Norman while the community waited for the burned out school to be rebuilt, and now she was back home, teaching within sight of where she had grown up in her parent's house up above the intersection of the Black Springs and Langley-Lodi roads.

Dad was driving the bus and I could have ridden with him every day, but that would mean leaving home at least an hour and a half earlier than I had to because he had to make his run over to the west end, turn around and pick up all the kids coming back from across the Little Missouri to school, then make the short run up to Norman Risner's place at the edge of the national forest before coming back through and picking up those kids. I preferred to sleep that extra hour and a half, thank you.

So I walked to school, an easy hike even for a first grader. Down the hill past another teacher's house, Allie Jones, back up a little grade and on past the Pate Marsh house up on the hill, and finally through the intersection and past the little store on the left that was owned by James and Flossie Lowery.

It wasn't as if there was a lot of traffic to worry about along the little gravel road. Chick had usually already sailed over the hill in front of our house by the time I hit the road, so that danger was past.

In really bad weather later on that first winter, I decided to ride the bus some, waiting long enough to catch the other bus that came from Lodi. It was driven by Floyd Cowart, another neighbor of ours who lived on down the road a few miles. Riding that bus was like stepping into hell for the fifteen minutes or so that it took to get on to school, or to return home that evening.

No matter where I sat on the bus, there was always one of the worst of the Lodi bunch sitting behind me just salivating at the opportunity to thump my ears until they bled. The fact that I was from Langley, compounded by being a teacher's kid, and further aggravated by being without a doubt the runtiest kid to ever attend school, left me completely vulnerable.

I soon realized that there was no such thing as weather that was worse than having to suffer through that pain. Mama didn't like it at all when she would see me get off the bus with both ears looking like they were about to flame up, and I would usually tell her which Welch or Duggan or Killian or Kirtpatrick or whoever had been today's culprit.

Mama also knew better than to raise a fuss about it. Next time they could do a lot worse, she knew, especially during the long recesses at school. So I went back to walking, and stayed with that plan even after we had moved over to the home place and the walk was closer to three miles than one.

In a few years I decided it would be better if I went ahead and rode on to school with Dad when he left in the school bus. I gave up a little sleep, although not much because the hike was closer to the hour and a half that I was losing by riding, but I also gained an extra hour or so of playing time by getting to school early.

By this time I had made friends with several of the Langley boys, most notably Mike Pinson, and he was close enough to school to walk so we usually had some extra time to play before the bell rang for classes.

Mike and I really hit it off from the first, but I also knew he had one thing going for him that had become a necessary requirement for anyone to become my friend. He had a bigger brother. Like I said, I was one of the youngest boys in school, and always one of the smallest.

That fact, plus being the teacher's/principal's son, along with actually being able to read and write, strongly alienated a certain segment of my classmates. To survive I had to have some help. It only seemed natural to me to gravitate toward someone of my age and size, like Mike, but someone who also had a big brother who was nearly always within hollering distance when we needed him. It didn't hurt a thing that big brother Pat was known to not be afraid to take on anything at any time, and was especially unfond of the Lodites.

So Mike became my best friend as we started school together. Later on I made friends with another kid who was also like me, small and very un-tough. Albert Lowery was the fourth offspring of Clark and Lula ("Luler" as she was known locally) Lowery.

Clark was occasionally spotted in the vicinity of Langley, but mostly the kids, especially after I got to be friends with Albert, were the sole responsibility of Lula. Somehow Albert had missed out on the inherited characteristics of his two older brothers, Herbert and Hobert, and even his sister JoAnn. They were all tall and angular, especially Herbert and JoAnn.

Hobert was big enough to take care of himself and came with a reputation that made folks avoid tangling with him. He was quiet and unassuming, which may have had as much to do with folks leaving him alone as anything, but Albert and I always thought he would protect us if need be. Albert was one of the few kids in school that was actually smaller and scrawnier than I.

He was a couple of grades below me in school so our friendship was based more on activities outside school time, while my buddying up with Mike was mostly at school. Mike lived over across the creek from Langley, up on the hill past the other Langley store that was run by John L. and Loney Jones. Albert lived on down the road toward Lodi about two miles past the turnoff to our place, so it was fairly easy for us to get together on weekends and get into some kind of daring adventure.

* * *

Now I know I have talked about the need for protection at school as if fighting and bullying were a serious threat. I don't want to overemphasize that point, but really, I don't think I can overemphasize it. I'm sure it had started many years before I came along when there had been a school at Lodi and a school at Langley.

Somehow, possibly after major bloodshed had been strewn across the landscape, the two schools had been combined into one. There had not been enough time, and really there never would be enough time, to recover from such trauma. In fact, the bad feelings that consolidation had caused would eventually be the very downfall of the school and, hence, both communities. Some people back in those days really specialized in carrying a grudge.

At the time I came along, it was just a matter of one bunch of toughs not liking another bunch of toughs, mixed in with the usual amounts of testosterone overdoses and family feuds that seemed to go back to the time of Columbus. I can barely remember any of the things I learned in any of the classes I had at Langley, but the fights that took place out in the fields on a regular basis have stuck with me like they happened just yesterday.

For example, someone would be playing marbles in the sand, a game that took place almost every day. The game would go on for a while and everyone would be calm, cool, and collected. There would be no particular warning.

Then one of the boys, usually one who was losing, and oftentimes Ray Davis, would yell "grab dakes!"(I swear that is what they said and no I do not have any idea what it means or where it came from) and start scooping up loose marbles as fast as possible. Someone else, usually one who was winning, and at least on one occasion, Burl Cowart, would take strong exception to this action, not surprisingly, and it would be toe-to-toe whaling away at point-blank range until one of the whalers could see that he was not only going to lose all the marbles he had grabbed, he was also going to lose considerable blood out of his nose.

Sometimes if they were not too busy having coffee down in the lunchroom or discussing the latest actions of their favorite baseball teams, a teacher might eventually show up in time to separate the fighters before too many lips had been split. But usually not.

Most of the time the fight went through about three stages: First, fisti-cuffs. That lasted about three furious minutes. Second would be wrestling. Another five to seven minutes. Third, and most often final, would be one person yelling for mercy to avoid being strangled in a choke hold. But mercy wasn't granted easily in these situations.

That last part of the fight almost always lasted considerably longer than the other two stages, while both protagonists gathered their wits and their wind and the loser tried to come up with exactly the right words to gain his release without being viewed as too much of a whiner, while the winner made sure it was obvious to everyone that mercy might or might not be granted this time.

Next time there would be no need to even bother asking.

***

Over west of Langley about five or six miles there was a long hill where the road went down a pretty good grade and at the bottom of the grade lay the crossing of the Little Missouri River. The Little Missouri headed far up into the Ouachita National Forest above Camp Albert Pike, which was the summer tourist hangout for folks from Texas and Louisiana.

At that point in the river there was a nice campground alongside a big swimming hole that stayed cool enough even during the hottest summer days that it would sometimes take your breath away when you first dove into the water.

On above Camp Albert Pike, as it was commonly referred to, the river turned back west past the Little Missouri Falls and another backwoods resort area called Bard Springs, finally winding around through the draws and hol-lers until it went into the ground for the last time at a spring somewhere just south and east of Wolf Pen Gap.

On the way down from there it picked up drainage from numerous sources including Long, Brier, Blaylock, and Sugar Creeks, each draining significant amounts of water from the high east-west ranging southern Ouachita Mountains. By the time the river got to the low-water crossing west of Langley it was a large stream, even in the drier parts of the summer.

The crossing at the river consisted of a long concrete slab that had been constructed to span about one or two feet above the stream bed, with support bases every ten feet or so. The slab was just wide enough for one vehicle to cross at a time, maybe twelve feet at most, sloping down toward the river slightly at each end before becoming flat.

During normal times of the year when the rains hadn't hit for a while the water ran mostly under the slab. But then there were the other times. And that was when the school bus driver earned his pay.

Southwest Arkansas receives over fifty inches of rainfall each year, almost none of which comes in the form of snowfall or drizzle. When it rains there, it rains hard. I believe the term "frog-strangler" was probably invented in North Pike County, Arkansas. The steep mountainsides that feed into the creeks and rivers shed these heavy rains quickly, sending the river over the banks in a short period of time.

After the first couple of years in school I had started riding the bus with Dad more and more, and almost always went with him on the evening run out west of school. His route in that direction crossed two streams that were always a threat to rise in a hurry after a rainstorm; the Little Missouri, which didn't take much of a rise to be covered because of the low slab over it, and Big Blocker Creek, which was right in Langley and was spanned by a bridge that rose four or five feet above the streambed.

There were many times when Dad would stop the bus at the edge of the river crossing on the evening run to take the kids home from school. The water would be swift and brown from a heavy all-day runoff upstream, and a lot of times the only way to gauge the depth of the water over the slab was from his knowledge of having crossed so many times. If the water level came up far enough to cover the slab as far up as the end of the sloping parts, he would know that it was a questionable decision to try and drive the bus across.

He still had several families of kids to deliver to their drop-off spots and there was no other way to get them across and home for the night other than at this bridge. I'm sure that Dad took some chances on those crossings, chances that no one would dare take today. I can certainly recall times when the water came well up into the area of the bus door, at least up over the first step.

Of course one of the major dangers he faced with this crossing was the force of the swift water pushing against the large, flat side of the bus. It always seemed that the water velocity increased dramatically the further out onto the slab he drove, until finally we would be past the halfway mark and it would begin to let up a little and everyone could finally exhale.

We only had to go another two miles or so before he dropped the last load off and we turned around to head back, but there was always the danger that the water would rise even higher before we made it back to the crossing, leaving us stranded on the wrong side of the river. That never happened to us, but there were times when we crossed on the return with the water even higher than it had been on the way over.

I can never recall a time when Dad turned the bus around and didn't risk the crossing, although I'm sure there must have been a few such situations where he knew it was too dangerous.

※

It was during these years of riding the bus with Dad that I more or less learned to drive. Now I don't want to say that I learned everything about driving behind the wheel of that old school bus, but by the time I was old enough to learn, I had a pretty fair grasp of what to do.

At first he would just let me sit in his lap and steer the bus after we turned around at the top of the hill and started back to Langley. Later on I would do it all, including steering, braking, and even shifting the old four-speed stick-shift-on-the-floor bus.

Naturally there was almost no risk to us or the bus because he was still sitting there ready to grab the wheel or hit the brakes if need be. And it wasn't like we ever met another vehicle on the road. Mostly the trip was routine. We would drop the kids off and stop at the Jones' store in Langley where I would usually get my treat of the day, a nickel bottle of Coca-Cola filled with peanuts. Sugar and salt; the perfect mixture.

On one occasion, however, we had a slight problem. Just as he was turning the bus around at the top of the hill above the Thornton road, Dad tried to shift the bus into second gear (first, or "granny," gear was only used for really hard climbs). I wasn't paying much attention until he said something like "Hey, would you look at this!" He was holding the shift lever in his hand and it was wobbling all around on the ball connection where it went down through the floor of the bus to the transmission area. When he moved it around it was obvious that something had broken because nothing was happening underneath.

It was in a forward gear, which was good. Otherwise we would have been faced with a real dilemma, traveling all the way back to Langley in reverse! But the gear it was in was not exactly ideal either, although it could have been worse. It was in third gear. That meant we could move forward at least, but not too fast. And we would not have much climbing power.

Fourth gear was the highest gear and was used for anything above about twenty mph. Second was good for starting off or climbing the two or three grades we had to go over. Third would have to do. It was all we had.

I was all set to get out and walk all the way back to Langley or try to catch a ride, which was unlikely because there was never any traffic on the road, but Dad said we would just give it a try and see how far we could make it. Everything we gained, he said, was that much less walking.

We started off at the top of the hill heading down toward the river crossing. It was downhill more or less all the way from the turnaround to the concrete slab, but then on the other side of the river the road started up a long climb of at least a quarter of a mile. The grade was such that he would always have to shift down to second gear to make it over the top. But now we didn't have that second gear to shift down to.

Dad started off down the hill accelerating as quickly as possible in third gear until he got the bus going at about all she would take in that gear. When the bus stopped gaining speed under power, he pushed the clutch in and we gained even more speed by coasting down the hill. We were going pretty good as he guided the bus onto the low-water slab and, still coasting with the clutch in, we started up the grade on the other side.

He had to pick just the right moment when the bus slowed enough so that he could then let the clutch out and flatten the accelerator pedal to the floor. We went over the top of that first long grade without too much strain, but we knew we still had one really steep hill to climb.

Just past the store at Langley the bridge crosses Big Blocker Creek before it starts up a steep grade for several hundred feet, flattens out slightly in front of Claude Lowery's house, then heads on up an even steeper section of road before leveling out after another few hundred feet.

I was impressed with our progress to this point, but Dad cautioned me not to get my hopes up too much. He thought we might have to leave the bus in Claude's front yard if we didn't make it up the second part of that hill. And not only that, if it stalled out on him we would end up having to roll back down the hill and try to make it either into Claude's yard or if not that, roll backward across that narrow bridge! That did not sound like fun.

When we hit the top of the hill coming into Langley we passed the Pinson place where Mike and his big family lived and went into full coasting mode right away. There was a long steady grade all the way down past the John L. Jones store to the creek crossing and when we flew by the front of Loney's store we surely must have been going at least fifty miles per hour. That just may have been top speed for that old forty-one Chevy bus.

We hadn't slowed a lick when Dad managed to center the narrow bridge and he kept the clutch engaged until we were just past Claude's house and starting up the second, steeper part of the climb. As soon as the bus slowed down just enough he let the clutch out and revved her up, somehow avoiding ripping the gears from underneath our feet as we got the last bit of power the old bus had left and we slowly crawled over the final grade where we could see the school grounds just ahead.

It had been quite a ride and I never forgot how we had laughed at the masterful job of driving we had done to get home that day.

I don't know if we were going so fast that no one had seen us when we sailed past the store in Langley or if we just got lucky and no one happened to be looking out the window that day. Either way, Dad never heard a word of complaint about how he had endangered the lives of downtown Langley proper by driving like a maniac with a wild-eyed screaming kid riding shotgun.

9

Leaving Arkansas for Amarillo, Texas would have probably been a deal-breaker if anyone had known what it would lead to down that long and winding road. As it was, it was mostly considered just a temporary whim. Something to humor him. Let a couple of years pass while he leans into that north wind and he'll come home.

And it certainly was a windy place. It had other features, but none that would grow on them. The job was a good place for him to start his engineering career; working with other engineers on a major dam building project on the Canadian River that would store water to be piped through huge concrete pipelines to a dozen cities and towns on the high plains.

He was trained in all phases of the work, starting with contract administration in the office, moving out into the field to learn construction oversight, and back to the office for design work. They called it a rotational training program, and he was happy with the amount of technical training he was receiving.

At home, life and marriage both were moving fast as well. A couple of years after the first son was born, along came the second. They enjoyed watching the babies grow into little boys, and the little boys playing together every waking moment it seemed. Every long weekend meant a flying trip back home to see and be seen by the grandparents. Christmases and Thanksgivings were always spent back "home" with the families.

They lived in a little rented house on the corner of Western Avenue and Richard Street in the southwest corner of town. A small shopping area lay across the road within easy walking distance, and they enjoyed spending their limited disposable income at one of the first discount chain stores they had ever seen: Gibson's.

Some of her grandmother's family had settled in the area south of Amarillo around Hereford, Texas, and one of them even lived in Amarillo, so they visited occasionally. But mostly it was playing with the boys and watching them grow.

They had been there about four years when word started going around the office that this project was winding down and engineers needed to be thinking about moving on to other locations. The agency he worked for had numerous projects scattered across the country, mainly in the west, so he started checking into possible relocation opportunities. A few places in Oklahoma that didn't sound too great. Southwestern Colorado might not be too bad, but that project wasn't really going yet.

Two of the major projects underway would mean a move to either North Dakota (too cold) or Needles, California (too hot). He managed to hang on for a while after the project received additional work and funding for adding a National Recreation Area, and he ended up doing most of the design work for this addition.

Working on picnic and camping facilities, and even access roads and boat ramps, seemed to be more fun than the water transmission and storage projects, which were the bulk of the agencies mandate. His design work with the recreation facilities put him in touch with someone in the park service agency, which had an office in Santa Fe, New Mexico. That sounded like a better place to them than Minot or Needles, but at the moment there was no job opening with the park service in that location.

They talked about options, not really wanting to fold their tent and move back to Arkansas where he would probably work for the state highway department, just as most other engineers had done. Time was running out and decisions would have to be made.

❊ ❊ ❊

While they lived in Amarillo they had already had a brief encounter with one of the places they were considering. He and his Dad had never done much hunting together when he lived at home because his Dad had always been too busy with work and other activities, but now that was changing. They had talked it over and decided they would like to try something totally different from anything they had experienced before: Elk hunting.

He had seen an article in the local newspaper that sparked his interest, announcing that New Mexico would be holding a general elk season in the fall that was open to everyone who applied for a license. They decided to give it a try. Since they knew nothing about elk hunting and even less about

New Mexico, it was up to him to find out as much as he could in the next few months.

First came a trip in the Spring with her and the new baby. They left Amarillo on a Saturday morning, drove to Santa Fe and on up to an area north of Santa Fe where someone had told him there was National Forest land where he could find elk.

On up through Espanola and El Rito, where they found a dirt road up into the mountains of the Carson National Forest, finally giving up when they discovered that the spring runoff from snowmelt in the mountains made the road impassable to their Oldsmobile.

Later that summer he and his Dad made another exploring trip, this time turning off at Tucumcari and going over the mountains from Las Vegas to Taos, where they took a short cut across the low bridge south of Taos to Vallecitos and finally down off a steep, crooked mountain road to find their elk camping spot in a little meadow just beyond El Rito Creek.

Thus began a lifelong adventure that would find him going back to this same little meadow for as long as he could make it. And it also meant a connection with his Dad that would probably never have happened without this decision.

So when the engineer from the Forest Service came to Amarillo and said he was looking to hire some folks away from the agency, the only question he asked was "do you have any jobs in Santa Fe or Taos?"

Two weeks later word came forth that, yes, there was a job opening in Taos. Would he like to have it? They had not been to Taos, and he even wondered what the job would be like. He hadn't even known that the Forest Service hired engineers. And they hadn't hired engineers for much of their past, but that was all changing.

They talked it over. By this time, there were two little boys to think about. One was not quite two years old. What would life be like for them in such a strange place? And they didn't even want to think about what her parents were going to say about them moving another three hundred miles further away from home.

They took the job, drove to Taos one weekend for their first look, fell in love with the place at first sight, and found the house they would be moving into…an old adobe set under some huge cottonwood trees in the southwestern part of the little village. About three acres of open field was fenced in with the place.

The engineer that he was replacing had moved out of the house already and the landlord, a fellow named Dale Shappel from Wichita Falls, Texas, was anxious to rent it to another Forest Service person.

They would never look back at Amarillo.

* * *

When the time came to pack up their belongings and move from Amarillo to Taos, there was one thing for sure. They agreed that they would move themselves this time instead of paying a moving company to do it. Their limited experience with moving companies had taught them a lesson. Never let your stuff out of your sight, and pay no attention to those TV commercials.

They really had no choice in the first move they had made from Fayetteville to Amarillo that summer four years ago. All they had was a car and she was eight months plus pregnant, and besides, when they had the movers come out and inspect their household furnishings, limited as they were, they were assured that everything would be well taken care of.

"We treat your stuff just like it was our own." It sounded so good, and they were so young and naïve and excited about the whole idea of moving out West to start a new job. The moving company had come out with a small truck and loaded their belongings into it, telling them that everything would go on the next big van that was leaving right away for Texas. They had only left themselves a few days between the end of the school summer session and the day he was to start his new job, so they asked repeatedly about timing.

Would everything be in Amarillo when they got there? Sure, they were told. Nothing to worry about. And don't be concerned about your new living room furniture, which they had only had a few weeks. We will protect it so that it arrives just like it is now, looking like new. It all sounded so professional and so responsible.

After the long hot drive to West Texas they immediately called the local moving van office. It was like they had never even heard about this

50

whole move deal. Furniture, what furniture? And who told you it would be waiting for you? They began to get the picture.

They called back to Fayetteville and for some reason they were unable to speak to the nice lady who had done all the assuring. But they did find where their furniture was located. Still in the warehouse in Fayetteville and still waiting for that next big truck headed for Texas.

The run-around they were given was that it was such a small load that they just couldn't make it a priority and were waiting for the right van to come along that was almost but not quite full already. But don't worry; your stuff is just fine.

He had made the flying trip back to Fayetteville to take the final exam for his correspondence course and since he was there he decided to go down to the mover's place and discuss the matter. That was when he found their furniture. The company representative reluctantly took him back into the warehouse to see it because he told the man that there was something he had to have from it.

For some reason he wasn't surprised to see everything piled up in a little heap out in the middle of the floor. Not one blanket or tarp or anything for protection. And to add insult to injury when their things did finally arrive in Amarillo, the company called them and told them that it was ready for delivery but before any of it could be unloaded they had to pay for the move: In cash.

They scrambled around and got enough cash to take care of it, the movers started unloading things, and naturally they quickly saw that their new furniture was no longer like new. Several deep gouges showed in the wooden arms of the couch and rocker that had left their house in Fayetteville without a mark on them.

They had protested, but to no avail. The driver showed them the estimate form they had signed back in Arkansas and over on the back in fine print was written "scratched and dented" where the form asked for the condition of the items.

So he talked around the office and found two of the guys who worked there in the drafting department who said they could use the extra money he was willing to pay them to help with the move to Taos. He rented a U-haul truck and when they couldn't quite get everything crammed into the truck, he also rented a small trailer that he could pull behind his pickup.

He drove the Dodge pickup and pulled that trailer, she drove their Oldsmobile, and the guys from the office tried to keep up in the U-haul truck as they rolled across the Llano Estacado, dropped off the caprock out west of Vega, and turned north at Tucumcari.

By the time they got to Taos and unloaded everything it was sundown, and Gary and Tommy were going to drive the U-haul back to Amarillo that night. They had just enough time to buy the boys a big steak dinner down at the La Fonda before they crawled into the truck and headed back to Amarillo on a long, lonely drive.

They spent that first night in Taos sleeping on one full sized mattress in the living room of the old adobe house that would be their home for the next few years and would be in their hearts forever.

They had left all of the world as they knew it far, far behind.

10

 One day I was living on top of the world (hill) and the next day Jack and Jill, my daily playmates and branch fishing partners, were gone to Rosboro and we had finally inherited the house that Uncle George built. Thus began what I still consider the times of my life.

As much as we all missed our cousins, the chance to move down off the hill and out of the deep freezer into a really nice place was just too exciting for us to bear. And it was not like we wouldn't see them again; Rosboro was only twenty-five miles away and we were counting on them coming back to see us regularly. They couldn't count on us returning the favor at the moment for one primary reason: We still didn't even have a car!

I suppose the job Dad took as a school bus driver had both a positive and negative effect on our lives. First of all, we did have ready-made transportation to almost all school activities, at least as long as the bus was running and we could make it up the steep, slick hill just down the road from our house.

But I'm sure the fact that we always had the school bus handy may have been at least part of the reason we were still without our own vehicle...the other reason being money.

After the places we had lived in up until this move, this house seemed like a mansion for sure. Real doors and windows, even screen doors, a working fireplace, and three actual bedrooms! The front porch was covered and led into a large living room which was flanked on the side by two bedrooms.

From the living room a doorway led into an open room that served as part bedroom, part dining room, with the big kitchen beyond that, and finally, out the back door onto another covered porch. The yard around the house was fenced in with a front and back gate, and the entire yard was covered with a smooth, soft coating of beautiful green Bermuda grass.

Down a little pathway from the front of the house lay the spring, which had been developed over time by earlier residents, and Dad quickly took things one step further by building a nice masonry wall around the entire spring area and covering it with a sloped roof.

The spring consisted of a concrete spring box in the corner, which Dad enlarged later, and as the cold water flowed out of the spring box it went into another rectangular-shaped concrete box that was large enough to keep milk jugs and other items cool during the summer months. We had a small icebox in the house but that depended strictly on keeping it filled with fresh ice, which was a problem since the nearest ice house was in Glenwood, about twenty miles away. And did I mention that we didn't have a car?

Of course the house did have one major drawback, but it was one that none of us even knew about, or at least thought about. There was no electricity. We were several years away from having such a luxury as electric power, but since we had all grown up without it, we didn't actually miss it. Life was just built around doing things without it. There had been talk of all that changing when the Corps of Engineers and local REA began discussions of a big dam somewhere on the Little Missouri River, but we all knew that such a thing would be a long time happening, if it ever did.

Even though we were now living in a new house and life on the farm seemed to be going great, some things never seemed to change. The Parks girls still came over to see us, or we to see them, on a regular basis. The Lodi boys and the Langley boys were still fighting during recess at school. And Mama was pregnant again. In November after we had moved down off the hill, Gayle was born.

I was beginning to feel a little outnumbered in the sibling battle, but when Jack and I were presented with a new bird-dog puppy from Uncle George, that kept me satisfied. His dog was a male and mine a female and we immediately named them "King" and "Queen."

I really don't know what ever happened to Jack's dog because he was off in Rosboro, but my Queenie, as she soon became called, was the constant companion that a boy growing up in the hills and hollers of that country had to have.

For the next dozen or more years she would be my friend and play-mate. I never went anywhere without her until many years later, long after we had left the farm and I had moved on to high school. I still remember how sad I felt that I hadn't been by her side the day Mama called me and told me she had been run over and killed.

* * *

I never knew how much moving back to the old home place meant to Dad until many years had passed. I knew he was happy there but just figured it was because we were so much better off than we had been anywhere else, with a great house to live in and the farm to occupy what little spare time he had between school duties.

But the real reasons for his feelings were not apparent to me until later in life when I began to learn more about our family history, and especially how we related to this piece of ground.

Dad never knew his Austin grandparents because they were both gone when he was born. Simeon Austin had come to Arkansas from Scott's Hill, Tennessee after the Civil War, some time in the 1880s as far as we know. His parents were James and Zilpha (or Zylpha) Austin and they had moved out of Anson County, North Carolina with several other family members around 1825, settling in the Scott's Hill country.

James Austin's parents were Richard and Sarah (Morgan) Austin, Scotch-Irish immigrants who stayed behind in North Carolina when James and brothers Charles, Morgan B., Jeremiah, a half-brother Pleasant, and a sister Isabella moved to Tennessee.

James and Zilpha had ten children of their own, including Simeon, who was born in 1831. Simeon had married Winnie (or Winney) Duck and they also, coincidentally, had ten children that survived to adulthood, with one girl dying at the age of six or seven before the family left Tennessee.

About the time Simeon and Winnie married, his father James passed away. Simeon's oldest son, James Franklin, eventually married a local girl and they were destined to be the only members of the family to stay in Tennessee when the rest decided it was time to move on.

Dad had heard some of the stories of the rough times they were having in Tennessee, how hard it had been for them to leave for unknown parts, and how much the parents, Simeon and Winnie, regretted leaving their first-born son and his growing family behind. It was a time of trial and tribulation because they knew they were not likely to ever see them again.

The Austins had made the journey, along with several other neighboring families, like the Ransoms, Simmons, Linvilles, and others in similar situations. They had ferried the Tennessee and Mississippi Rivers and finally ended up in Pike County, Arkansas around the confluence of Self Creek and the Little Missouri River (later called Daisy).

Winnie had died about fifteen years after they arrived and Simeon, along with his son Newton and daughters Sarah, who had married Harris Ransom, and Fannie, also married to George Reed, had filed homestead claims on land between Daisy and Newhope, just north of where a road turned off to go to Langley. They had worked these homesteads for the next ten years or more when they heard about a similar homestead being available about ten miles further north.

Somehow Simeon and Newton managed to sell their acreage and they, along with grandfather Fate, ended up securing the place that we would always know as the Austin home place, the place where we were now living.

Simeon lived there until he died in about 1908, while Newton and his family lived there until after Dad was born in 1912.

Originally the family had owned much more than the current one hundred twenty acres; probably over twice that much. But hard times came on after Fate died and when the long depression settled in it forced grandmother Tamsie to parcel off forty acre pieces to survive. Somehow she managed to get by with three young children and when I had come along a year or so before she died, she still hung on to enough of the land to pass forty acres each on to those three.

I had no idea at the time just how much blood and sweat my Dad had put into this old farm. Although Simeon was gone when Dad was born, he had been living there until just before Dad's birth with Fate and Tamsie when their first child was born, Jewel Gracie, in 1906.

The household at that time consisted of Fate, Tamsie, the new baby Jewel, as well as Simeon and one of Simeon's daughters, Ellen, who had not married at that time. Dad always talked about how there had been a "spinster" daughter, Aunt Ellen, and it would be many years later before it was discovered that she had actually been married briefly to a man named Elias Hinds from Murfreesboro.

Dad did know that Ellen was buried alongside Simeon and Winnie in three graves marked with simple concrete posts in the Mt. Joy Cemetery near Daisy.

❊ ❊ ❊

I had no history of place at the time. All I knew was that I was exactly where I wanted to be in the time I wanted to be in. Growing up in the woods and streams surrounding the home place made for some kind of life for me. Every day was a day of discovery and adventure.

My fishing experience quickly grew from catching chubs on tiny hair hooks in the branch below our house to treks down to the real streams with different family members.

We called one of those streams Rock Creek. I would learn many years later that we were wrong. Officially. The maps that were put together by folks who had never wet a line in our part of the country labeled it as "West Fork." West fork of what, I wondered.

Well, I suppose it had to be the west fork of Self Creek, which was another similar stream that headed up around Lodi and ran into the Little Missouri down by Daisy. And on looking closer at those maps, it was clear that, yes our Rock Creek did join up with their Self Creek just before the two of them ran into the river. Okay, but why not make theirs the "east fork" of our Rock Creek?

Whatever the name, we fished it hard from the earliest days of living on the farm. We took an old road that ran along the south boundary of our farm down to the east where it went by one of the forties that had originally been in our family but had been sold to "Uncle Thaddie" Miller.

An old house still stood there in a little clearing where we walked through on our way on down to the creek. From the old house place we took a trail across the hill and down a draw to cross the branch that flowed from our spring into the creek, finally coming in to the main stream at a place we called the "Old Stump Hole."

This was just one of the many places along the stream where enough water gathered between riffles to be called a "hole," and these were the places we went back to each time we fished.

If we didn't catch anything much at the Stump Hole, or if we thought we had caught enough out of that spot for one day, we might move on down to the next spot. Rock Creek had many named places, including the "Long Hole," the "Old Train Hole," and others with similar names attached to them.

Sometimes the names were well known by everyone in the community, but sometimes the names were just a way for our family to identify a place. "Whur'ja catch alla them fish?" "I caught most of'um outta the Train Hole."

Rock Creek trips were usually done on the spur of the moment and were not a major commitment of time since it was within a fifteen or twenty minute walk. Other fishing excursions were longer. Some might even involve going in a vehicle, or in the early days on the farm, taking a horse and wagon.

In particular, we fished on the Little Missouri River a lot. There were three places that were reasonably accessible for us; the "Mouth of Blocker," which was where Blocker Creek entered the river; "Caney Bend," a place where the river made a sweeping turn from the east toward the south; and finally, the "Cat Den Bluff."

This latter place was especially fun for us kids because the only way to reach the river from our side (north) was to scale down a hundred foot bluff where the river had eroded away at the hillside and now ran swiftly right up against the rock wall at the base of the bluff.

This was not a place the adults fished much because it was so inaccessible, but some of us kids loved to go there because even if we didn't catch a single fish, which was often the case, we had still had the pleasure of surviving the descent and climb back up the Cat Den Bluff!

It didn't take me long to find my niche in these fishing situations. I soon figured out that the grown-ups were in it more for the sport than anything else, while I thought we were trying to catch enough fish to eat.

So while the adults set out their trot-lines in the river trying to catch a big catfish, or loaded up their cane poles with a sunfish or horny-head minnow hoping to land a passing largemouth or smallmouth bass, I went to work catching supper (no, we didn't call it "dinner;" we had already eaten that meal around noon before we left home).

Finding just the right spot alongside the bank of the river, an art that I quickly picked up, I would be filling a stringer with big slab-sided yellow perch or bluegills before the others would figure out how far out to toss their baited hooks. My reputation as a catcher of fish, as opposed to a fisherman, soon earned me a sure-fire invitation to any potential fishing trip. And it didn't take much praise to get me to work hard at honing my skills.

By the time I was old enough to do some serious fishing, my grandparents from Lodi, "Dock" and "Tennie" Brinkley, had moved in with us at Langley. Papa and Granny had moved back from West Texas where they had lived until the drought of the dust bowl and depression days dried up all of the farming country out that way. Papa had been a sharecrop farmer most of his life but had managed to buy a little farm of his own down at Lodi after first settling down on the Rock Creek Cutoff between Salem and Glenwood.

He had raised cotton on twenty acres of hillside hardpan, had a few cows and chickens and a work horse or mule, but when our family grew to four children and it became apparent that both Dad and Mama were going to have to work to make a living, Papa sold out and they moved into the house with us.

This move seemed natural to us kids at the time because now we would have someone at home with us any time our folks were at work, which was a lot of the time. Mama had gotten a job as a cook at the school, and of course Dad was teaching, serving as principal, driving the school bus, and in his spare time, coaching the boys' basketball team. At the time, only Judy and I were in school, while Sandra and Gayle were still staying at home.

Although this crowded us up a little because they had to occupy one of the bedrooms, it seemed to make life easier for everyone. And the farm, which had pretty much lain dormant except for a little bit of a garden that Mama planted every year, would soon begin to show signs of Papa's hands.

He planted corn in two of the three bigger fields, raised a good peanut crop in another, and was soon pulling stumps out of a "new ground" field out behind the barn. The garden doubled in size with Granny there to work it every day, and we soon had half a dozen milk cows and calves to sell or butcher, along with a full pen of hogs.

My chores also increased dramatically with all these farm activities. My job was to drive the cows in from the fields every night so I could feed them in the barn, carry the day's food waste ("slop") out to the pigs, and shuck enough corn to run through the corn-sheller in the corn crib to scatter for the chickens.

These were the daily chores. When harvest time came I was in the middle of it all, whether it was gathering corn from the stalks and tossing it into a wagon or shaking the dirt off the peanut plants before we hauled them up to store and dry in the barn loft. Later on when we joined the rest of the local farmers to plant cucumbers to sell to a pickling outfit, I joined the rest of the family to pick the cucumbers every day for hauling to Langley for sorting and weighing.

Papa was the ultimate farmer as far as I was concerned. He always had a plow horse for use in the fields, along with an iron-wheeled wagon that was our main mode of transportation until we finally acquired a car of our own several years later.

As I look back, I realize more and more how much of a sense of humor he had, but at the time I didn't realize that his names for his horses were basically family names. "Old Pearl" the mare died and was replaced by "Old

Maude," another ill-tempered mare that hated me almost as much as I hated her. I didn't make the connection at the time, but Papa's two sisters who lived out in Paris, Texas, just happened to named "Pearl" and "Maude."

Having a family name didn't seem to bother him that much when he needed to admonish his plow horse, at least from what I could hear every day that he was behind the plow. I don't know about the girls but I know I learned all the vocabulary I needed in all the situations I encountered for the rest of my days. And some I still haven't had occasion to call upon.

But I did practice quite a bit anytime I got caught out in the space between our back gate and the barn or, more often, our outhouse. The toilet was about two hundred feet from the fence and gate that kept the livestock out of our back yard.

Old Maude spent a lot of her resting moments in that part of the farm, usually up around the barn, which was another two hundred or so feet to the west. She almost always allowed me to go freely to the outhouse, which was considerate of her. But invariably as soon as the toilet door opened and I was ready to go back to the house, I would see her ears perk up and her eyes widen noticeably.

I tried every tactic I could think of, from seeming to ignore her and walking slowly and deliberately, to bursting out of the two-holer at full speed. Nothing seemed to deter her. She came at me like a mad zebra, mane laid back, teeth bared, and feet throwing dirt and gravel into the air behind her, and had the distance been twenty feet further I am certain that I would have been trampled to death.

As it was, I would be forced to SLIDE feet-first under the bottom of the wire gate at full speed just in time to avoid her as she screeched to a halt right at the fence line.

Papa tried to teach me to operate the plow behind Old Maude but it just didn't work out. I used all the words that he had taught me, plus a few of my own that I had learned at school or made up on the spur of the moment, but she just wouldn't pay me any mind at all.

She might plow two or three straight rows for me just to make me think I was finally in charge, but then for no apparent reason other than to aggravate me, she would suddenly take off on her own to destroy whatever rows had been started, only stopping in time to avoid whatever sweet gum pole Papa had gone after her with. We finally called off the plowing lessons, but the barnyard chases went on until I left the farm.

It was sometime along about this part of my life that I got a real shock. Dad came into the house one evening from school and said simply, "Well, Grady shot and killed Raleigh today."

II

You know I was thinking about something.

He was talking...and she may have been listening...as they drove the long highway again.

Do you have any idea how much time we have spent on this road?

They were traveling from Oregon to Arkansas, a trip she knew they had made so many times but she had never thought about his question. When she didn't answer right away, he told her.

I've been going over it in my mind the last little bit, and would you believe that we have spent about a year-and-a-half of our life driving this highway?

Are you sure? She couldn't imagine that much time spent just going from home to home and back home again. That doesn't seem possible. But he had figured it out.

Think about it. We've made this trip at least twice a year, on average, for almost forty years now. Three days going and three days back. That's six days for each time we've done it, and we've done it somewhere around eighty times, give or take half a dozen. Eighty times six, that's four hundred and eighty days!

She seemed less than impressed, as usual.

Which road are we on now? she said, looking out the window on her side.

He explained that they were taking the highway that went through Moab and across to Albuquerque, then on the interstate to Amarillo. We've probably used this one more than any, he said.

Well it doesn't look that familiar to me, she answered quietly. I don't think I could find my way across here by myself if I had to.

He wondered why she had never paid more attention to the roads they had traveled. He guessed it was probably because he always did most of the driving. She would drive for an hour or two if he got tired or sleepy, but she always worried that she might take a wrong turn somewhere while he was dozing. Don't worry about it, he would say. All these roads will take us to the same place eventually. Some are just longer than others.

Where are we stopping tonight? she wanted to know.

Probably in Moab, or maybe Cortez, he answered. Depends on how we feel when the sun goes down.

Are there some good places to stop there?

Don't you remember that nice Holiday Inn Express we stayed in last year? He was puzzled because he could always remember all of these places but she never seemed to know where they had traveled before or where they had spent the night.

Well, she finally said, laying her head back on the pillow, all of these places look the same to me after all these times. I wonder how the kids are doing today?

She was soon asleep and he liked to see her lying there all warm and comfortable. It seemed like she slept better while they were traveling than any other time.

To occupy his mind and make the trip go faster he began to think about some of their trips they had made in the past. There wasn't much scenery that he hadn't seen many times before so he couldn't get too excited about that. He knew her favorite was the Wyoming route, but they had long since decided that was only good during summer trips.

After they had moved to Oregon they went to Arkansas for Christmas for the first five or six years, mainly because the kids were not happy being away from their grandparents at Christmas time. But they had always had so little time to make the trip back then, and the weather was always at its worst during that time of the year.

It was probably their first trip back for Christmas that they turned at Ogden and went across Wyoming, having left Baker at daylight on a Saturday morning three days before Christmas. She was teaching and school kept her there until Friday so they were going to barely make it home in time for Christmas. They could make the two thousand mile trip in three days of hard driving, and this first day was one of those hard days.

At least they were comfortable traveling in the big Oldsmobile Delta Eighty-Eight that her parents had handed down to them just before they had moved to Oregon. The three kids were fairly well spaced out in the roomy back seat and the Olds was handling the north wind that blew steadily across their path.

Somewhere out past Rock Springs or Green River, he had felt a little hesitation hit the steady sound of the engine. At first it didn't bother him. He figured maybe just a touch of bad fuel. Maybe it would go away. It didn't.

The occasional misfire became a regular thing and he began to look for a place to crash land, not really wanting to suddenly be stranded on the side of the freeway with the temperature well below freezing and the wind approaching nasty. The first opportunity came at a truck stop wide place called Wamsutter. He pulled in to the service station and was glad to see a sign that read "Mechanic On Duty."

After waiting around for an hour or so it became apparent that the mechanic, if there actually was one, was occupied with one or more of the big rigs that were idling in the parking lot. They discussed their options, which were two. Go on and hope to find something in a bigger town, or go back toward Ogden.

Going on meant taking a big chance because it was a long way to the next town of any size, which was Rawlins, and finding a garage that was open on a Saturday afternoon would be a miracle. But going back probably meant going home for Christmas, with the lost time that would be involved.

So they had gone on, finally limping in to Rawlins to find that the only place that was even open was the American Motors Dealer. They had no choice, and after a couple of hours of waiting around while the mechanic replaced a cracked distributor, they were back on the road. The car ran fine the rest of the trip and they were happy to get out of Wyoming. The north wind had turned into a real gale force during the day and they saw the roadside littered with big trucks that had been blown off the highway, some even overturned.

That would be the last trip they would take through Wyoming in the winter, and also the last trip for the big Oldsmobile. It was getting a few years on it and although it ran fine, they chose to sell it and get a newer vehicle. They would make several more trips home for Christmas, with every trip seemingly more life-threatening than the last. They stopped going through Wyoming and opted for a more southerly route down through Salt Lake City and across to Albuquerque, but that route involved some serious bad-weather stretches too.

One part of the road in particular was always a challenge; from Provo over the mountain at Soldier Summit to Price. They never failed to catch a bad storm either going or coming, and sometimes both ways, on that fifty mile portion.

On their last Christmas-time drive they had caught blizzards in both directions. He shuddered when he recalled how they had thought they were almost home free after driving across Idaho in an icy, freezing fog when they had barely been able to see the tail-lights of the car a hundred feet in front of them, up over Soldier Summit in a driving snowstorm, and finally into northwestern New Mexico a little after dark.

The weather looked decent for a change and they needed to make it on to Albuquerque before stopping for the night. As they drove down the highway from Farmington the road climbed steadily and suddenly they topped over a hill and looked down the grade ahead of them and saw car lights shining off in all directions.

He pulled over into a wide spot at the top of the grade and when he got out of the car he fell hard to the ground. The pavement was a sheet of ice. Cars coming up the road ahead of them had slid off into ditches or spun out right in the road. Some were putting chains on, which he decided he needed to do also.

As he was lying on the ground putting chains on the rear-wheel drive Buick, he looked back up the road behind where they were parked and saw a horrible sight. A delivery truck was headed right toward them, sliding sideways and obviously totally out of control.

He didn't even have time to jump up and move out of the way. He lay there for the next five or ten seconds thinking about what was going to happen next. The truck was going to slam into the back of their car, still sliding sideways, and it was going to roll right up over the car and smash them all like a pancake. It was the most helpless feeling he had ever felt in his life.

He could still see what happened next, and he still could not believe it had played out like it did. Somehow the truck tires caught some kind of traction as they slid off the pavement and across the gravel in the wide spot, and just as it looked like there was no way it could miss them, the truck turned ninety degrees and went straight across the highway and rammed into the bank on the other side from where they were parked. He hoped she and the kids hadn't seen it all, but she had seen the ending at least.

After they drove the next forty miles with chains on, they broke out of the ice and made it on to Arkansas fine. He didn't remember much about how their Christmas had gone that year because the trip back to Oregon had been enough to wipe the past from his memory. This time they had made it all the way to Idaho before they hit a blizzard.

Coming across from Salt Lake City through Snowville (an aptly named place if there ever was one!) they had been driving in a light snowfall all the way. They thought about stopping at Twin Falls for the night but it was New Year's Eve and they figured they might not be able to get a room. Besides they were hoping to get home that night so they could watch football all day the next day. Let's go on, he had insisted.

Just after they passed the last town and started into the long stretch of nothing between there and Mountain Home, the snowstorm became serious. The wind picked up and was blowing the drifts across the highway so hard it was almost impossible to see. He saw that there was no oncoming traffic, and very little even going in their direction, so he made a quick decision at the next overpass.

He told her he was turning around, which she gladly agreed to, and pulled off the road to go back over the freeway to head back toward a town, any town. As they went over the overpass and pulled onto the on ramp, the snow had drifted up on the ramp and he saw that they were in trouble right away. If they got stuck in the drift they were really screwed. So he did the only thing he could think of at the moment; he stepped on the accelerator and gunned the Buick through the snowdrifts.

Back out on the freeway it was snowing even harder as they tried to decide if they could make it back to Twin Falls, which was about thirty miles, or if they should just stop at the first chance. They took the first chance and pulled off the freeway at Wendell.

There were no motels by the freeway so they drove down toward the few lights that were showing. There were no motels there either, but there was one old two-story hotel on the corner of the two-street town. The lights were on so they stopped and went inside, finding that the hotel was mainly a bar, but there was one room available upstairs if they wanted it.

They didn't hesitate. It was a long night, but it was shelter from the storm. The five of them slept in one old creaky double bed, and sleep was a little tricky, not just from the cramped bed but also from the all-night New Year's celebration that came up through the thin walls from the bar below.

That would be their last winter trip, and the kids would always feel bad about not being "home" for Christmas. They knew the grandparents were sad too. But they never regretted missing out on the dangerous journey. He wondered how many of those trips she remembered, as he looked at her sleeping peacefully.

Sometimes it seemed to him like maybe he had been traveling alone all these years.

* * *

Do you think the grandkids will still want to go to Fly Creek?

He knew she didn't know the answer to that, but wanted to talk about the possibility of keeping that part of their life alive.

No, I don't think they will, she answered. Not after this year.

Their oldest grandson was getting ready to go off to college. Things would not stay the same after that, they knew. He already had a girlfriend and that would change things too.

They hated to think about losing that part of their family time. It had been so much fun for so many years now, and the grandkids had all looked forward to going back every year. From the moment they left for home each time, they started planning what they would do next time they were there.

The first time they had camped there had been when their grandson was almost a year old. He wasn't walking yet but had taken a few first steps there in the grassy area where they had camped. But they hadn't made it a tradition to go back every Memorial Day weekend until the last grandchild had come along, and that was when it became such a strong family connection.

Every year was somewhat the same but always different, as they watched the little ones grow. They marveled at the progression that could always be seen in the final picture of the four kids standing in the same spot on the little bridge across Fly Creek. He made sure they took that picture each year to record not only how the kids were changing, but also to show, in the background of each photo, what they had done that year.

They had played most of the daylight hours while in camp in the little stream that at that time of year was always just slightly above freezing because it was mostly snowmelt. But that didn't bother the kids as they waded up and down the creek, looking for fresh-water mussels, rode their rubber raft under the bridge and around the bumpy rapids down to a take-out spot just below camp, or mostly just dug and worked to build something on and around the little island that lay just upstream from the bridge.

It had started out as just the usual stone dams or walking paths across the water from the bank to the island, but then it became a little more of a project each year. One year it had been a "dock" that they placed along the bank of the island, constructed of large rocks interspersed with smaller stones and sand and finally covered with mud and sod.

They were pleased to see that a major part of their dock was still in place when they went back the next year. So they added some complexity, this time building a little wooden pole bridge that was covered with reeds and dirt, shored up in the middle with a stone pier, allowing them to actually walk from the shore to the island.

Another year had been spent putting up a lodgepole pine lean-to on the island, covering that with heavy sod from the sides of the stream. Their last project had been a serious pole bridge that was much heavier and longer than anything they had done before.

They had anchored it on the island end with a huge stump that was wrestled out of the ground nearby and tumbled down across the stream, which was running high and swift that year because of the heavy snowmelt. The bridge was strong enough to hold all four of them when they finished.

After that was done they had dug a hole in the sand of the island, built a small warming fire, and talked about whether or not the bridge would last until they came back next year.

The campout was not just for the grandchildren, though. All of them had enjoyed being there together. They had brought camp trailers and tents and always worried that they were going to be asked to leave the little meadow above the creek where they camped because it was actually on private land and even though it adjoined the national forest, they knew the landowner could tell them to leave. But they had never been bothered for over a decade.

There were other things to do while they were together, as the adults fished some, rode bikes, but mostly just watched the kids play. There would always be a group hike with everyone going along sometime before camp was broken. And he would take the grandkids on four-wheeler rides on the old logging roads in the area, taking turns with them and trying to take them to new places each year.

She prepared meals in camp or brought things she had already cooked at home, to save more time for playing once they got there. And she worried about the grandkids getting sick from playing in the icy water, or getting dumped out of the raft in the two foot deep creek.

Nights were for the usual campfire activities; roasting marshmallows after dinner was mandatory. One game they played brought them great pleasure for several years. Everyone played as they sat around the campfire at night, with one person starting a story by telling a few lines about a situation.

The next person around the circle would add his or her take on the tale, and this would go on around the group for several cycles, usually ending either when everyone had laughed as much as they thought they could stand, or in a few cases, when the final addition to the tale just could not be improved upon in any way.

Some of those endings had even become legendary among the family on different occasions, the most famous being the tale of the midget zither-playing gypsies with twins Spanky and Juan plus the girls Olga and Svegrid and not to forget the youngsters Bobby and OJ, culminating in a wild ride in a runaway semi at the border where the only thing left to do was to "Mash on that thing. Run 'em over!"

Wiffle-ball games that involved everyone there in the meadow, skeet-shooting contests, and a few drives on over the mountain for a swim at Lehman Hot Springs were just a few of the fun things they did. At night inside the trailer they might play a board game or, more likely, something like Balderdash. Everyone was always involved and by the time the sleeping bags were rolled out, the kids were always ready for some rest.

But now they worried that this particular fun time might be over. She said she hoped that they might still go back every once in a while, maybe with some of the kids and grandkids, if not everyone. They knew it was unlikely that they would ever be there with the entire family again. It was both sad to think of it ending, but also nice to remember all of the fun they had had while it lasted.

We couldn't have done anything that the little ones would have enjoyed more, she said.

I know. He thought about how they had looked around for a place that would be a good substitute in case they ever had to move from that spot, but every spot they had gone to with the grandkids had been vetoed by them. It had just been the perfect place in the perfect time.

You know, he added, sometimes when I think about how fast the time has gone by, it seems to me that it is just like a dream. Or that it didn't even happen at all.

12

There were a million things on her mind, and almost that many that she knew she needed to do now that James was gone. But fortunately for her now, he had taken full responsibility for everything that he could do to make her life go on without him as smoothly as possible.

They had wills and a trust and she didn't have to worry about her financial well-being. The life insurance policy was also there and that would help too.

And he had laid out a road map for her to follow to help her get through the immediate time, almost in the same way he had always planned their trips. Day one, his yearly planner for her read: "Get over me." She smiled when she remembered that notation, and how she had done her best to make him know that she never would be able to follow that order.

But he wanted her to go on with her life and at least not dwell inordinately on their life together, which had ended. That was fair because she knew that he understood her well enough to know that she wasn't one to stay behind when everything called for going forward.

There was also one more trip back to Arkansas that needed to be discussed with the children. She and James had picked out a headstone for the gravesite and it would be ready by late Spring. They had all talked about wanting to go back together when it was placed.

She knew they were doing that mostly for her benefit, but that was okay. They would want to do it for their father too, and the way she had planned everything was for the stone to be placed in time for Decoration Day. She remembered how important that Sunday weekend in May was for the people in the hill country.

And now she wanted it to be just as important for their family too, as she knew it would have been for her husband. She knew the days would come when the feelings of the certainty of it all hit hard. After the initial phase of having too much to do and very little extra time to think about anything except taking care of everything that needed to be taken care of, the letdown came.

13

 We were all sitting out on the front porch that evening after supper. Papa rolled a Bull Durham cigarette and lit it. The glow from his cigarette looked just like the tail end of the lightning bugs that filled the air around the yard as dark came on.

We kids were silent and still for a change, knowing that this wasn't the time for ripping and romping around the front yard, stirring up dust and entertaining ourselves. We didn't even catch any lightning bugs to store in a pint fruit jar to watch them light up our bedroom later that night.

Granny sat on the porch, rocking steadily and looking across into the darkening space that lay between our house and the only neighbors we were close enough to see. The Cowarts lived down across the branch and over in a little house tucked back into the woods. I figured they were also sitting outside somewhere, doing about what we were doing, which was nothing.

The summer air was still hot and sticky, which would have been enough reason to postpone going into the house. But the news about Grady shooting Raleigh had put an extra damper on things for that day. Things like that just didn't happen. Not around these parts.

Oh sure, there was trouble between folks at times, and it wasn't unusual to hear about family feuds breaking out into fistfights or threats of such. But most such feuds were settled in the time honored tradition of country folks everywhere. Folks would go on the non-communication list. Sometimes that would last for a day, usually more like a few months, but in some cases, forever.

But to have someone just up and shoot a father-in-law? That was news we didn't really know how to even think about, let alone talk about. Of course the kids knew they had probably already been told all they needed to know. Any real discussions would take place later that night behind closed doors.

Granny only paused from her steady rock about every tenth motion forward to spit her snuff into the flower bed down in front of the porch. I can still hear the sounds of evening settling in over that little home's front porch. Somewhere off to the south a dog barked sporadically, just barely within hearing.

Probably one of the Dowdy's squirrel hounds still looking up into an oak tree and wondering if Nolan was going to come along and shoot the big red fox squirrel that was cutting acorns up toward the top. Neighbors were heard in the distance with their "suuk,,,,suuk,,,,suuk, Jersey" calling in of the cows for the evening feeding.

Frogs croaked from the spring house all the way down our part of the branch, ending with a huge bass bullfrog somewhere in the edge of the deeper pool down on the main branch where the road crossed to go over to Leander's house. It was a locust year. Cicada's seemed to fill every tree and the cacophony of legs rubbing together seemed to overwhelm every other sound and threatened to even drown out my thoughts.

What happened between Grady and Raleigh, I wondered?

I knew I would never know how it had come to that end, but the rumors and gossip tidbits that slipped out the next few days seemed to point toward the common bad blood between a father who thought his daughter was not being treated right and a husband who thought it best for the father to stay out of the fight.

Raleigh York was a close neighbor of ours, father to the daughter who had married Grady Morphew. He was also the father of our friend, the fast-driving "Chick" who had entertained me with his horn back over by the old school. They had another younger daughter still living at home, while Chick had married my first grade teacher, Marie Marsh and they had built a house up the hill a few hundred feet from his folks' house.

Grady and his wife lived a quarter of a mile on up the road toward Langley, across Little Blocker Creek, in an old house that I would become familiar with later on after my friend and playmate, Albert Lowery, and his family had moved into the house.

So about all I remember learning about the incident were the basics. Grady and his wife "Evy" had a fight, probably on-going, and Raleigh had come down to the house to see if he could straighten things out (the word "intervention" hadn't been invented yet, and probably wouldn't have applied in this case anyway).

When Raleigh left the front door after his discussion with Grady, Grady had shot him dead with his double-barreled twelve gauge shotgun before Raleigh reached the front gate. I assumed the gun was loaded with double-ought buckshot. At least that was what I imagined, based on the limited amount of information I had been given.

There was the obligatory trial for Grady down at the courthouse in Murfreesboro, which I was not allowed to attend for some strange reason, although I figured the trial would be quick and decisive after which Grady would be hauled off to Tucker Prison Farm never to be heard from again.

Much to everyone's surprise, the trial was not as cut and dried as we had all expected. Seems Grady's family somehow got wind of a semi-famous trial lawyer out of Little Rock and had scraped up enough money to bring him down to Murfreesboro to defend Grady. Still, we all thought, what excuse could even a big-city lawyer come up with to explain what appeared to be obvious guilt?

Well, it was soon clear that this lawyer was worth his salt as he managed to convince the jury that Grady had simply succumbed to a severe case of temporary insanity brought on by, of all things, a case of syphilis that Grady had been carrying around since his younger days.

The lawyer made it sound like only a fool or a country boy would fail to understand that such a disease could seriously affect the brain at any time, and it had chosen to creep up into Grady's noggin just at the exact moment when Raleigh had walked down across the creek to interfere with a marital dispute. Never mind that rumor had it that Grady had gone up to a neighbor's house several hours earlier to borrow a couple of loads of buckshot for his twelve gauge shotgun.

The sentence was not, as most of us had expected, a long and lonely life raising peanuts down at Tucker Prison Farm. Fifteen to twenty, with time off for good behavior, or some such was what came back to us. I calculated that the lawyer had somehow managed to place more sons-in-law on the jury than fathers-in-law. One stipulation that did come out of the verdict was that Grady could never return to Pike County so I never heard anything else about him after that.

But occasionally when I would hear a dog barking off in the distance just before dark, or a whippoorwill chanting "chip the widow's white-oak," I would wonder if Grady was ever sorry that he shot Raleigh.

I always guessed not.

***

For every tiny second of bothersome happenings, there were so many days of sheer joy and pleasure to be had there on whatever fork of whatever creek branch we lived on, days when there was nothing that kept us from just playing all day and into the night. If there wasn't a game to be played, we invented one.

I could go for days on end with nothing more than a tin can nailed to a short piece of two-by-four that was thus magically transformed into my truck that hauled my dirt and built my roads in the sandy soil under one of the big post oak trees that ringed our yard.

There were bridges and tunnels to go along with commerce of hauling sticks from one side of the imaginary city to the other, with stones going back in the other direction.

When cold weather or summer rains kept us inside, I joined the girls with a game that was simply called "paper dolls." Every kid from the country during that time played paper dolls, and the boys who claimed they would never play a sissy game like that were either liars or their family had used all their Sears and Roebuck catalogs for other, more mundane purposes.

We took great pains to carefully cut out all the family members we needed from catalogs that were passed along to us by the adults. Little did we realize that they knew well what a perfect toy they were giving us and how little danger there was that we could hurt ourselves with this game. To make sure there was zero danger, we were even given little round-nosed scissors with which to do our cutting.

Playing consisted mostly of two phases. First and foremost was the careful choosing of the characters that would be our family. After the people were trimmed from the pages, we would set about furnishing our home. No expense was spared as we all looked for the best pictures possible to place around the many rooms of our new families' homes.

The game was pretty much winding down as far as I was concerned by the time every possible imaginary acquisition had been pulled from the pages of the catalog and placed around the various rooms. There didn't really seem to be much that could be done in the way of interactions within or between these perfectly groomed and clothed model families.

Occasionally the girls would take the game to another level by pretending that something worthwhile had happened or was about to happen to one or more of our people, but by this time I was usually ready to finish my part of the game by scooping up my people and my furniture or whatever and putting them all back in the shoebox.

I played a lot of games all by myself, a few with my three sisters, but many more with cousins or neighbor kids who came to visit. Outside games were always in order during daylight hours, or sometimes even into the darkness. There were the usual games of hide-and-seek, or modifications thereof such as knock-the-can (I never heard it called kick the can because we didn't kick the can to get to go back out and hide again, we knocked the can as far as possible with a good sized stick), or pig-in-the-pen-wants-a-motion.

We had a perfect place for playing such hiding and finding games because we could hide all around the house to the back, down by the spring house, up behind the storm cellar, and behind any of the numerous huge oak trees close by.

Another outside game that was played was one that was always more of an adult game than a kids' game. I don't know if it was played at other family homes or not, but I do know that at our house and at the Cowart's house across the branch, each family had a set of stone marbles that came out of a box almost every summer Sunday afternoon.

These marbles were something to see, consisting of at least five larger stones that were about one-and-one-half-inch in diameter, ground perfectly round from some kind of extremely hard but not too brittle stone such as marble or granite. These larger "ring" marbles were placed in a square drawn out in the sandy yard, with one marble at each of the four corners of the square and one in the center.

Four players each chose a "taw," a shooting marble that was about half the size of the ring marbles and were used to try and flip across the yard hard enough to knock one of the ring marbles out.

Sides were drawn up, two players to the side, and all four players would stand by the ring to start the game, roll ("lag") their taw at the taw line, which was a line drawn in the sand about fifteen feet from the square or "ring." Closest one to the taw line got to shoot first, and partners then alternated shooting after that.

Usually a board or boards would be placed at the other end of the yard to stop the opening shots to keep the marbles in the yard because shooting from the taw line would mostly consist of flipping the taw with the thumb as hard as possible, trying to dead center one of the marbles in the ring.

If anyone hit the center marble and happened to knock it out from the taw line, it was game over. That team won. Otherwise, the first team to knock three of the five out won. A simple game for sure, but one that afforded many hours of entertainment to the men who played and the women and children who watched.

For a few hours on a hot summer afternoon, the cares of the fields were forgotten as partners became lifelong friends over a child's game. Each player always had their favorite shooting taw, and nothing was more likely to squelch an afternoon of fun than seeing one of the shooting stones split in half by what was usually an exceptionally accurate, but devastating, shot.

When I left the farm all those years later, Papa entrusted me with his precious set of stone marbles. I have kept them in the box they were stored in and I'm still waiting for Papa or Preacher Cowart to tell me they are ready for a game.

We also played horseshoes and pitched washers into holes, or holes with tin cans sunk into them. And when daylight was gone and chores done, supper finished but bedtime still a few hours away, we played inside games.

In those days Dad and Mama were so busy working and so tired from making a living to allow us to survive that they usually didn't join in the games at night. It wasn't that they didn't enjoy these games. They just needed a little more rest than the rest of us.

I don't know if there was a game ever played on a board or a table that Papa hadn't tried, learned, and usually mastered. I am pretty sure that I have forgotten many of the games he taught us to play, but the number I recall surely ran well into the dozens. Every possible kind of domino game, from what we called "plain" dominoes, to matador, moon, and forty-two; games he had learned mostly in his time in West Texas.

We played card games of every kind, such as pitch, hearts, casino; and I am still amazed when I think of how good he was at checkers. I know he wanted me to be as good as he was, and I know he thought the only way I would get that good was for him to never give an inch when we played.

I could tell that he was driving Granny crazy because he would never just let me win. I had to learn enough to earn it, and that bothered her. I'm sure if there had been a way for her to teach me a trick or two so I could beat him, she would have done it in an instant. I didn't keep count of all the checker games we played. If I had the tally would most surely read something like this: Papa won eleventy thousand or so; John didn't.

One more outside game was played with a soft ball of some kind with two people standing on opposite sides of the house. We called it "Annie-Over" for some reason. The person with the ball would call out "annie" and the other side would answer "over." Once the ball was thrown over the house the object was for the other person to catch it and sneak around the house to try and throw the ball at the person who had tossed it over, thereby winning that round.

Our house was pretty good for the game because of the straight line pitched roof that was uniform on both sides, except for one minor drawback at the chimney on the south side. The ball could get caught behind the rock chimney and temporarily stall the game.

I was the only one agile enough to scale the side of the chimney to get the ball. The only drawback to the way the house was built as far as this game was concerned was that the floor stood about a foot above ground all the way around and was open underneath so that by looking under the house we could usually tell which way the person with the ball was coming from and head in the opposite direction.

That worked both ways though because it was easy to feint one direction and turn and run full speed in the other to catch the opponent coming around a corner right into the path of the ball.

Of all the games that I played the ones I remember most were the games I made up to pretend I was playing major league baseball. One such game involved standing just outside the back fence behind our house in an area that contained a lot of slatey rock. I would cut a persimmon pole that was about an inch or so in diameter and maybe three feet long. It would always be a little bigger on one end than the other so the smaller end would be where I held the bat as I tossed up a small rock and took a swing.

The barn was just about where centerfield should be, and the corn crib was deep left field. The chicken house was a little closer but since it was standing in for right field and would normally require that I be swinging from the left side, that was okay.

I made up my lineup for the two teams that were playing, and the favored team would always be my own favorite, the Detroit Tigers. Usually "we" were playing against the hated Yankees or semi-hated Red Sox, but occasionally one of the other minor American League teams would come to town. It didn't matter.

I knew the full lineups for all eight of the teams in the American League, including the normal four starting and one relief pitcher. In those days before free agency spoiled the game forever for us real fans, the same lineup might play for several years and only change with age or serious injury.

A full nine inning game was almost always played unless there was an interruption caused by such thoughtless acts as Mama calling on me to do something unnecessary around the house or some such. One side would bat from the right, which being my normal stance, usually ended up being my team.

The other guys had to bat left, which placed them at a noticeable disadvantage the first few months but after a while I began to see enough improvement in "their" batting that some of the games actually ended up being fairly close. There was almost always a dramatic home run from one of the heroes late in the game if it happened to get a little too close.

I can still hear the sound of those sharp-edged flat-sided pieces of slate rock buzzing as they sailed up and away toward the bleachers beyond the corn crib or barn. And just to make sure my throwing didn't take a back seat to my batting, I devised a second game that consisted of pitching and fielding.

In our front yard the gate stood about thirty feet straight out from the porch steps, which were three risers up from the ground, meaning that to go from the yard to the porch required us to step up onto two flat steps before stepping onto the porch. That meant there were three vertical boards that I could aim at to bounce a ball back to where I had constructed my "mound" in the middle of the front gate. I marked the edges of the strike zone and began announcing another nine innings.

It wasn't just practice on hitting, pitching, and fielding that interested me. I was also making sure that the game was being properly broadcast for the "fans" out in the hinterland.

Pitches that centered the strike zone area and came back off the vertical boards were strikes. Those same pitches that were outside the zone were balls. Anything that bounced back along the ground from above or below the strike zone was a ground ball that required that I field it and throw it at the steps in just such a way that the ball would bounce up and back to me without hitting the ground. Otherwise it was a hit. Pitches that hit the intersection of the horizontal and vertical boards just right would come back out at varying heights as fly balls.

Oh, there were some magnificent games played on those summer days. For the life of me I just could never figure out how my Tigers could not do as well in real life as they always did in my made up games. All I could think of was that it must have been that the umpires favored the hated Yankees or Red Sox.

**

There was one place on the farm that I really didn't like at all. I mean really didn't like. As in hated with a passion. Funny thing is, it was probably the one place where I was the safest, although even that seemed like a mixed bag to me.

One reason I disliked it so much was that I never went there during daylight or good weather. It was almost always in the middle of the night when we would be in a deep and dreamy sleep when (usually) Mama would stick her head into our bedroom and announce with a hurried tone in her voice that brought us to wide-awake status immediately.

Get up! She'd always start with that so there was no doubt what our first move had to be. It's storming. We're going to the storm-house. Right now!

She would be out of the room in a second and we would be scrambling toward the back door where at least Mama and Granny would be lining us out for the quick sprint from the back porch through the side gate and down the three or four steps into our cellar. I don't know if it was early macho-ness that most times kept Dad and Papa in their warm beds, or if they just figured they could outrun a tornado when the time came and would rather take their chances with that option than where we were going.

The cellar was a dugout sunk four or five feet deep into the slate bank just outside the back fence. The floor was dirt and so were the walls up to where the original ground level had been. Above that a few logs had been laid around the sides to raise the height a couple more feet.

On top of these side logs were piled more logs across the top to form the ceiling/roof. The height of the ceiling was just enough so that most of us could stand up underneath it, but Dad and Papa would have to stoop over to keep from banging their heads on a log.

The ceiling logs were overlaid with random boards that were meant to keep the dirt which was then piled over the top of the structure from falling down into the hole. The boards did a fair job of keeping out the dirt, but there was still a fine sifting of dry, powdery soil that had to be swept off the top of everything, including the old frame bed where the kids would pile up as soon as we got inside. A couple of rickety chairs and a bench along the sides provided a place for the adults to sit.

Granny would light a kerosene lamp that was kept in the cellar at all times and that would at least provide enough light for us to look around and check all the places where a snake could be hiding out, waiting for one of us to sit or step too closely.

Most of the time the snakes that frequented the cellar were harmless enough, although for us kids there were really no good snakes. But the black snakes, king snakes, coach whips, and such normal-headed snakes actually

did us a favor by crawling into the cellar and cleaning out the smaller creatures that would have otherwise soon filled it completely. We saw very few
mice or frogs in the cellar and we knew that could only mean something had
been doing a good job of cleanup.

The main kind of snake we had to watch out for was the secretive but
deadly dangerous copperhead. There were a few big diamondback rattlesnakes seen around the farm on occasion, but they seemed to prefer the drier,
rockier places that were found in the hills and on up into the mountains to
the north.

Most of the ones we saw were just passing through and they were very
happy to announce their presence with a loud rattle any time a person or
dog got within close range. And the other venomous monster that we had to
avoid, the cottonmouth water moccasin, lived closer to some kind of standing water.

So that left just the copperhead, but that was definitely enough to keep
us on our toes. They were especially nasty because they had the reputation
of being ill-tempered and prone to think that wherever they happened to be
at the moment was "theirs," leaving them free to sink their dirty fangs into
the rear-end of any other warm-blooded mammal that made the mistake of
sitting on them.

Granny would always shake out the bed coverings thoroughly after
she had the lamp going, partly to clear off the dust but we also knew she was
making sure we weren't lying down with a serpent.

But that wasn't all we had to watch out for. There were other things
living in this dark, dank hole in the ground that were pretty much immune
to being eaten by anything else, other than perhaps each other. Black widow
spiders being the worst. There was just no way to get rid of all of them, or the
two other crawly critters that kept us from ever sleeping soundly in the cellar.

We had scorpions that were hideous little poison darts that loved
nothing better than to throw their barbed tail into a human hide, leaving
a stinging shock and reddening, rising swollen place behind. Centipedes
were not as potent as scorpions but were bad enough in their own right,
sometimes reaching a length of several inches and able to leave a mark on
bare skin with every one of the "thousand legs." Other than those minor in-

conveniences, the storm-house was a marvelous place to wait out a tornado.

The cellar must have saved us because we were never blown away. Actually, our farm must have been in a lucky place because for all the years we lived there, and for all the history we knew of before, a tornado never hit close by.

Based on all the horror stories we heard, we would do our level best to act like we felt honored that the adults felt so strongly about our safety that they would even let us continue to sleep in the cellar after the storm threat had blown over and they had all slipped out and gone back to their real beds.

14

 Taos in the Sixties was a sight to behold and an experience to live through. It seems that they had arrived two summers before the official "summer of love," but from the looks of things around town you wouldn't have known it.

There was the new job of course, and that occupied his mind and his time during the week. New people to meet, a new place to go to work in an old adobe office next door to the post office, things to learn about life in a forestry agency that was just beginning to understand that they might need an engineer if they were going to be doing all those engineering projects.

He designed roads and trails, worked with other people who had skills in such areas as timber and range management, recreation planning and development, landscape architecture, watershed protection, and all the technical areas that the growing work of the national forests required.

And there were other areas that he had never thought about and had he known about them, he might have had at least a touch of doubt about where he was moving to.

Law enforcement was a big thing in Northern New Mexico in the late

1960s. Their timing was not exactly perfect as they had moved to Taos right in the middle of a land dispute that spanned over a century now.

It seems the Spanish land grants that had been passed on to the Spanish settlers from the King of Spain had somehow been rudely ripped from the hands of the secondary owners (the first being of course the indigenous natives).

That action had caused some serious bad feelings and those bad feelings had begun to come to a head as a charismatic orator took to the courthouse steps and rallied his people against the Anglos who were now mostly in control of the land. One special target just happened to sit squarely on the back of the big national forest where he had gone to work recently, totally unaware of the possible tensions that were now being faced on a daily basis.

A month before they arrived in Taos to begin what they thought would be an extended vacation in paradise, a group of folks had occupied a forest campground near Ghost Ranch and had "detained" some of the forest service rangers and other folks who had attempted to regain control of a really nasty situation. Bloodshed was averted on that day by mostly pure luck, but there were still plenty of opportunities for that in the coming months and years.

Bad blood continued to show up throughout the area but he was able to avoid the conflict himself. Most of the long time forest personnel who worked out in the woods or on the ground attended training to improve their skills in law enforcement. Crash courses in speaking the language common to the area, Spanish, were given to all who needed or wanted it.

None of these issues really seemed to bother them though, as they did their best to find their way into a totally new culture that was Taos. They lived in an adobe house with white painted wood floors and peeled log vigas in the ceilings. A corner fireplace provided them with a challenge every time they attempted to fire it up in the same way he had always built a fire back on the farm.

One of his first attempts at stoking a fire in it ended with him having to open the turquoise painted windows next to the fireplace and tossing the smoking Pinyon firewood out into the front yard. Otherwise the entire house was going to be filled with dense, acrid smoke before the flue ever warmed enough to draw.

In that front yard the two little boys learned to play with their Spanish neighbors, Ernie and Frankie. Coming in across a cattle guard from Carabajal road into the front yard, a yard that was ringed by the house on one side, the garage straight ahead (almost), and a large, one room studio or (for them) storage house stood on the other side.

Right in the middle stood the biggest cottonwood tree either of them had ever seen. It was so big and so close to the middle of the yard that to get into the one doorway of the dirt-floored garage, they had to drive around the tree, angle back to the left, and then turn sharply back to the right to enter the garage. Out past the cottonwood tree they had set up the swing and slide set they had brought with them from Amarillo for the boys to play on, which they did every day until the snows came.

Also in the area on each side of the entry road were two or three wonderful apple trees that they grew to appreciate more and more each year. They were old fashioned apples of some kind, probably a red delicious derivative, and never failed in all the years they lived there to bear prodigious amounts of juicy, sweet fruit. The apple trees and the swing set would also be connected in their memories forever after one summer day of play.

He came home from work and found that the youngest boy had a couple of bandages on his head. One was on his forehead and the other near the crown. What happened?

Well, she said. It happened like this, more or less.

They were trying to knock apples from the tree and the bigger boy tossed up a large rock or brick. It came down. Naturally it landed where the smaller one happened to be standing, looking up, expecting an apple but catching a brick in the noggin instead. She took him to the doctor's office and they put a butterfly bandage on it to hold it together and help it heal.

A little later in the day they decided to play on the swings, and somehow they both got their swings going pretty high and in the same direction at the same time, and guess what?

The swing set tipped over, nailing the little one in the back of the head and also knocking him down into the dirt face-first, where he managed to undo the butterfly bandage on his forehead. Another run to the doctor, this time for butterflies in both places.

Naturally she was blaming herself for not watching them more closely.

*＊＊

Who were those people riding with what's his name?

They were driving to Santa Fe or Albuquerque from Taos and had passed an old Blue Ford Bronco when they noticed that the hippie-looking guy driving it was Dennis Hopper. He had moved to Taos after filming a lot of his latest movie there. She noticed that it was him and wondered who his friends were.

Whoever they were, they were being thoroughly entertained by Dennis as he was waving his arms animatedly as he tried to keep the Bronco on the narrow, crooked road heading south toward Embudo.

That's the way life was in Taos in those days. Dennis Hopper hadn't brought the summer of love to town, but he had certainly come along for the ride. He bought Mabel Dodge Luhan's adobe mansion in the heart of Taos and was undoubtedly inspired there to begin a long and successful career in art himself.

They knew why he bought a place there in Taos because it was an amazing, fun place to live at that time. Sure, there were riots going on across America and big cities everywhere were getting nasty. But it was peace and love as far as the eye could see in Taos.

They soon found out that living in Taos meant having lots of visitors for them, too. Everyone they knew seemed to want to come out for a few days. Parents, siblings, even cousins that they had not seen much of since leaving Arkansas were suddenly in town for the tour.

The tour would usually start with a walk around the Plaza, through some of the many local art galleries and gift shops, a walk through the Kit Carson or Governor Bent museum, followed by a trip out to Taos Pueblo. The pueblo was always a highlight as the southerners were exposed to a culture living in the eight hundred year old pueblo in ways that hadn't changed much in all that time.

After the pueblo, another must-see stop would be out to the high bridge that spanned the Rio Grande Gorge a few miles west of Taos on the road to Tres Piedras. Every visitor was left as speechless as they had been the first time they drove out across the flat sagebrush plains to suddenly come onto a quarter-mile wide gash in the granite that dropped down to the river six-hundred and fifty feet below.

They would park on one side or the other and walk gingerly out onto the beautiful steel arch bridge to stand on one of the pedestrian view-points that jutted out from the sidewalk several feet. It was always a little scary just walking onto the bridge, and would seem even scarier when a vehicle would drive by and make the bridge shake slightly.

Pictures were taken of all the company that came. They might drive on over to Tres Piedras and even up to Hopewell Lake on the new highway that went through the National Forest where he worked. Sometimes they went up north to Questa and Red River and he might show them the big Molybdenum mine that was gouging out huge chunks of mountainsides to pipe ore down for milling in Questa.

Or they might go on up into Upper Red River to see the scenery around the summer cabins that the Texans had built along the river. Leaving Red River they could come back to Taos the same way they went up, or they could make the loop on around through an old mining town of Elizabethtown, where cabins and sluiced out hillsides still showed evidence of the early gold mining.

At Eagle Nest they would often take a side road up to a new resort that had been built at Angel Fire, with big fancy homes overlooking the ski area and golf course, turning around there and heading back up over Palo Flechado pass and down Taos Canyon and back to their house.

They wasted no time adjusting to the local food, acquiring a taste for green chile and sopapillas that would stay with them for the rest of their lives. It seemed there were no bad restaurants in town. At least none that they found, and they tried about all of them with all their company, although she quickly became adept at serving her own favorite dishes at times.

Soon after they had moved there, they drove by the local car dealership one day and noticed a shiny new car in the showroom window that really caught their eye. It was a Nineteen-Sixty-Eight Dodge Charger R/T and it would follow them home to replace their Oldsmobile.

He and the little boys especially liked the way it roared as he tested the 440 Magnum engine out on the straightaway beyond the high bridge. And they loved the sleek lines of the racing green and black-striped body, with the buckskin vinyl top and the red R/T emblems on the hood and tail panel.

They thought it was the ride of a lifetime. To her, it was just another nice car.

15

 I clearly remember when I had the chicken pox. Not that I was very sick or anything, although I did get to stay home from school for at least one day. The reason I remember staying home is because Granny took me fishing that day down on Rock Creek.

She knew full well she wasn't supposed to take me anywhere near the water, and I knew she knew that. But what we both knew was that we could pull it off and Mama would probably never know a thing about it.

I was feeling nothing more than a little speckled that morning when everyone left for school, but I also had something else on my mind. It was late Spring and the bass were running like crazy up out of the new lake down by Murfreesboro. We would even see some of the smaller bass as far up as our spring branch below the house, and Rock Creek was teeming with them.

I had been down to the creek several times already with Papa and Granny and we were really sacking them up on our cane poles and hooks baited with minnows we had caught or seined out of the creek branch. Most of the time we had been able to catch all we wanted in the first two or three holes we fished. The old "stump hole" was especially productive and some-times that's as far as we would have to go to catch a good mess of bass.

The last time we had gone we had seen something unusual that really got us excited. We still were not sure what kind of fish we had seen, but what-ever kind they were, they were huge. They were definitely not bass. Bass did not act the way these fish acted. We had been sitting there quietly watching our bobbers dancing around with a live minnow on the line, waiting for a bass to suck it under so we could set the hook and haul them out of the water.

I don't know who noticed them first, but whoever it was probably said one or more bad words, followed by something like "did you see that?" As we sat quietly watching more closely, a few minutes later a dark shadow rose slowly up out of the deep water almost to the surface before sinking back into the depths of the creek.

As we kept watching the pool of water, which was about twenty feet across and maybe forty feet long, we could see more of the shadows floating up toward the surface. That show went on for a while but just as suddenly as it had started, it ended. We saw no more of the mystery fish that day.

So when Granny asked me if I thought I felt like going fishing, it didn't take me long to answer. Yes. I had to promise her only two things. First, I absolutely had to avoid getting wet at any time. She was afraid that might cause a flare-up of my pox and make me really sick. The second thing I already knew about. We positively could not tell anyone about our trip. Especially not Mama. Ever.

Papa certainly wasn't about to miss out on another crack at the mystery monsters that were hiding out down there at our fishing spot, so he very quickly filled the minnow bucket from our springhouse cool water live-box where we had stashed enough horny-head minnows for a fishing trip and off we headed down the road with our cane poles.

We followed the old road running due south from our house along the west side of the branch down past Uncle George's new ground where it intersected the east-west road that went from the Black Springs road all the way through to hit the Lodi road down close to the Joe Lawless place. We only had to walk about a half mile on that road before turning off on a foot path at the Uncle Thaddie Miller place to go down to the creek.

We hit the creek just above the place where we planned to start fishing, the stump hole, and this was where the trail crossed the main creek in a shallow set of riffles that were easy to wade. Normally I would have been the first across the creek here, but today was a different story.

Granny didn't have to tell me. I stopped while she bent down and let me crawl onto her back, then she slowly and carefully waded the creek. Papa carried all the poles and minnow bucket so she could hold onto a stout pole that she used to keep her balance. We both knew it wouldn't be smart for her to lose her balance and dump me off into the water now.

We soon had our cane poles set out on the bank awaiting some action. And it wasn't long before we began to catch a few bass. For some reason, catching bass seemed to be a little dull. What we wanted was to snag one of the big dark shadows that were again sliding almost close enough to the surface for us to be able to see what they were.

But try as we might, we could not get them to even offer to take a minnow. That was very frustrating. We knew they had to eat something sometime, but what and when? Papa decided to try something different.

He cut a couple of long, straight Alder poles from along the bank of the creek, making sure that he had some that were stout enough for whatever we were going after. He tied a line on each of the poles and we put a hook with a very small sinker on, baited the hook with just a tiny piece of earthworm that we had with us, and started easing the bait along close to the surface where we were seeing the shadows floating.

Nothing happened at first and I began to think that these were just ghost fish. That thought had just entered my mind when all of a sudden I felt my line go taut. Something had taken the hook and was going to the bottom. I looked over at Papa to see if he had noticed, and I saw that he had one on too!

We set the hooks at about the same time I guess, because all I remember in the next few minutes was a lot of hollering and maybe even some random cussing while Granny scrambled around frantically trying to get the cane poles and lines out of our way.

Papa yelled something particularly blasphemous and Granny and I both knew his fish was gone. So was his line, which had snapped off before he could even catch sight of what he had hooked. My fish was still on but I was not in control of the situation at all.

I looked at my Alder pole, which I had calculated to be strong enough to handle any fish that swam in this water, but I saw that it was bent almost double. I hauled on it harder, trying to get some movement out of my fish which seemed to have anchored itself to the bottom of the world. I finally felt him give a little, and then I felt him coming slowly to the top.

Now I have caught a lot of fish in my life since that day, but nothing has ever topped that one. I don't know how big he was and I never really found out for sure what he was, but when he rolled his big, black back on the surface and headed back to the bottom, he snapped my pole in half like it was a matchstick!

I fell backward on the bank of the creek, shaking like a leaf, not knowing whether to laugh or cry. Granny was laughing so hard she was crying, so I just joined her.

We heard rumors later that summer that there was a big fish coming up out of the lake that was called a Blackhorse sucker. They wouldn't take a bait of any kind but some folks had managed to catch them by using a snagging or treble hook.

We never managed to hook another one after that day, which was okay. The important thing was, however, as far as Granny and I knew, Mama never found out about this fishing trip.

* * *

Whoever came up with the game we played most of the time at school should have received the Nobel Peace Prize for Schoolyard Diplomacy. Of all the fights over marbles, over girls (or between girls), and all the other playground disputes that took place on a multi-daily basis, I can never recall a single incident that came close to being a problem when we played work-up ball.

Maybe it was the amazing simplicity of the concept that made it work so well. Or it could have been that we all secretly desired one thing in our lives that wouldn't be a threat to our health and welfare.

For the first few years after the new schoolhouse was built, we had no gymnasium and the basketball court was a hard-packed clay dirt court out behind the school building. I remember watching games there before the gym was built and I know that Dad had grown up and gone to school playing on such a surface, but by the time I was in school most places had some kind of indoor basketball court.

There were five towns in Pike County with schools: Glenwood, Kirby,

Murfreesboro, Delight, and Langley. Langley was the stepchild of the bunch for sure, being smaller and poorer in every way, including playing basketball on a dirt surface. So as soon as the school building proper was paid off, or maybe even before, a new gymnasium was built.

It was a nice building, also rock masonry, although not nearly as beautifully built as the schoolhouse. But it had a smoothly finished oak floor with painted lines and the echoes rebounded from far up in the rafters when a ball was bounced inside with no crowds in the bleachers. The court was only slightly smaller than the building, especially at the ends, with only about three feet between each end of the court and the wall.

On the sides the court was about that same distance from the first row of bleachers. Bleachers consisted of about four rows of seats along the sides of the court, with another four rows located upstairs in a balcony. Upstairs seating had to be fairly steep for the folks sitting in the back row to be able to see all of the floor below.

As proud as we were of the new gymnasium, and especially proud of the fact that Langley was about to be chosen to finally host the big county tournament that would be the culmination of that year's basketball season, we had lost something in the process. Our baseball field.

That had always been where we spent much of our recess times before losing it, and now it was sitting directly underneath the new gym. One of our neighbors came to the rescue though, as Claude Lowery cleared off a spot in one of his fields that was adjacent to the school ground, even leveling it up to make a decent baseball field for us. That's where our work-up games were played.

As I said, the game was very simple. Four people became batters, usu-ally chosen arbitrarily but almost always decided by who got out to the field and grabbed a bat first. Catcher, pitcher, and the four infielders were also occupied on pretty much a first-come, first-served basis.

The outfield was filled with everyone else, with no limit on numbers who could be in the outfield. Fortunately for our purposes, we usually only had enough players to fill the required positions, with no more than half a dozen extra outfielders.

The object of the game was simple. Bat as long as possible. And the way to do that was to not get put out during your turn at bat. A strikeout, put-out at a base, or caught fly ball meant you were done. That batter went immediately to the back of the line, which was the outfield.

The new batter who would replace the one who had been put out came from one of two methods. If the batter struck out or was put out on a base, all the infielders moved up one place, with the catcher taking his turn as batter. If, however, the out was made by someone catching a fly ball in the infield or outfield, then whoever caught the ball took the batter's place.

The game was fraught with potential conflicts over things like strikes and balls, ground-outs that might have been close calls, and even which outfielder was actually in line to move in to third base after a put-out. But I remember this game as being carried out in a particularly civilized manner, probably as close to an honor system situation as ever existed at the Langley school.

For one thing, there were no winners or losers as such, no Lodi against Langley groups or teams. We also knew that when the bell rang for classes that game ended, but another one would take up at the next recess.

It would be a few more years before I began to play more serious baseball on one of the many sandlot and other teams that I played for over the years, but I don't think I ever enjoyed the sport any more than during those recess work-up games.

And baseball would occupy a big portion of my life from those days forward.

16

 Summer comes on slow at seven thousand feet in elevation in Northern New Mexico. By May they would be wanting to get out in the woods, and sometimes they would brave up and head out somewhere on a sunny Saturday, but they always ran up against the snowline or high spring runoff and ended up eating a picnic lunch on the side of the road before heading back to Taos.

But finally the high sun drove the cold on up into Colorado and summer would be there.

The best times were the summer weekends when they didn't have company. It was always nice to have the folks out for a visit but that meant entertaining instead of exploring, and exploring is what they enjoyed most. He would start loading the Dodge pickup on Friday night if it was going to be a full weekend camping trip.

The old green tent, foam mattress pads, the big double sleeping bag that stayed zipped together for most of their lives, and the two smaller bags for the boys. She would get the food ready, maybe fry a chicken to take along for the first meal, and pack a few clothes in a duffle.

Saturday morning would find them rolling out of Taos heading in any one of the cardinal directions, but usually west, sometimes north, but rarely east or south for camping. The mountains east of town were higher and steeper and far less accessible, plus they usually held the snow pack until at least the middle of the summer. And they were close enough for the other kind of exploring they liked to do, which was one day drives into the woods.

Across the Rio Grande at the high bridge, or sometimes down river on the low bridge above Pilar where they would drop down the steep grade to the river and climb back out to go over through Carson to Taos Junction. From there they could head down to Ojo Caliente and back into the national forest toward the old settlements that were scattered across the landscape.

La Madera, El Rito, Vallecitos, Petaca, Las Tablas, Servilleta Plaza…the names themselves invited nothing if not investigation on a warm Saturday afternoon. They would stop along the way at one of the old country stores to buy any last minute items they needed, or maybe a cold pop for the four of them, marveling at the way time had stood still in these establishments that had served the native people so well.

They would pass several campgrounds along the way, from primitive little roadside areas to fancier spots where camp trailers might be seen mixed in with a few tents. These did not interest them in the least. The boys (and he) would have gone back home before they would stay in such a place. If they couldn't find a spot that was all theirs, they just hadn't gone far enough back into the boondocks.

So it was that they usually drove the pickup to the very end of the road, or maybe even just a tad further, before settling on a particularly inviting looking flat spot under perfectly arranged Ponderosa Pine trees with maybe even a tiny trout stream running nearby that would be theirs alone to fish and putter in.

Such places included the end of the road camping trip they took one weekend when they drove up through Vallecitos to Canon Plaza, then instead of staying on the main road that went back out to the highway and Tres Piedras, they kept going up into the forest where they crossed the Rio Vallecitos, drove on through a small piece of private ground called the Jaramillo ranch, and ran out of road up against the boundary of the huge Tierra Amarilla land grant.

When they had their tent set up and were ready for the evening, he hiked down through Escondido canyon to the east of camp and came into an area that was called the Vallecitos Box. He never saw a better fishing place than this anywhere.

The river was not that big but here it was hemmed in on both sides by sheer rock walls that made travel up and down stream impossible except by clambering over the huge boulders that littered the bottom of the canyon and formed waterfalls and pools where he took huge cut-throat trout on flies at every cast until his arms were too tired to lift the rod any more. He kept a half dozen of the nicer fish for dinner that night and they put them in foil with butter and laid them on the coals of the campfire. She fried a pan of potatoes and they knew that nothing could taste better than such a meal as this.

The next day the boys played on the old logs lying around the area from a past timber sale, rode slender aspen trees to the ground and bounced up and down on them like they were riding in a mighty rodeo, and afterwards they all hiked a trail far down into the upper reaches of the river canyon. When they stopped to eat their picnic lunch they could hear the roar of the water below and he promised to bring the little ones back some day when they were big enough to fish with him.

Similar trips were taken on almost every free weekend during the summers they spent in Taos. And most weekends were free. It was what they enjoyed the most and only cost them a few dollars in gas. They might break down once or twice a year and drive down to Santa Fe, or maybe even as far as Albuquerque, to see a movie or do some shopping, but those were rare occasions. They always felt like they had lost a weekend if they didn't go to the woods.

And it seemed like every trip ended up with some memorable moment that they would always look back on with pleasure. They took several long camping trips across the high bridge to Tres Piedras and on up past San Antone Mountain toward a series of little lakes far back on the edge of the national forest. The general area was called Lagunitas.

One such trip ended a day early when they drove down into a canyon where the Rio San Antonio was small enough to step across at any spot, but where he caught six-to-eight inch rainbow trout on every cast.

They had a perfect camp site right on the bank of the creek and the water in the creek was cold enough to make the watermelon they brought along taste so good after they left it to cool overnight.

The next morning after breakfast they planned to go on a brief hike back down the old road they had driven in on, but they had only gone a few hundred feet when she saw something in the sand that changed everything on that trip. There, plain as day, was a huge bear track.

The old bear had walked right up the road in their fresh vehicle tracks. He didn't try to talk her into staying the second night, knowing full well he had no good argument.

Another trip on the other side of the Lagunitas road resulted in them camping on the top of a rock bluff at the end of a two-track road that dropped off into a place called Cruces basin. One of the most beautiful spots they found to camp, their tent was sitting on a hill that looked down into a fisherman's paradise.

Three smaller streams came together just upstream from their camp, and they could see all three meandering for a mile up through the wide meadow. The larger stream that was formed below this confluence was the Los Pinos River, a fairly good sized stream that runs in and out of the New Mexico-Colorado northern boundary all the way down to Antonito.

The creeks were named Beaver, Diablo, and Cruces, and he couldn't wait to fish all three. Camp was a couple hundred feet in elevation above the streams and there was a good, if steep, trail down to the meadow where he would start fishing. She said she would hike down with him and let the boys watch him fish a while, then she would take them back to camp as he fished on up one of the creeks.

They crossed the creek at the bottom and he started fishing right away. The boys played along on the bank and in the creek below where he was fishing, and after he had gone about five hundred feet upstream, she decided it was time to go back to camp.

They had seen an old dim road or cow trail that cut across the meadow and headed back toward camp, so he suggested that she and the boys take that path to camp instead of wandering back along the creek bank. It was a shorter route and they could see camp all the way from the trail they would be on.

She and the little boys left him to his fishing and went out of sight for a few minutes over a little rise, and then he was startled to hear a scream. It was definitely her voice, but that wasn't all! He heard two more smaller screams. They were all yelling at the tops of their voices!

He threw his fishing rod to the ground and ran full speed back up on the bank and around the corner so he could catch a glimpse of what he thought surely would be a bear dragging the three of them off to his winter's den. What else could it be, he thought, as he wished for something larger than the twenty-two pistol he had strapped on his belt?

He saw them standing in the meadow in the middle of the cow path, and as far as he could tell, there were no bears around. But he did notice that both boys were as high up on her hips as they could get, and they were still trying to climb higher. The screaming subsided somewhat as they saw that he was running as fast as he possibly could in his wading boots. What is it, he hollered as soon as the noise had died down enough that he thought they might hear him? The boys were both pointing at the deep grass along each side of the trail, and she had calmed down enough to utter one word. Snakes!!! Everywhere, she finally added.

He looked along the ground but didn't see anything. Knowing it could have been rattlesnakes since they were close to some rocky ground, he got a long stick and started poking around in the grass along the edge of the trail. Soon he saw what it was. Garter snakes.

And there really were quite a few of them, as he could see as they slithered away from him as he walked along the trail in front of them. But as far as she and the boys were concerned, they may as well have been huge diamondback rattlers. They weren't going anywhere without an escort back to clear ground.

That wouldn't be the last encounter one of the boys would have with a snake, as another camping trip back across the road on another weekend found the oldest one playing by himself inside the tent during the warm afternoon. She was sitting in a lounge chair reading a book and the smaller boy was sleeping on a blanket beside her. The older boy had zipped the entrance fly on the tent and had been playing quietly inside, but suddenly she heard him yell and when she turned around he was frantically unzipping the fly as fast as he could.

He barely got enough of an opening to fit through before launching himself out of the tent, white as a sheet. It seems a big garter snake had also liked the warm, dark green tent and decided to invite itself inside. This time she and the boys took care of the snake with a shovel while he kept on fishing.

All of their fun wasn't limited to their camping trips though. Even the day trips to the woods could end up being an adventure as well. Like the Friday afternoon after work on one of the long summer days when he figured they had time to make a two or three hour run out south of town and up into the mountains on an old logging road that they hadn't explored before.

It was called the Bear Wallow Road, a romantic enough name, and it headed back up into a section of the national forest that had only recently been added as some kind of land swap after the private timber company had logged it over pretty heavily. His friend Sabino Trujillo had told him about the road and said it would be a nice trip some evening after work.

The road turned off the highway up into the forest about five miles out of Ranchitos and they had jumped into the pickup that evening without planning to take anything along with them since they would be back in time for dinner.

It was a fun road, climbing into the forest quickly and going along the north slope of one of the main ridges that ran back into the old Pot Creek Land Grant. It seemed to be a well-constructed logging road, not too steep, and even had several "water-bars" constructed into it to keep the rain water from running down the ruts too far and eroding the surface.

But it was one of those water-bars that did them in that night. They were zipping right on up the mountain when they went over a pretty good hump in the road that was the lower end of the rolling dip or water bar, and just as the front of the pickup dove into the mucky wet mudhole on the upper side of the hump, he knew they were in trouble.

The pickup was front-heavy at best, and tonight it was worse than normal because all four of them were sitting in the cab of the truck while the bed underneath the canopy at the rear was mostly empty. There was a shovel back there, which he always carried, and a couple of folding aluminum lounge chairs that had been left in for some reason. That was about it.

At first he thought they could surely back out of the mudhole because the road sloped back down behind them fairly steeply. But even with the positive-traction rear end on the Dodge, which kept both rear wheels spinning at all times, it was no use.

The front end was buried down to the axle in the soft area that had been doing such a great job of diverting water away from the road during rainfall, but was also just in the right place to hold all of the water that had seeped out of the steadily flowing spring on the upper side of the road.

He shoveled and pushed while she tried to drive the pickup out, but the more they worked, the deeper the hole became. There was nothing to do except admit it. They were stuck, seriously stuck. And he knew one other thing. There would be no good-samaritan come along to help them out tonight, nor tomorrow. Nor probably even in the next two weeks. This was a very lightly used road, which was one reason he had chosen it. But now he wished for a little more company.

They ate the small bag of cookies she had stuck in at the last minute and drank the coffee which was still hot in the thermos. That was it for food. He looked around and found a semi-level spot off the road where he built a little warming fire and set out the two lounge chairs.

They would have to spend the night here for sure. There was no other good option. It was a good five miles back out to the highway and he knew they wouldn't want to make that hike and still have to try and catch a ride back to town for help. It was almost dark and would be before they could get down to the highway and he surely wasn't going to hike out alone and leave them there in the dark. That wasn't one of the options.

So they would spend the night. No problem. At first they sat around the campfire enjoying the evening just like a normal camping trip. Then it started raining! They moved into the pickup and spent the rest of the night there sitting in the cramped cab, trying to sleep a little, or at least trying to stay comfortable.

He started the pickup engine occasionally to warm the engine enough to keep them from being too cold. Luckily the weather was fairly mild that night, in spite of the rainfall, and they managed to make it through a very long night.

At first light he hit the road and walked back to the highway where he quickly caught a ride into town and borrowed a four-wheel drive jeep. Back up on the mountain he easily pulled the pickup out of the mudhole and turned it around, but knew she would have to drive it back to town since he would be driving the borrowed vehicle.

The problem was that the pickup was not only a stick-shift, which she had never really learned to drive very well, it was a Dodge stick-shift. Meaning that the clutch was horribly touchy and had not one ounce of forgiveness for the uninitiated. She reluctantly took the wheel.

And she made it just fine down off the mountain and even back through Ranchitos and into town. He was in a big hurry to get the borrowed vehicle back so he drove on ahead. He worried a little when he saw that she had caught the stop light coming up the hill into town, but he went on to return the jeep.

That stop light just happened to be located in the middle of a steep little hill, meaning that she had to stop the pickup, push in the clutch and hold it, and hold the brake to keep from rolling back down the hill.

She managed to take care of that part okay, but when the light changed to green, she now had to execute the most difficult part of stick-shift driving.

Put the truck in gear, let off on the brake, and at the same time, <u>ease out on the clutch</u> until the vehicle moves forward. This nasty little maneuver is tricky at best, but when combined with the worst clutch setup ever to come out of Detroit, it could frustrate even the most expert stick-shift operator, which she wasn't.

He hurried on up to drop his borrowed vehicle off a few blocks on up the road, waiting there for her to come pick him up. He waited. And he waited some more. Surely she knew where he was going to be waiting, he thought. Why isn't she here?

Why she wasn't there was because she was back down at the stoplight trying to get that (numerous bad words strung together) Dodge pickup to cooperate! By the time she finally showed up, it was obvious to him that it would be a while before she would be in the mood for another quick trip out to the mountains.

She parked the Dodge on the side of the road when she met him, slamming the door to emphasize her unhappiness with the whole idea of what he had left her with.

He never did find out for sure if she managed to lurch the beast on up the hill or if some poor soul who happened to be stuck behind them had offered to help her out of the jam. At the moment she was not in the mood to volunteer that information, and he knew that he had pushed his luck way too far already that weekend to even think about asking for additional details.

But there was one thing he was pretty sure of: She would never get behind the wheel of that old Dodge pickup again.

***

Why do you keep this old thing?

She always asked him about the Blazer, knowing that it would get a rise out of him. Especially if they were riding in it at the time, which they were now. He liked to drive it occasionally just to keep the battery charged, and to make sure it still ran okay. He wasn't too worried about how it would be running. It had never failed him yet.

Well, I used to think I would keep it so I could be buried in it.

He laughed, but she didn't think it was that funny. That idea had been squelched by the oldest son's comment.

Not gonna happen, he had said emphatically.

We might prop you up behind the wheel for the visitation, but you're going in the ground without "my" Blazer.

He was actually pleased to hear that one of them might feel almost as attached to the vehicle as he was. Almost, but not quite. He could never fully explain what his feelings were about it, but he knew it was about all the times they had spent together as a family, all the times he had spent with his Dad on their hunting trips, and all the other memories that were connected by one common thread. An old yellow 1971 Chevy Blazer.

She always told people when they asked about it that he would have their yard filled with all the old cars and pickups they had owned if she would let him. That was partly true, of course, as he still cringed when he thought about selling off their 1968 Dodge Charger with the 440 Magnum engine.

The boys had even talked him into restoring one of those old gas burners after he had retired, and he had enjoyed working on it for a while, but then it became a job and he lost interest and sold it to a real car nut who could do it justice.

And of course he always wished they could somehow have parked her first car in a shed back in Arkansas so they could still have it. It was a 1956 Chevrolet, which is a fairly common antique car still today. But this one was not a common model at all. It was the 210 Sport Coupe model, a relatively rare version that he had not seen at any of the car shows in all the years since.

But he had managed to hang on to the Blazer, even doing some light restoration work on it over the years although it had not needed much because he had pampered it and kept it garaged most of its life. The yellow ochre paint faded after twenty five years so he had it repainted, using the original factory paint.

And a friend of his who was a mechanic had completely restored the engine from the bottom up, replacing any moving part that might possibly be worn at all. So it was pretty much all original and ran and drove about like it always had. That was good and bad.

He thought about how they had come to own it in the first place. It was when they were living in Albuquerque that they had seen a for sale sign in the window of the vehicle one Sunday at the church they were attending. They had a car, the Charger, and he had his Dodge pickup which had been a very good truck for their camping trips and his hunting trips.

But even though they had built a home-made canopy for it, put in a platform bed and an intercom in the back so the boys could ride back there part of the time on longer trips, they knew they needed something with a little more room with another baby coming along real soon. She was eight months pregnant at the time.

So they sold the pickup and bought the Blazer. The owners were Alberto and Kaye LePore, a very nice older couple who lived in another neighborhood and happened to go to the same church. Alberto was a real estate salesman and he said he had bought the Blazer thinking it would be good for taking his clients around to the various real estate holdings that he was involved in.

He probably couldn't have bought a vehicle that would have been less suited for such a task. It was a very nice vehicle with top of the line for that year amenities, but it was still just basically a four-wheel drive utility rig. Two people could ride comfortably in the front bucket seats, but to get into the back seat, the passenger side seat had to be tilted forward and the rider had to climb up into the vehicle to sit in what was a fairly small bench seat.

That rear bench seat was perfect for three small children, but not particularly suited for an adult looking to buy a lot or a house from Alberto. He quickly recognized his mistake after only a few months and a few thousand miles, and they were happy to take it off his hands for several thousand dollars less than the original retail price. She even made the claim that owning the rough riding, short wheel-based bouncy Chevy had caused their daughter to come into the world earlier than planned.

But they had put many miles on it before leaving New Mexico for Oregon, and many more after coming to the Northwest. He still told people about one of their first trips they had made in it up to meet friends on a weekend camping trip at the elk camp site:

His parents were visiting them at the time and they had driven their car behind the Blazer as they traveled north from Albuquerque up to Santa Fe and Espanola. He decided to go on around through Canjilon instead of turning off to El Rito, planning to show them some different scenery along the road up past Canjilon Lakes and over the Mogote divide where they would drop down to meet their friends who would be waiting at the camp.

As they turned off the highway at Canjilon, he noticed a very dark cloud hanging up over the mountain ahead but the road was still dry so they went on. Not long after driving out of Canjilon they left the semi-paved road behind and he began to sense trouble. Rain began to pelt the windshield and the road was soon wet and becoming very slick.

The road surface consisted of two types of material: First there were the boulders. Then came the glacial till. There was nothing in between. So traveling the road now became simply an exercise in trying to miss the larger boulders while maintaining enough momentum to keep from sliding off into the ditch on the left side, or worse, sliding off the hillside on the right.

He was pulling their tent trailer with the Blazer and made it fine up to the spot where the roads forked, with one branch turning left to go on up to Canjilon Lakes, which was a very popular fishing area. Since this was a holiday weekend there was a lot of traffic heading up toward the lakes. They had seen several other vehicles coming along behind them after they left town.

The other fork of the road went straight ahead. For some strange reason that he could never quite understand, the road from this point on up to the lakes was actually paved, even though the five miles of road back down to town was just mud and rocks.

The road on over the top, a climb of another four miles and several hundred feet vertically, was more mud and rocks. Except worse. They pulled over onto the pavement at the lakes turnoff and talked it over.

He knew they were in trouble but it was getting late in the day and if they turned around and went back around through El Rito it was going to be very late when they got to camp. But if they tried to go on up the road they might spend the night in the ditch up there somewhere. Not very good options.

Probably more to stall off the decision than anything else, he and his Dad decided to unhook the trailer from the Blazer and drive on up the road toward the divide to see how bad it was. He didn't tell his Dad that the four-wheel drive wasn't working on the Blazer at the time because he had snapped a bolt off a few days earlier when trying to force it into low range. That problem became much more serious than he had imagined when they clawed their way up through the black gumbo-like mud until they finally could see the top.

One of the main problems with the road was that the forest service had chosen that particular time to grade the road. He figured it had probably only been graded about every ten years or so, but now the freshly bladed soil filled all the old ruts and he was having trouble staying out of the ditches.

Luckily they had not met a single vehicle on the way up the side of the mountain. If they had, it would have been disastrous because there was no way to meet or pass on this road under these conditions.

He breathed a sigh of relief as they came to the top of the hill, but his relief was very short lived. When he stopped the Blazer on top to decide what to do next, he felt the rig begin to slide sideways. He was totally helpless at that point and they could do nothing to stop the inevitable drift off into the ditch.

It was some relief to see that the ditch was only a couple of feet deep. But it may as well have been bottomless because when he tried to drive out of it they were totally stuck. No movement forward or backward. The tires were completely covered with several inches of black muck, and only the rear tires had power due to the transfer pin problem.

Well, what else was there to do except get out and hike back down the mountain to join the women and children in the Polara?

About the time they were ready to abandon ship, they saw a vehicle coming up the road in front of them. The only other person they had seen since leaving the campground turnoff came driving up in an old Jeep pickup. He not only pulled them out of the ditch with ease, he managed to help them skid the Blazer around to head back down the hill in the other direction.

They were not looking forward to going back down the way they had come up because he knew the traction would be even worse going downhill than up. But the Jeep made a nice straight rut in front of them, which they got into and stayed with until they made it to where they had left the car.

He quickly hooked up the trailer and they started back down the road to Canjilon, thinking they had slipped out of the noose. But when they came around the first turn in the road, the sight they saw looking down the road ahead was as ugly as it gets. At least half a dozen rigs of every kind were hanging in ditches on one side or half off the hillside on the other.

Some people were pulling large camping trailers and these were almost all jackknifed and hopelessly stuck. They were going to be on this road a long time, that was for sure. Maybe all night, the way it looked.

But to their amazement, the Lone Samaritan in the old Jeep pickup started hooking onto first one then another rig, and in a surprisingly short amount of time, everyone was turned around and headed back toward Canjilon.

They hit the pavement somewhere above town but didn't get out of black mud for at least another couple of miles because every vehicle had carried about a hundred pounds of the stuff back down off the mountainside.

When they finally pulled into camp around midnight, their friends woke up long enough to say hello and tell them that they had already decided that someone had made the bad decision to come through Canjilon instead of El Rito.

He fixed the transfer case lever when they got back to Albuquerque, but of course they never needed it any worse than that rainy Fourth of July weekend.

"Those were the days my friend
We thought they'd never end
We'd sing and dance
Forever and a day."
—Mary Hopkins

17

 Looking back, I don't see how I could have been interested in playing anything other than baseball. Not only was baseball the primary professional sport that was available for the country folks to listen to on the radio, it was the main occupation every weekend from early spring until late fall.

Almost every little community put together some kind of baseball team and I started playing with the adults, some who were Dad's age or older, when I was still too young to play basketball on the school teams. In fact, when I started playing on the local team, Dad was playing along beside me, usually at first base by then because he didn't run too well and his throwing arm was about shot.

Dad had his own baseball story which I didn't know much about. All I knew was that I had heard rumors that he might have played a little professional ball before I came along. I did find out a few of the details one day as Dad and I were driving back home together from a trip to Little Rock.

It seems he was home one weekend during his stint with the CCC (Civilian Conservation Corps) and a friend was visiting relatives in Langley (Claude and Lavelle Lowery). This fellow told Dad that one of his main reasons for coming to Langley was to contact him with the news that he was about to receive a contract from the Siloam Springs baseball team, which was a member of the Class D Arkansas-Missouri league. The league at the time consisted of six clubs, three in Arkansas (Siloam Springs, Fayetteville, and Rogers) and three in Missouri.

The friend, a fellow named Pete Parker, was playing with Siloam Springs that year and had told his manager that he had a friend in Southwest Arkansas who could make the team. Shortly thereafter a contract arrived in the mail from the parent club, which was the St. Louis Browns, and Dad said he was so excited that he hesitated to mail it back for fear of it getting lost in the mail somewhere. He even thought about hand-delivering it.

So after signing on with the team and playing for awhile, he said he was disappointed to see that there were sandlot teams around Langley that could have competed with any of these "professionals." A few weeks later he said they found out that Rogers Hornsbys' brother had come down to look the situation over and everyone knew something was up. One of the Missouri teams had folded and a team from Northeast Oklahoma was supposed to take their place if they could reach an agreement with some major league club. No agreement was reached and with only five teams left, the league disbanded.

Everyone on the team was offered a tryout with the Class C Muskogee club for the next year, but since he was already twenty-five years old Dad said he knew there was no reason to continue. Thus ended his brief tour in professional baseball, but I always wondered how life would have turned out differently if he had been given such a chance when he was younger.

Dad had told me some of this as we were driving home one weekend after my own aborted effort at playing baseball at a higher level than the sandlot leagues I had been playing in so far. The Kansas City Athletics had held a tryout in Little Rock and somehow I had been invited up, along with a couple hundred other boys, to let some of the local scouts look over the potential "big leaguers."

I had gone up with my spikes and glove and an old ratty uniform that came from one or the other of the local teams that I had played for.

Things started well for me that Saturday morning as all two hundred of us lined up for the first activity, which was a sprint from the first base dugout area to the left field fence and back. I should have signed my contract right after this event because I was fast, only losing this speed contest to one other guy by a few steps.

But coming in second in the foot race was the only thing that went right for me that day. The next thing the scouts did was to send about half the two hundred of us to the outfield where they proceeded to "fungo" one long fly ball after another in our direction. I think about six guys ended up fighting over every ball while the rest of us stood by and watched.

After an hour or so of that seemingly worthless exercise they rotated my group into the infield area where the boys who had been taking infield practice then moved out to take fly balls.

I was looking forward to something that made a little more sense to me, plus I had played a lot of infield during my early days. And it started out okay for me. We lined up on the sidelines and took our turns going out to shortstop where a guy sent a couple-dozen grounders out for each of us to field and throw to first base. I liked the looks of that exercise.

But then disaster struck, as I took my place and took quick care of the first two or three ground balls that were sent my way. My throws to first were accurate but not that strong. I was getting prepared to put a little more zip in my next throw when the guy doing the batting miss-hit the next grounder and instead of a ground ball, he hit a sharp line drive right at me.

Normally that would have been no problem for me at all, but I guess I was already a little nervous and in my desire to make doubly sure I didn't miss an easy liner, I used both hands. When I did the ball caught my right (throwing) hand dead straight on the end of my fingers! Ouch.

I knew I was in trouble right away, although I had caught the ball and no one could tell that it had caught me too. But when I went to make that zippier throw to first, I could barely grip the ball tightly enough to throw it at all.

Here is where I was just too timid to get myself out of this pickle. Instead of admitting that I had completely numbed my fingers on my throwing hand and asking for a relief fielder until I could regain the feeling in my fingers, I just kept right on scooping up balls and tossing them to first with almost nothing on the ball.

Dad didn't even know what had happened until later when we broke for lunch and I met him up in the bleachers where he was watching the action. He was as disappointed as I was I'm sure, but he understood what had happened. He thought perhaps I had hurt my arm trying to throw harder than I normally would have, but I showed him my fingertips which had turned a nice shade of purple under a couple of nails.

We stuck around that afternoon through one round of batting practice and when I pretty much flunked that too because I couldn't grip the bat that well, I told him I was done with the big leagues. He wanted me to stay and participate in the final trial, which was a simulated game, and I always felt bad that I gave up so easily.

Later when he told me the story of his brush with the big leagues, I understood why he had been so disappointed in the way the day turned out for me.

* * *

Mama hadn't exactly had an easy life herself, although she never really talked about it. She did have her folks living in the house with us now, and what I knew about her family at the time consisted of yearly visits back and forth between Arkansas and West or South Texas, where her sisters lived with their families.

All, that is, except for Aunt Nora Brooks, who lived fairly close by at Newhope, just twenty miles or so down the road.

Nora and Tom, along with Cousin Alice, lived in the back half of a little house right across the road from the store in Newhope. The front half of the house was where Uncle Tom did his cobbling work. In those days, this was a pretty decent way to scratch out a living.

Shoes were bought to be worn a long time and most of us only had one pair at a time so they received a lot of hard wear and tear. Tom had all the tools required to keep those shoes in shape for a few more years. There were heavy steel shoe lasts of each size standing over against the wall. These lasts were used to take a worn out sole off and replace it with a new sole, or to add a "half-sole" if the original wasn't too far gone.

There were various cutting, trimming, and polishing machines that would be used to finish up the leather work or to make the new soles conform to the original shape of the shoes. Heavy duty sewing machines would be used to stitch the leather as necessary and the house always smelled strongly of linseed oil or whatever he used to soften and preserve his work.

Nora and Tom were both deaf and we all learned enough sign language from them to be able to communicate. Granny, Papa, and Mama were all able to carry on the animated conversations that usually occurred whenever we were around Nora.

Alice helped us kids learn to communicate because she was not hearing impaired at all and would usually speak her words as well as sign them when she was talking around folks with hearing, unless she wanted to keep a secret from someone. Then she could be as tricky as the best signer!

Nora had gone away to the Texas School for the Deaf in Austin when they had lived in West Texas. Papa worked as a sharecropper on farms around Snyder in those years and Granny spent most of her time taking care of a house full of young girls, including Mama.

There were five of the girls, including the oldest, Nora, and there had been one other girl, Lorene, who had died before her first birthday about ten years before Mama came along.

But there had also been a little boy. Mama and the sisters still talked about their brother, Cobert. I wondered a lot about him myself because he seemed to have had a life very much like mine, the only boy among five sisters; similar to my life with three sisters.

From what I gathered, he had enjoyed life just like I was enjoying it in those days. Granny always seemed sad when any mention was made of Cobert, and I knew that Papa didn't ever talk about him at all. What I didn't know until long after they were both gone was just how hard it had been on them when he died.

Aunt Nora was very sentimental and kept everything. After she died Alice gave Mama two letters that Nora had saved all those years. They were from Papa and were written to her while she was away in the Deaf School in Austin:

"Snyder Tex R#4
2-14-26

Dear Nora,
    This will let you know we have had to give up Cobert. He died this morning at 2 o'clock. We wish you was hear but he will be buried when you get this. 'Tis sad indeed to part from him, but 'tis sweet to know he is in a better world. The rest are all well. Hope these few lines will find you well.
    With sadness from Papa"

And the second letter:

"Snyder Tex

Feb 15, 1926

Dear Nora,

I am sending you some of the flowers that was put on your dear little brother's grave. We are so lonesome we can't hardly stand it. It was hard to give him up, he wanted to get well so bad. Cheer up dear and just put your trust in the good (lord), he will give us peace. Brother McDerment said the Lord knew best. I will write often. From your lonesome Mother and Father to our dear little Nora."

Cobert had come down with pneumonia and was buried in the cold hard ground near Dunn, Texas at the age of eleven. I wished I could have known him. I think we would have had a lot of fun together.

* * *

I had a friend, Albert, who was there to play whatever games we dreamed up on the weekends, and my friend Mike was there to fill my recesses at school with fun and some protection from the bullies. All I needed now was someone to teach me a few of the finer points of the outdoor life.

That's where Nolan came in. Nolan Dowdy lived across the hill to the south of us with his parents and a sister, and he was the best woodsman I ever met, bar none.

We had big woods all around our place and even on the three forty-acre parcels that we were living on. Off to our north between our boundary and the main road from Langley to Lodi was a half mile stretch of mostly large southern yellow pine that was owned and managed by the Dierks lumber company.

In those days the only type of logging the company did was called selective harvesting, which meant they would come in every ten to fifteen years and take out a percentage of the larger pine trees, leaving the medium sized and smaller ones to grow. So the woods were always heavily timbered but mostly open underneath the big tree canopy.

In addition to the logging practices another thing that kept the woods clean and open was the habit of burning off the underbrush every few years. This wasn't something that was planned and done by the company. It was purely a matter of long standing practice by the natives living in the country, primarily to keep some new shrubs and grass coming up every year that would serve as food for the cows and hogs that might be roaming freely on company land.

The company didn't seem to mind the practice because in general it suited their purposes just fine. Without the fires and grazing, the underbrush would have quickly taken over and robbed the pine trees of nutrients as well as preventing pine seedlings from getting started.

Fire was actually required to open the pine cones and activate the seeds that were needed in naturally regenerating the forests. The days of clear-cutting and hand-planting seedlings were not even imagined.

On over to the west of our place was an area more suited to small game animals such as squirrels and rabbits. A hardwood flat ran from the west boundary of our farm all the way down to the Black Springs road. And to the south and east were more pine covered hills owned by the timber company and hardwood sections still owned by private individuals, most of whom had long since left their old homestead places behind.

These hills and draws were nothing but a paradise to Nolan and me as we took every opportunity to hunt and trap, and when we weren't hunting or trapping, we were hunting some other place where we could. My Dad was far too busy with school stuff to spend time hunting, even though there would come a time when we would make up for lost time.

Papa enjoyed hunting and fishing as much as anyone, and he did spend a lot of time with me doing both. But he was also responsible for trying to make the farm produce a little income and as much food for the family as possible. That kept him out of the woods during a lot of the prime hunting periods of the year.

The chief objective of our hunting activities was usually squirrels. Deer had pretty well been killed out during the depression and it was rare to even see a deer track. Most of the deer hunting in those days took place far up north of Langley in the Ouachita National Forest, or over west of Athens in some of the hill country where a few small bunches of deer had somehow survived the starvation years.

There were always plenty of squirrels, both the gray squirrel, which was smaller and tastier than the larger, red fox squirrel. We ate every squirrel we killed, of course, but Nolan and I were more in it for the sport so we didn't pass up any squirrel that we saw just because it might be a little tough to chew.

Some serious squirrel hunters in the country kept a little feist dog for treeing squirrels but we never had that luxury. My little bird dog companion, Queenie, was always by my side any time I was in the woods but she never caught on to the looking up part of the squirrel hunting. But that didn't slow Nolan and me down.

We became masters at what was truly "still hunting." I guess I should actually say that Nolan was a master of the technique. I was more of a dabbler.

Still hunting required one of the many traits for which I would never be famous: Patience. I can still see Nolan sprawled on his stomach under a group of big oak trees, not moving a muscle while he waits for the squirrel that he knows is up in the top of one of the trees to flinch and forget that someone is lying down below with a twenty-two rifle ready to shoot the noggin off, or better yet, bark the tree right by the squirrel's head and knock it unconscious and unmarked to the ground.

I have come upon him in these circumstances in the woods and one thing that always impressed me was that there would be at least a ten foot circle where every leaf or twig would have been slowly moved out of the way so that any movement he made would be silent.

Nolan had the only good squirrel gun either family owned, a little single shot twenty-two. We usually shot only "shorts" in it because they were cheaper and would do the job just as well as the bigger "longs" or "long rifles." And there was no such thing as wasting a shell on a practice shot.

I would sometimes carry Papa's squirrel gun, which happened to also be his deer gun and every other needs gun. He had a heavy old twelve gauge L. C. Smith double-barreled shotgun. It kicked so hard, even with the lighter squirrel-shot loads, that I would usually defer to Nolan's twenty-two unless we were in a situation where I had no choice.

At times we had to pull a complete surround job on an especially wary old squirrel, which meant one of us (usually Nolan because he could stay still and quiet) would take a position on one side of the tree, while the other, me, would go around to the other side and make enough noise to get the squirrel to want to wiggle around the tree away from the noise.

That usually meant coming into view of Nolan, and the twenty-two would crack and down would come supper. Sometimes the squirrel would simply stay put and hope that we either couldn't see him or else couldn't get a clear shot. They might be lying across a big limb where only the tail would show but everything else would be hidden by the limb. The shotgun came in handy at times to dislodge one from such a perch.

We pretty much hunted spring, summer, and fall, but when winter came, it was time for trapping. Nolan and I both had a half dozen small traps and the word was out that animal skins were bringing a pretty penny. Actually they were bringing just a little more than a penny, but enough to make us want to learn another life skill. Trapping 'possums.

We didn't necessarily intend to specialize in opossums so much as that was what was available to the semi-skilled trapper. There were plenty of raccoons and even a fair number of the ultimate hide animal, mink. But 'possums were plentiful and they were easy to catch, while raccoons required a lot more skill.

I never even heard of anyone in our school catching a mink, they were so wary of traps. And there was one other animal that could be trapped, although we never actually set out to catch one on purpose. That was a skunk, or as some called them, polecat.

We soon had our territory pretty well figured out so that we had located many of the old snags that had rotted out near the base of the tree where we could set a trap inside the opening and place a small piece of rotten meat behind the trap. That set usually resulted in catching an opossum, or occasionally a skunk.

Raccoon sets required that we place our traps along the edge of a stream where these critters liked to catch crawfish or other types of water bugs, and we would invariably find our traps thrown but no raccoon in sight.

There were mail-order places where we could send a stretched and dried hide. The average price paid for an opossum hide was ten cents while raccoons brought between twenty-five and thirty-five cents, depending on the size.

Skunk hides actually paid about the same as raccoons, but required considerably more skill (or less concern for one's personal aroma) than a 'coon. Not in the catching, mind you. In the follow-up activities.

We had heard that a mink might bring as much as three or four dollars a hide, but we figured we would find a gold nugget lying in the stream before we would catch a mink.

It turns out that the catching in the trap part of trapping was actually the easiest part. After that came the difficulty. It's probably better that I don't describe in too much detail the method we usually used to put the little fellers to sleep (kill them) so we could remove their fur (skin them).

Suffice it to say that there was usually a strong pole across the back of the neck (the critters) involved, on which one stood, while some significant lifting in the hind leg area occurred until either the pole or something else (the critters' neck) snapped.

Skinning was done with the utmost care because any nick or tear in the hide essentially made the skin worthless(er). Hides were stretched until completely dry and bundled up in special sacks for mailing to the hide buyers.

It was a good day for me if I was lucky enough to run my trap lines early in the morning and still get to school on time. Nolan and I had traps set all up and down the banks of the streams below our house and on down toward Rock Creek. I had to get up at least an hour earlier than usual to be able to check my lines before school. But it would not have been smart to wait until after school because that would have meant leaving the occasional catch in the trap all day long.

If I was lucky I might find a 'possum or two on my rounds, bringing them in so they could be skinned when I got home from school. And I soon learned that I was really, really lucky if I could go to school without smelling like the polecat (skunk) that I thought I had shot dead, only to watch helplessly as he came to life as I was carrying him "tail up" back to the house! Of course I could blame it all on Nolan. The rascal had claimed he only had one shell for the .22 rifle he loaned me that morning (times were tough and I believed him).

That bit of bad luck would have kept me from having to come up with a major fabrication that morning at school when my classmates so callously threw me out of the room, not buying for a second my argument that I had (really) finally caught a mink. I had heard rumors that mink had scent glands almost as bad as skunks.

One other skill that I hadn't quite mastered at the time was being a good liar, especially under the pressure of a room full of skunk odor (mine) intensified greatly by twenty or so kids standing around a hot stove in a tightly closed classroom on a cold winter morning.

Even though it quickly became obvious that I wasn't going to get rich with my trapping efforts, I convinced myself that I could always look forward to the day when I would be walking down the streets of Hot Springs or Little Rock and I would run into some rich lady with a big, happy smile on her face because she just happened to be wearing a beautiful and familiar-looking 'possum-skin coat.

18

 She watched as he crossed the right-of-way fence and walked away from the freeway. They were traveling to Portland to see the kids on a beautiful summer day when he had suddenly pulled over into a wide spot along the highway and stopped the car.

What are you doing? she looked up from her paper and asked.

You know how I've always felt like I've been here before, he answered. Well, I just need to take a few minutes and see how it feels to be here today.

He walked over to stand along what looked to be an old abandoned stretch of pavement that was grown over with weeds and fenced off from the high speed interstate that had replaced it so many years before. They had dropped off the hill out past Boardman and were now looking down at the Columbia River that would be visible the rest of the way to the city.

After passing Blaylock Canyon and before they got to Arlington, the old highway was visible in several places, sometimes coming right up next to the freeway where stretches of it had obviously been buried beneath the more recent highway construction.

It had been along this stretch of road that he had felt some kind of memory from his past.

I just know I've been here before, he would say. Sometimes to her, sometimes just to himself. There had been a trip long ago and he could see sketchy pieces of it in his mind, especially now as he stood there in the middle of a road that probably hadn't seen a vehicle since not long after he had been on it. If he had really been on it, he kept reminding himself.

Glancing down at the river he noticed a tugboat guiding a big river barge toward the Pacific. Probably loaded with wheat from Pendleton or wood chips from Boardman. Either way the load was headed for another world, most likely China, via one of the freighters tied up at Astoria.

Across the river the grassy hills rose quickly up from the river level to top out in a windmill farm that was bringing power to the growing cities of the Northwest. The big dams had not been enough to satisfy that need. And the long-abandoned nuclear plants had not been the answer either.

He could see the white-capped peak of Mount Adams to the Northwest, and looking back into the sun of the west, there stood Hood. Somewhere on down the big river was a high bridge that carried traffic north and south to join Washington and Oregon.

There had been an earlier time when the bridge had not been there. He could still see the full moon shining through the back window of the little Chevy coupe he was riding in as it floated across this river on a ferry.

Just after landing on the Oregon side they had driven on up the road for a few miles, pulling off into a wide spot where they could park for the night and get some sleep. It had been a long day already and they still had two thousand miles to go.

Well, she said, as he got back into the car. What do you think?

I know I have been on that road before, he said quietly.

The strangest part of it is, I felt sure that I had been on it before. But I was never sure that I was on it today.

**

It was time for the Perseids meteor shower and they were ready. They had the perfect place to watch for the shower of little blips of light streaking across the southeastern sky.

Sitting in the hot tub with the lights off in the tub and in the house to darken the sky as much as possible. Just enough ambient light to make it easy to see the glasses of Ste Chappelle Reisling she had brought out for the event. He heard her munching on a bit of cracker. She had to have some cheese and crackers with her wine. Always.

They had been watching for over half an hour and had seen maybe a dozen tiny flashes that last no time at all. He thought she might be losing interest and ready to go in. The wine was about gone and the warm water and wine together made it easy to think other thoughts.

Wow! Did you see that? He glanced quickly over at her.

Yes, she said. Wasn't that bright. Do you think it hit the ground?

He didn't know, but it had been as close to a real fireball as they had seen. And it surely could have gone from meteor to meteorite somewhere in the high desert down past Rome or Frenchglen. They sat silently thinking their own thoughts for a few minutes.

You know when I see that it always makes me feel like that is the way our life together has been. So bright and clear for an instant, but then just gone completely. Vanished forever. No way to know what it really was like, he said sadly. And no second chances.

She didn't know how to answer. It always made her feel funny when he said things like that.

Do you think it was as big as the meteorite you told me about? The one you found on your home place at Langley? She thought maybe this would get him to talk about something she could deal with.

I doubt it. That was huge. Probably weighed a good ten or twelve pounds and was just like solid iron.

He had found it just across the spring branch one time, just lying out in the open in a grassy area down below the huge red oak tree. It was more flat than round, extremely dense and heavy, and looked like some kind of metallic ore that had been through a furnace.

All the edges were melted and rounded smoothly, but the inner parts where there were holes down into the stony ore were sharp and clearly not burned.

She remembered how he had told her all about meteors, how this one tonight was called a fireball since it was so bright. And how they changed from meteors to meteorites if they actually survived the burning trip through the atmosphere and hit the earth somewhere, like in the field out by his house.

The one he had found, he thought, would have been classified as a "siderite" because of the amount of iron that was in it, instead of the more common stony type, called "aerolites."

I wish I hadn't left it, he said. I know it had to be a meteorite. What else could it have been in that location? And I wish I knew where it came from.

That's why I feel like I need to tell our grandson my story, he said quietly, after several more minutes had passed. I want him to know how little time there is, really, and how he needs to know how quickly that time passes.

More importantly, I think he has to understand how quickly everything can change if something bad happens. In the blink of an eye, just like these little space peas.

It's so important to me. He will be going off to college soon and I need to talk to him before then. There was an urgency in his voice that she hadn't heard before.

Okay, she responded. I understand. Maybe you should just tell all of them.

No, he said quietly. I know if I tell him, he will pass it on to the others. That's why he is who he is. He will know he has to. They will listen to him when they might not listen to me.

The way he was rambling she thought maybe he had enjoyed the Riesling a little too much.

19

It wasn't that I was so afraid of the dark. I just preferred not to be left alone with it for too long at a time. Especially in creepy situations. Like in a dark alley with a drunk hobo. Three of my major fears all rolled into one. Drunks, hoboes, and dark places were not things I looked forward to as a small boy.

Fortunately we lived a long way from the usual haunts of hoboes, such as near railroads or bigger towns. We did have plenty of drunks around, and for some reason I never quite felt comfortable when I heard someone saying things like "I 'moan kill you! I 'moan kill you a million times!" I guess I figured they might actually get started on that promise even when they usually couldn't get up enough courage to even get up.

Once or twice in my lifetime I actually did see a tramp wander through the Langley area. It was a hard time for everyone and for lone wanderers on a country road looking for a handout from folks who barely had enough left after a meal to keep an old hound dog from starving, there wasn't much to entice them into our part of the country.

I was just as glad. My imagination couldn't contain thoughts of the hard choices they had been forced to make already and the harder times they knew were ahead. It seemed to me that there wasn't much space between where they had come from in life already and anywhere they chose to go next.

But I was exposed to the dark as a matter of course, living on a farm with no electricity and no reason to waste precious kerosene on unnecessary lamp lights. Most of the time if I was in familiar territory I had no problem with the concept of assuming that there were no special creatures roaming around in the dark that were not there in daylight. But sometimes it just didn't work out to be that simple.

I think I was about nine years old when someone managed to secure a movie projector and screen from the state for use at the school. The excuse for the equipment was, I suspect, to indoctrinate us kids in the latest government propaganda for our eternal benefit.

I'm sure we all got to see how healthy and happy we would be if we made sure we let the county nurse poke as many holes in our arms every year as possible. Whatever the official reasons, it wasn't long before a deal had been worked out whereby we would be able to see an actual real movie every Saturday night.

Dad seemed to be in charge of the operation, which included ordering a movie from the seemingly endless supply of titles listed in a catalog that was sent out, showing the movie every Saturday night, and then returning the movie with the next order. Every week starting with the Sunday after the last movie that was shown the night before, we would pore over the catalog that he brought home trying to choose the next selection. It seemed like an almost impossible task due to the endless choices.

I don't know if there was a charge for these movies or not, but I suspect it was part of the effort to extend the amenities that were beginning to be taken for granted in the more populous areas out to the hinterlands. It surely was a welcome addition to our limited entertainment venue, and proved to be immensely popular with both the school kids and even adults in the community.

To make it work there had to be some transportation provided, so it was decided to run the school bus on the regular route on Saturday nights so folks who had no other means of getting to the school would not be left out. That included me.

I have no idea what system was used to decide on the movie to be shown each week, but whatever the process used, it could not have failed. We were so starved for entertainment that any movie would have worked. Most Saturday nights were filled with some combination of cowboys, Indians, horses, and/or pretty but helpless women.

You couldn't go wrong in those days with Lash LaRue and his sidekick Fuzzy St. John, Hopalong Cassidy and his partner Gabby Hayes, Red Ryder and Little Beaver, The Cisco Kid and Pancho, mixed in with an occasional Charley Chan ah-so-ah-saw-who-dunnit. And it really didn't matter what the main feature was, most of us would have come back just to catch the next installment of the weekly serial!

The serials were nothing more than weekly come-ons blatantly intended to make us want to find out how the hero or heroine managed to wiggle out of the surely inescapable situations they were left dangling in week after week. Those were simple times and it was easy enough to grab the attention of folks who had spent the week being entertained by the never-changing view of a mule's butt.

So things rocked along pretty smoothly. I rode the bus to and from the movie every Saturday night, got off in front of Jimmy Dunson's house, and walked the half-mile through the pine woods to our house. Always in the dark but it never seemed to bother me. I would still be thinking about how the Lone Ranger had managed to jump out of that two story window and land on Silver and still be able to say "Hi-Ho Silver Away!" without sounding like Johnny Weismuller doing his Tarzan yell.

And then came the night they showed "Frankenstein Meets the Wolf-man." I don't know if I would have actually skipped going to the movie that night if I had known what Dad had in store for us or not; probably not. After looking forward to the next show for a whole week, and also hearing all the potential escape scenarios for the serial hero on the playground that week, I'm sure I could not have stayed home.

But I knew I was in a mess of trouble when the movie opened on that scene with the townspeople of Transylvania clomping over to the mausoleum at midnight with their one little carbide light, crawling in through the open window to slowly raise the creaky lid to the coffin to disclose...nothing! The coffin was empty! That can't be good.

And sure enough it wasn't. The rest of the movie went from bad to worse to horrible. By the time it was over I was absolutely sure that the old farmer sitting one row up in front of me did not start out the night with that much hair sticking out from his shirt sleeves!

I noticed when I reluctantly boarded the bus, knowing that after three miles I was going to have to get off, alone, that there didn't seem to be as much of the usual laughing and joking around. Or maybe I just couldn't hear any noise because my heart was still pounding so hard.

I pondered my options as Floyd drove up the road from Langley, stopping a couple of times to let someone off. Lucky people, I thought. You only have to walk a few hundred yards to your house. I am facing a long half a mile. Through the woods.

I considered just hopping off with whoever was getting off ahead of me just so I would have some company, but I didn't know exactly how I would explain the sudden urge to spend the night with Myrna Jones or Faye York, since they were both several years older than I was.

Maybe I'll just stay on the bus until it goes all the way to Lodi and back and when Floyd gets home I'll tell him I forgot where I lived and he will have to drive me home. I quickly discarded that idea when I realized that he would not get back to his house until much later that night and if he refused to go along with my lame excuse I would then have another mile to add to my walk at a time when the midnight hour would definitely be too close for comfort.

I knew there were many, many more big trees down that way where Lon Chaney could be lurking, growing hairier and fangier by the minute and getting ready to let go with that god-awful howl at the first sight of a little feller like me.

These thoughts were running swiftly through my brain when the bus stopped and Floyd opened the door to let me out in front of Jimmy's place. I had no choice now. I glanced over to see if maybe there was a light in the Dunson house, thinking of how I could convince them to take me in for the night. Nothing but darkness. I didn't need that.

Stepping down off that bus seemed like the longest three steps I had ever taken. But they were certainly not nearly the quickest. That would be the next two, or three, or five hundred. Actually, I remember telling myself that there was absolutely nothing to be afraid of. It was just the same half mile stroll through the woods that I had done dozens of times, especially since the movie showings had started.

I even listened to myself for the first hundred feet or so. But then I got out of sight of Jimmy's house and into the deep woods where suddenly those big pine trees growing right alongside the road took on a whole new meaning. And of course, there was that dang moon. Totally full and totally creepy to look at up through the pine needles, just like in the movie. I tried whistling at first, but couldn't make a sound. How can my mouth be that dry when I'm sweating bucketsful, I thought?

I started skipping along the road. Not so much to go faster, but just so my mind would have something else to work on besides images of claws growing out of places where fingernails should have been. I almost tripped over my feet trying to skip along the dirt road and realized that the last thing I wanted to do right now was find myself lying on the ground, stopped still, with something big and extremely hairy hovering over me. I took it up a notch, going into a crisp jog.

Now I discovered that there was one disadvantage to jogging. It was more difficult to look behind me. It had already been somewhat of a problem to make myself turn around and look over my shoulder, but so long as I was walking or even skipping, I had done it a couple of times. Not expecting to see anything, but just double-checking to see if that warm breath I was feeling on the back of my neck was anything I should be concerned about.

Ok, I thought, after a few long seconds of loping along at a casual pace. If I am going to be moving so fast that I can't even look back for fear of hitting a tree, why heck, I might as well just go ahead and RUN! I took it up several more notches. In fact, I skipped all the phases in between a jog and my best impression of a runaway train.

There were two mud holes and two little stream branches along our road. Usually the mud holes were pretty wallowed out and nasty, especially if we had been having a lot of rain. The mud holes would get upwards of twenty feet long and hold water to the point where it would be necessary under ordinary circumstances to walk over into the edge of the woods to avoid the mud or the water. These were not ordinary circumstances.

I don't even remember seeing those mud holes, let alone going over them, and I know I didn't touch water when I cleared the streams. All I do remember is not getting anywhere close to the edge of those woods.

I was sticking strictly to the center of the road and still gathering speed when I hit the front door of our house. Everyone else was already in bed asleep, for which I was thankful. I didn't really want to have to explain why I had run through the front door with hair standing up on the back of my neck and sweat pouring off my whole body.

I crawled into my bed and pulled the covers up over me like it was the dead of winter even though it was a hot summer's night. At first I was just still sweating from the record-breaking half-mile moonlit sprint, and then when that went away, I began to sweat from the thought of how close I had come to becoming the first werewolf in our family.

It was good daylight when I was able to finally stick my head out from under the covers. I had tried a few times during the night but every time I peeked out all I could see was a dark, hairy shadow coming through one of the windows that were suddenly way too close to my bed.

Even worse, I was sure that once when I was almost able to drift off to sleep, I heard some kind of god-awful howl coming from back over in the woods where I had just recently set a new land speed record.

The Saturday night movies would continue to be shown for a couple more years at least, but from that night forward I made sure that I inquired well in advance to find out what movie Dad had picked out for us that week.

I must not have been the only one who had trouble sleeping that night because I don't think we ever had any more Lon Chaney sightings around Langley.

* * *

Once Albert and I got our bicycles we branched out quite a bit in our rambling around the countryside. I don't know how Albert secured his bike but mine came to me through my usual deviousness.

I didn't have to do too much to convince Mama and Dad that the fur trapping business was beginning to look like a fairly slow way to get ahead, especially since it only took one polecat encounter to basically blow my entire wardrobe budget for the year. So I proposed an alternative. If they would buy me a bicycle, I would start my very own paper route.

The "Grit" newspaper was an ingenious idea for those times before television. No one could afford to subscribe to a magazine but for ten cents a week they could have a copy of the Grit delivered directly to their doorstep every Saturday. That's where I came in.

But first I had to have a bicycle, and that's where the deal-making came in. I should remember what that brand new Schwinn Flyer cost my folks, but due to the circumstances surrounding my failure to live up to my part of the bargain, the price has long since been stricken from my memory. I am sure it was well past whatever small amount of discretionary spending they had planned on for the entire year.

I made a decent effort at first. Step one of the process required that I basically take on the task of going door-to-door and securing a commitment from people to promise to pay me my dime if I delivered their paper.

I rode my bike from our house out to the road and started with our neighbors, Jimmy and Ellie Dunson. They were in and I headed west to knock on doors on up through Langley proper and finally as far over as Floyd McGee's place about three miles past the Jones' store.

I may have picked up a dozen commitments, which was actually a pretty decent percentage considering how few houses there were along the road. At first I was excited about the prospect of providing such an important service to our neighbors and friends, especially since I was going to get paid for simply riding my bike approximately ten miles every Saturday. Why, I convinced myself, I would probably be doing that for nothing anyway.

It only took me about three of those ten mile trips, which started to feel more like thirty miles when I found out that I HAD to go regardless of whether or not there was a ball game or a fishing trip or some other reason to make me want to skip it. I also woke up one day and realized that my cut of the paycheck, which was a nickel out of every dime collected, was going to take a long time to pay off my debt on that new bicycle.

And I discovered another thing about myself. It was a lot more fun riding my bike with Albert when we were just riding along for fun than it was when I had to actually ride it to deliver those dang heavy newspapers. That was turning into something more like work than I had counted on.

One good thing about my lack of commitment, I told myself as I slowly backed away from the newspaper business, was that at least I hadn't stayed with it long enough to get anyone seriously hooked on the Grit.

So Albert and I rode our bikes a lot. We rode all the way down to Caney Bend and the Cat Den Bluff to fish the Little Missouri. We rode up to Albert Pike once or twice just to prove that we could. We just about wore the tires off those two bicycles, and we only had one real problem on any of our rides.

Anytime we rode past "Chick" York's place, which we did on a regular basis, we had to deal with his dad-gum bike chasing, kid hating feist dog. We tried every trick we could think of to sneak by without having to pedal for dear life to avoid having our ankles chewed off by that bleary-eyed little devil-dog, but nothing worked.

He always lay out by their mailbox which was right on top of the hill in front of the house, and from his perch he could see for a quarter of a mile up or down the road in each direction. There was just no way to get past him.

We could make it pretty good if we were going from east to west because we had a flat grade approaching the dog, with a good downhill run all the way to the bridge across Little Blocker creek after we got by him. That meant we had to start pedaling as fast as possible about a hundred yards before we reached him, zip by on the opposite side of the road from his lair at full speed, and hope to leave him in the dust as we roared on down the hill.

He learned fairly quickly not to put too much effort into a chase going in that direction. He was not only vicious. He was also a smart little sucker.

It was only when we had to come back by the house from the other direction, which was inevitable, that we paid the full price. We tried the speed approach, but soon found out that we were no match for him because by the time we had pedaled to the top of the hill, which was right where he was lying in wait, we had run out of steam and were easy prey.

We tried to act calm and unafraid, having heard somewhere that the way to deal with a mean dog was to ignore them. He wasn't buying any of that, obviously never having even heard of such a stupid theory, so we abandoned that technique right in the middle of one almost fatal trial.

It seemed the only solution, if it could actually be called a solution, was that one of us had to sacrifice for the other each time we made that ride. Someone was going to have to ride on the dog's side of the road and take the full brunt of his attack so the other person could get by safely.

We actually got fairly good at pedaling down the road with one foot on the pedal while the other foot was raised up about handlebar level to avoid being snapped off at the ankle bone. And we managed to divert his attention from our own flesh and bones by dragging a burlap bag ("tow sack") along behind the bike, although that almost ended up with Albert being eaten alive once when the dog sank his fangs into the sack and stopped Albert and the bike dead, almost literally, in his tracks. After that we learned to let go of the sack instead of tying it too tightly to the bike.

***

The summer was rolling along pretty fast and Albert and I were spending a lot of time together. He came over to my house often so I don't really know what it was that made Leander Cowart suspicious of us that one weekend. Maybe it was just his sixth sense that told him that there were two boys who were acting a little too nonchalant and he better be on the lookout for trouble. And maybe, just maybe, he should be especially watchful of his watermelon patch.

I had been eyeing Leander's watermelons all summer. His crop was all the way over in his south field which was over a pretty good hill from his house and right across the barbed-wire fence that separated his land from Uncle George's new ground where Papa had planted corn that year.

Any time I was over in the corn field I would look across the fence and check to see how those melons were progressing. And boy were they progressing, getting bigger by the day, unlike our little patch of midget melons that were still just sitting there taking up space.

It always seemed like our family just could not grow good watermelons. Little puny things that were never quite sweet enough and were full of seeds resulted in one of the few regrets I had about my childhood…I never really got to eat all the watermelon I wanted. But it seemed like most of our neighbors had the gift of growing a bumper crop of big, juicy red, or better still, yellow-meated melons.

I know Leander couldn't have heard us scheming that day because we didn't even want my folks to know what we were up to as we devised our plan, a plan that seemed totally foolproof. Leander's watermelon patch was a half mile away from our house, over to the south and east of his house.

We could see his house from our house but it was certainly not close enough for him to be able to hear us cautiously whispering our plan of attack. We played around the house for a while, nonchalantly pretending that it was just another day on the farm, and then we began to stroll out past the barn and all the way out to our west field, which was in the opposite direction of the watermelons.

As soon as we got to the west field, we veered back south and hightailed it on over through the patch of pine timber that Dad had planted when he got his forty acres. From there we circled back down along the ridge to the southeast toward the cornfield, staying out of sight all the way.

We were still a good half-mile from the melons and had stayed hidden in the woods all the way down to the creek, which we crossed and went directly up a little hill into the corn patch. The corn rows ran in just the right direction for us to go down the middle of a furrow and come out right at the fence line, on the other side of which lay the biggest watermelons we had laid eyes on in our short lives.

The day was perfectly still and quiet as we stood there hidden in the corn field for as long as possible, looking all around to make sure that our plan had worked. Not a soul was in sight so we crawled under the bottom wire of the fence and quickly made our way over to search out the biggest of the prized monsters.

There was no reason to rush. We could take our time and not just take the first ripe melon we saw. May as well get something special after all that waiting and planning, we figured. The best ones appeared to be out closer to the middle of the patch and we made our way out to them, stopping occasionally to thump a particularly nice looking one.

We both saw the one we wanted at about the same time. And boy was it a beauty, so big that we knew it was going to take both of us to heft it over the fence and down to the creek where we could take our time eating our fill of it. We moved over to the trophy and I had just bent down to pinch it off the vine when I heard what I thought surely had to be the very voice of the devil himself.

I didn't want to know what it was, and could barely bring myself to look up, but when I did I saw it was not the devil. It was a lot worse. There stood ol' Leander, not more than twenty feet away from us. And we were looking right up into the end of his double-barreled shotgun that was pointed in the general direction of the watermelon in which I was suddenly no longer interested. I'll never forget what he said then if I live to be a hundred:

"Why don't you boys just pick <u>two</u> a' them watermelons and bring 'em on up ta' the house so's we can all have some!"

Somewhere between the words "you boys" and "to the house" was when Albert and I simultaneously cleared the top of that barbed-wire fence at full speed, knocking down several rows of Papa's prized sweet corn as we thrashed our way back down across the creek.

We didn't look back and we didn't stop running until we were totally done for and hiding in a pine thicket as far out in the west field as we could go.

I ate a lot of watermelons after that day, many times right out of someone else's field where I found them because that was where they grew and also because we never learned to grow decent ones. But I can definitely guarantee all the remaining Cowart descendants, heirs, and assigns that I never was the least bit tempted to go back to ol' Leander's melon patch again.

20

Where are we going? She asked the question like she thought she already knew the answer.

He just laughed and said, you'll know when we get there.

They had spent an evening dining in the Geiser-Grand Hotel and she was all dressed up to enjoy the celebration of an anniversary. It had been exactly forty years to the day since they had left Kirby in a rainstorm heading west all the time.

The honeymoon trip had brought them up through Oregon and they had often wondered what they might have noticed but long since forgotten about the town they now called home, Baker City.

The little trip log they had kept in the Nineteen-Sixty-Two Chevron road atlas showed that they had bought gas at a Union Seventy-Six station in Baker, but they were not even sure where that had been. There was no Union Seventy-Six service station left and they had never inquired to find out where it had been.

Leaving Salt Lake City after a couple of nights there they had driven across southern Idaho and into Oregon late in the day and they could remember that the sun was setting across the fields of Baker Valley as they came to the little town called North Powder.

It had been no more than a few houses and stores, the same as today, but there had been a newer looking motel so they had stopped for the night. The name of the place was identified in their diary as the Elkhorn Motel, named after the small mountain range branching off from the main Blue Mountains.

She had always laughed about how she would tell her typing students in high school about how she spent a night on her honeymoon at the North Powder Motel, which was the current name. The kids always thought it was funny that she had stayed there on her honeymoon and were really surprised when she told them that she had come all the way from Arkansas to do such a thing!

So she had figured out where they were going that night as he drove out of town and hit the freeway going north out past the rest area. He had come up with the idea of taking her back to North Powder a few days earlier and had driven out to take a look at the motel and to make a reservation for their anniversary night.

Not that a reservation was needed. Although there were only about a dozen rooms, only a few of them looked occupied, mostly by fishermen who were staying in the area. But he didn't want to take a chance that it would be full that night and spoil his little surprise.

When he talked to the fellow who was running the motel and told him what he was planning, he also asked jokingly if the price would still be the same as it had been that first time forty years before. About six dollars was what showed in their diary. He found that wasn't really much more than that now.

As they drove along the interstate from Baker City to North Powder they talked about how much fun their trip had been and how fast the time had flown by since then. They both wondered at the way life had turned out, bringing them back to live where they now lived, close enough to relive part of their honeymoon in a place as far away from Arkansas as North Powder, Oregon.

She loved the surprise. He loved this day and night, and wished they could relive all their times just like they had this one.

His champagne toast that night in the honeymoon suite at the North Powder Motel was a simple one: If this truly is only a dream, please don't let me wake up.

* * *

Where will you go?

It was three or four hours past the middle of the night but he knew she was awake. They often woke up like this in the darkness of the early morning, even when they went to bed late, as they usually did.

She lay there for a while, hoping he would go back to sleep. But she knew he wouldn't.

What do you mean? She turned over toward him and let him roll closer. He liked lying close and she was okay with it as long as she wasn't trying to sleep.

I was just wondering what you will do after I'm gone, he said quietly. What will you do with this place?

I don't know, she answered softly. And he knew it was an honest answer.

I really think you will need to move somewhere else. Find a new house that you love and leave a lot of this stuff behind.

She wasn't sure how to respond to that. She knew they were different about things, and even places. He was always so attached to any house they ever lived in, it seemed, always ready to go back and see them again, or talk about them.

And they had been in this place for so long now. She knew he had poured his soul into everything around them. The house had been new when they moved in but over the years they had added on, remodeled, built a big shop and storage building for mostly his things.

I'm not like you, he said. I would stay for as long as I could, but there's no need for you to worry about doing that. You need different things. You're not so close to places and you don't feel the same way I do about little things. I can't even bear to think about not being able to walk out and look at the trees we've brought in from other places to plant in our yard.

She knew he was right.

But you'll be happier if you live in a new house with all the things you like. Some place a little warmer maybe. He knew that moving away was going to be a problem. The kids were always going to be up here in the northwest. She would not want to be very far from any of them.

I don't know what I'll do, she said again. I don't know where I'll go. I wish we didn't have to think about it.

He held her close and smoothed her hair, kissing her on the forehead.

I know. But remember what the song says: There comes a time when we have to put away childish things.

Who said that? She never could remember singers.

James McMurtry.

Oh yes. Wonder if he's as weird as his dad? She had started out loving to read Larry McMurtry as much as he did but had left him because, as she always said, he had no compassion for his characters. They always died. Usually after much suffering.

I doubt it, he answered. But then, I don't think Larry is weird. I think he just tells the truth about what it's like to be a human.

They lay quietly for a long time. Finally he spoke again.

Remember when we lived in Amarillo and they filmed one of his first books out at Claude? "Hud" had always been one of her favorite movies.

Yes, I know. That was really good. She had stopped reading McMurtry sometime after "Terms of Endearment", or maybe "Lonesome Dove", and seemed to be pretty determined not to take up the habit again.

You should read this last one I just finished, he said. It's the end of the Duane Moore saga, and you really liked those.

I hated "Duane's Depressed." She wouldn't give in.

I know, it was a real downer, but then, that's what I mean about telling the story like the story happens. He was still trying.

Duane dies in this last one, but it isn't really that sad. He's lived a fairly happy life, even being surrounded by what he was surrounded by. Mostly family. I enjoyed it.

Of course if I were Jeff Bridges I wouldn't read it. Every line in the book seemed straight out of Jeff's mouth. I think Larry got trapped after they filmed the first two books with Jeff as Duane. From then on, I think Jeff became Duane.

She was hoping he would drop the subject, and other subjects as well, so she could go back to sleep.

I really need to sleep a few more hours, she said, rolling over to her side of the bed. Wake me up when the coffee is ready.

They had been to "Thalia," Texas, where Duane had roamed all of his life They had stood on the corner of the street where Sonny and Duane fought over Jacy. And they had sat in the balcony of what was left of "The Last Picture Show" movie theater.

Of course Thalia was actually Archer City, but the name didn't change anything. The whole story was depressing because it was just so true. It seemed especially true in the darkness of this hour of the morning.

He couldn't get Duane out of his mind for some reason. He tried to convince himself that Kate Wolf had it right when she sang about the great divide. He thought about her words, hoping they would help him sleep, or if not, at least understand.

"The finest hour...I have seen...is the one...that comes between... the edge of night...and the break of day...that's when the darkness... rolls away."

That didn't help.

Okay, he said. I'll bring you some coffee when it's ready. He had one more thing he wanted to say, whether she was listening or not.

I just can't help wondering what you will do and where you will go? And what will happen to all my stuff, my photographs and my books? Will all of that just end up in some dusty old box in an abandoned attic somewhere in a house that no one ever lives in again?

She was breathing deeply, asleep again, and he knew he was talking to himself. It seemed to make his point.

I think that's the real sadness of life. Not dying, but having all your stuff mean nothing to anyone else.

21

I have been asked many times, why the Detroit Tigers? For me it came somewhat naturally, transferred directly by bloodline from my Dad to me.

I didn't need to know at first how he came to be such a die-hard Tigers fan, but over the years he gave some explanation. First of all, it was partly his defiance of the natural order around the baseball times he grew up in.

Everyone in Arkansas, except for a few heretics like Pete, was expected to be a St. Louis Cardinal fan. After all, one of their own true hillbillies by the name of Jerome "Dizzy" Dean had gone on up to the Cardinals and became a huge success. If anyone doubted how big a success he was, all they had to do was ask him.

But there was another Arkansas native playing in the major leagues back about the time Dad was starting to listen to a few games on the radio. His name was Lynwood Thomas "Schoolboy" Rowe. Although Schoolboy was actually born in Texas, his family had seen the light and moved to Arkansas and he always talked of Arkansas as his home. When he died he was buried in Arkansas.

About the time Dad was getting serious about his own baseball playing career, Schoolboy had joined the Tigers and quickly led them to two straight World Series appearances in 1934 and '35. Those games were some of the first ones that Dad listened to as a young man and he would go on to become a lifelong fan of the Detroit team that would bring occasional joy, but a lot more heartache, to both of us.

So I was introduced to the Tigers early and often, and by the time I was of an age to be reading the box scores and keeping track of the statistics of my favorite players, another wonderful Arkansas native was leading the Tigers again. George Kell came out of Swifton up in northeast Arkansas and although he ended up playing for several teams in the American League over his fifteen year career, clearly his best years were with the Tigers.

I was a little too young to pay attention when the Tigers went to the World Series again in 1945, but they were still very competitive with the hated Yankees and the very good Cleveland Indian and Boston Red Sox teams of the late 1940s when I was old enough to keep up with them on a daily basis.

My strong support for Detroit met the stiffest test it ever encountered, however, when the Tigers did the unthinkable and traded my hero, George Kell, to the Red Sox. That trade even sent me into such a funk that I spent the next year or so doing my level best to convert from a Tiger fan to a Red Sox fan. The conversion failed miserably and I was soon back to my normal self, living and dying with the up and down Tigers.

One other thing that helped put me solidly into the Tigers corner was the fact that they owned the farm team that played in Little Rock, the Travelers, and Dad and I would get to see Detroit play every spring when they would swing back through Little Rock on their way north out of Spring Training camp in Florida.

We never missed these annual exhibition games and were thrilled to get a chance to see our favorite team in person, even if it were only a practice game against the minor league farm club in Little Rock.

The chance to watch some of the great names in Tigers history was a thrill of a lifetime for me, as I watched not only our own George Kell, but the superstars from Detroit's championship teams of a few years earlier. "Prince" Hal Newhouser was drawing close to the end of his career by then, but he was the greatest pitcher in Tiger history by the time we got to see him toss an inning or two with his smooth southpaw delivery.

The soft spoken Newhouser had carried the Tigers to that 1945 World Series and had pitched three games, winning two, as Detroit beat St. Louis four games to three that year. Most of the other big name players from the war years, such as Hank Greenberg, Rudy York, and Paul Richards, were gone by now. Charley Keller had been an outstanding player for many years with the Yankees and was finishing up his career with Detroit. Joining Hal Newhouser as pitchers for the Tigers during those years were Virgil Trucks and Paul "Dizzy" Trout, along with a promising newcomer named Art Houtteman.

Dad always got us seats behind the first base dugout where the Tigers were located and because it was an exhibition game, the players always spent an extra hour or so visiting with the fans, signing autographs, and making sure they entertained the youngsters in the crowd.

Somewhere in a foot locker at home after one such trip with Dad, I stashed my copy of the program for that day. On that program I had the autographs of two rookies, Harvey Kuenn and Art Houtteman along with the prize of all prizes, George Kell.

The game would be played eventually and the outcome was usually as pre-determined as a Harlem Globetrotter exhibition. The Travelers were expected to put up a good fight but in the end, the major league club was not going to lose to a bunch of youngsters and has-beens.

One other given was that the big name stars were always expected to put in a token appearance early in the game before retiring to the dugout and letting some of the younger players take over. It would not have been good business to have the fans drive from all parts of the state to see their favorite players, only to have to watch some rookies and bench players play the entire game.

So it was that the day I remember best saw the starting lineup of regulars, including the Swifton Swifty, George Kell, play the first couple of innings before giving way to the substitutes. I have no idea what kind of score was run up by the big boys but we all noted with some disappointment when Kell stayed in the dugout along about the third or fourth inning while some no-name rookie went out to third base to take his place.

There was no booing or anything of the kind because the fans were far too polite for that, and besides, we all knew the situation. The stars needed to rest up for the long season ahead so it was only natural to play the second stringers.

I don't know who the kid was that had taken over at third base, and it wouldn't have mattered what his name was because the first batter that came up for the Travelers smashed a screaming line drive right down the third base line.

The ball sailed about ten feet over the head of the new third baseman and was by him so quickly that all he could do was wave his glove in the general direction of where the liner had disappeared.

The batter was brushing himself off at second base when one of the old farmers that was sitting down in front of Dad and me leaned over to the farmer sitting next to him and said matter of factly: "Ol' George'd had that-'un."

❋❋❋

Dad and Mama were working themselves to death at school and on the farm and we were still not gaining much of a foothold on the prosperity that was still "just around the corner" for most of the country folks in the 1950s.

They had to try something different, and that something was about to take place right after the graduation ceremonies had ended at Langley school in the summer of 1951. They were going to Washington to pick apples.

Now folks around Langley had long been traveling up to Indiana in the summer for years to join migrant workers from all around the south and Midwest during the tomato harvest.

Mama had already done that once or twice, riding all the way to Indiana and back in an old cargo truck that Leander had thrown together for hauling people, suffering through the seven hundred mile journey sitting on some old wooden benches fastened to the sides of the truck.

But this Washington trip was a different story altogether. That was a good two thousand miles from Langley, with no way to avoid the Rocky Mountains. Just the kind of adventure an eleven-year old boy did not want to miss out on!

I'm fairly certain that the real discussion between my folks and my grandparents, who were staying behind on the farm to work and look after my three sisters, was mostly about where would I be less likely to be more trouble than I was worth. Losing that argument meant that my folks were going to take me with them on this adventure of a lifetime to Wenatchee, Washington.

Earl and Eunice Crump had made this trip before and knew where they were going, where we could stay when we got there, and more or less where we could possibly find work. They also had a car, which was a major plus. I don't think Dad could have used the school bus for that particular trip. They also had a son, Gene, who was about my age and in the same class as I was in school, so Gene and I would be forever linked to the "Austin-Crump Apple Harvest Expedition of 1951."

It was well over in the afternoon that Sunday when the graduation ceremony at Langley ended and we loaded four adults and two nearly-grown boys, plus a couple of suitcases of clothes and assorted necessities, into Earl's Nineteen-Forty-something Chevrolet sedan, and pulled out for the great northwest.

Traveling thru the dark night well over into Oklahoma before we finally pulled over on the side of the road so the drivers, Earl and Dad, could sleep, meant that the trip started off in total mystery for me.

By the time daylight came we were somewhere out in the panhandle country of Texas where it really didn't matter whether I looked straight ahead from my back-seat perch between two adults, or out either of the tiny side windows, it was all the same; flat, treeless prairie ground that I could just as easily sleep through.

We stopped for the night at a roadside "trailer court" in Dumas, Texas, where we were able to get out of the car for the first time for any length of time, and also have a chance to sleep on a bed. After a short night and an early morning departure, we went on up over Raton Pass and turned west at Pueblo, Colorado, heading for what had to be pretty much the highest pass we could choose to cross the Rockies: Monarch Pass.

I was totally amazed when we finally ground our way up the steep, winding, highway, stopping about half a dozen times to dip a jug into the cold water running down off the side of the mountain to pour into the overheated radiator of the hard-working Chevy. Long before we reached the summit we were in deep snow.

We had left Arkansas in late May where it was already well into summer and close to ninety degrees during the daytime, and now we were driving along with snow banks higher than the top of the car.

Earl stopped for the night again on the back side of the divide in Montrose, Colorado, and from there we would not stop again until we made it all the way to East Wenatchee. Driving on down off the back side of the Rockies through Grand Junction we hit the desert country of Eastern Utah, turning back northwest at Green River.

Another winding, mountainous road took us up over the Wasatch Range at Soldier Summit and finally down into the Great Salt Lake Valley. I was looking forward to seeing the huge salty lake that I had read about but we would not get close enough on this leg of the trip as we went on up through Ogden and took the highway across into Idaho, skirting around the lake to the north.

The road across Idaho was fairly unimpressive after what we had seen already, being mostly down in the sagebrush flats of the southern part of the state. We crossed the Snake River a couple of times, the last time just at dusk on the Oregon-Idaho border, and from there we drove on through the night across Eastern Oregon to cross over into Washington finally somewhere west of Pendleton.

Although the road we were on went right through the middle of a little town named Baker, Oregon, I must have been asleep at the time, or possibly just numb from all the sights I had already been exposed to. At any rate, I never remembered being in this town.

Normally the final leg of the trip would have been a fairly easy two day drive with the two people trading off like they did, but somewhere after we had crossed the Columbia River Earl took the wrong road and we wandered all the way up around Grand Coulee and maybe even Okanogan before finally turning back south toward our real destination, which was a little clump of cabins across the Columbia from the main city of Wenatchee.

Dad said he had been napping while Earl drove and when he awoke he heard Earl mumbling something about being on the wrong road and if they didn't turn around they would end up in Canada. We finally pulled into our migrant camp just after daylight on the fourth day out from Langley.

After being packed in the old car like sardines for that long, especially during the last two days and nights, we all staggered around for a while trying to regain our legs.

The family that owned the cabins had originally moved out from Arkansas so the Crumps knew them well and had been staying there during their previous trips. Their name was Walker.

We were quickly assigned our own little one-room shanty that we would call home for the next three months. Looking around where we had landed, it was obvious that East Wenatchee was the migrant worker compound for folks from all over who had come up for the apple and cherry harvest.

The main town of Wenatchee was directly across the river, which seemed immense to me since at that time the largest stream I had seen was the Little Missouri, a mere creek compared to the mighty river just yards from our little cabin.

As soon as we had deposited our meager baggage in our assigned cabin, Gene took me over across a little dirt road and showed me the river up close. It was an awe-inspiring sight. I figured it would swallow a dozen rivers the size of our Little Missouri and still not rise more than a few inches.

It seemed to be half a mile wide at this spot, as we quickly determined that we were definitely not going to be able to sail a rock anywhere close to the other side of this big boy.

Work for the adults was fairly easy to find and they were soon traveling around to the local areas on a daily basis to begin the first phase of the annual harvest, which was to thin the apples from the trees.

We went to places like Cle Elum and Leavenworth, up river to Entiat, out to the beautiful little orchard town of Cashmere, and along the roads in every direction where there seemed to be an endless supply of well-groomed apple or cherry orchards.

The work was steady but not much fun, consisting of constantly moving and climbing on tall step ladders to thin the thumb-sized apples to just the right spacing, usually around six to eight inches apart. Gene and I started out thinking we would contribute our part to the actual thinning effort but we soon found other more enjoyable ways to spend our time.

One of our main jobs, once the adults figured out that they couldn't count on us for much else, was to bring fresh drinking water from the nearby houses to our parents so they wouldn't have to stop working and waste time going for water. We usually managed to carry out this part of the bargain without too much difficulty, although I'll admit there were times when we got sidetracked and probably would have been fired if we had been working for anyone other than our folks.

Once we were working in a big orchard up toward Chelan when Gene and I were sent up to bring back jugs of water and when we got up to the house we found something that neither of us had ever seen before. Sitting out in the middle of a yard filled with immaculately manicured green lawn were some gadgets attached to the end of water hoses that were spraying water all over the yard in a circular pattern. Sprinklers.

We had never seen such a thing before, and for the next hour at least, we cavorted around through the spraying water like we had nothing else to do. When we finally remembered that we should be filling our jugs and getting back down to the orchard, we were both soaked thoroughly. I always wondered if, somewhere up in one of the upper story windows, the owner of the big mansion was watching our every move.

Another diversion we invented to avoid any involvement in actual work was to slip away from our parents with several hands full of walnut-sized green apples that had been trimmed from the trees so we could try another method of spanning the big river.

We would find and cut ourselves a long, slender willow or alder switch that was about an inch in diameter and five or six feet long, sharpen the smaller end so we could skewer a green apple on it, and thereby gain considerable momentum in our attempts to sling an apple across the river. Although we did improve our distance compared with simply throwing something, I doubt that we ever really threatened to put one on the opposite bank.

Back in East Wenatchee, the summer flew by swiftly as far as I was concerned. Gene and I played ball out in the field between the cabins and the highway, sometimes with the Walker's daughter, a girl who was a few years older than we were and who would later marry the Crump's oldest son, Jack.

A couple of the other men from around Langley, Charley and Joyce Markham in particular, came in one evening with some huge fish that they had caught below the Rock Island dam, which was just downstream from Wenatchee.

Now this activity was discussed in hushed tones around the camp because it was rumored to be frowned upon by the local authorities, which probably explained why the Arkies had thought to do it in the first place. From what we understood, there was absolutely no fishing of any kind allowed within a half mile of the dam because the fish were pretty much trapped there on their migration upstream.

The story we got from the perpetrators was that all they had to do was toss a weighted treble hook out into the swirling pool below the dam and when it was retrieved they would snag a big Salmon on almost every cast. It was just a matter of getting in and out as quickly as possible, which was an art the folks around Langley had been taught since the early moonshine liquor days.

None of us had ever seen a Salmon and we were amazed at the size and color of the huge fish they displayed in the back of their car. For the next few days the smell of baking fish around the camp was so strong that I worried about the police showing up and hauling us all off to jail. But what a treat we enjoyed as we learned to cook the big slabs of pink-fleshed fish.

One of the big events we were treated to on a few special weekends was when Dad took us over across the river into town to the ballpark where we got to see the local minor league team play baseball. Although it was only a lower level club, probably what would have been called Class B back in those days, it was still professional baseball to us.

We watched as a mixture of very young rookies played alongside much older men who were obviously on their way back down through the many levels of minor league baseball. A few names were even familiar to Dad as guys who had spent a little time in the big leagues.

As the summer wore on toward July and August, the work became harder and harder to find. There was clearly a fairly big gap of time that had to elapse between the end of the thinning jobs and when the actual harvesting would take place.

From what we found out, there would be some cherry harvesting available in late summer, but for all of the apple varieties it would be later in the fall before they were ripe enough to pick. That left the folks with somewhat of a dilemma, one which I suspect they had not fully examined before heading out from home with the Crumps.

The Crumps could stay as late as they wanted to, even though Gene was in school. It wasn't uncommon for families to let their kids miss several weeks of school if they needed to stay on a job somewhere, and Earl and Eunice had pretty much committed to staying at least through a lot of the cherry harvest in August and early September.

Dad could not do that. He was due to be back in school and as teacher, basketball coach, bus driver, and other duties, and there was no way he could miss the first month of school. Even though Mama's job as cook in the school lunchroom wasn't as critical in terms of the school folks, she knew if she wasn't there when school started there would be a new cook when she did get back home. We couldn't make it without her salary in those times.

**

When Dad drove in to the camp one day in a little Nineteen-Forty-One Chevrolet Businessman's Coupe, I knew we were headed home soon. And what a thrill for all of us. We finally owned our very own car! I was ready to roll any time they were now.

The car was a little tan two-seater that had a perfect arrangement for me to ride home in. There was no back seat, but in place of a seat there was a bench where I could sprawl out and have all that space just for myself. Mama put a couple of quilts down over the wooden bench and I was ready to head for home.

I don't know if Dad and Mama made it home that summer with any extra money at all, but the trip was obviously worth it for all of us just to be able to come up with the three hundred dollars that little car cost.

We said goodbye to the Walkers and the Crumps, as well as the other Arkansas families in camp, and pulled out of East Wenatchee heading south. All Dad knew was that he didn't want to retrace Earl's final route and go almost up to Canada before hitting the right road, so we drove down the Columbia, staying on the north and west side of the river until we came to a place where we could cross over into Oregon.

Our route took us to a spot on the Columbia where we found that there was no bridge across the river, but there was a ferry that would get us across. Another adventure.

I can clearly recall the feeling of Dad driving that car out onto the ferry after dark that night, and how we floated slowly and smoothly across the wide river as the full moon sparkled in the water alongside our raft. I was sure this must be exactly what it would be like to float through space.

The ferry took us from somewhere near Maryhill, Washington across to Biggs, Oregon, and after we had crossed the river we drove on east along the river until we found a wide spot alongside the road where we pulled over and slept that first night.

The next morning I woke up at daybreak and when I looked out the window of my special compartment, I saw a world that I would never forget. I tried to capture everything I could see to take back home with me because I never expected to see this spot again.

The trip back home seemed to go much faster than on the way out. Of course Dad did all the driving this time and I could tell that he and Mama were very pleased to not only be heading back home, but to be doing so in our little Chevy coupe.

And even though I had the perfect place to sleep on my rear seat platform, I slept very little while we were traveling. Dad must have known how badly I had wanted to see the Great Salt Lake because, after traveling once again through eastern Oregon (and that little town of Baker, which I still didn't notice), on down through Boise, where we stopped in the middle of town on a very hot August afternoon and ate a big, juicy watermelon in the park, he took a different route somewhere down past Mountain Home.

This time we stayed along the Snake River and saw an area called the "thousand springs" where the water gushed out of the sides of steep volcanic cliffs before dropping down into the river below.

And we were soon driving right through the middle of the hundred mile long salt flats that lay alongside the big lake out west of Salt Lake City. The sunlight reflecting off the pure white ground intensified the feeling of being on another world, as I imagined again that my space ship had just landed on some distant planet.

We crossed the Rockies in the same place as before but this time the snow was mostly all gone. By the time we made it down off the mountains into the lower country we soon decided that traveling along during the middle of the August days, when the temperatures were well up into the high

Nineties or even over One Hundred degrees, was not only hard on us, it was hard on our car too.

Dad had stopped in Pueblo at a garage and had the oil changed on the car, which he said had probably never been done. This decision almost caused a serious problem because the mechanic who was doing the work could not figure out how to remove the oil filter and after trying for half an hour to pry it loose with a crowbar, finally realized that it simply unscrewed from the filter compartment.

I hate to think what a problem we would have had if he had broken a part. We were already on a very tight schedule trying to get back to Langley in time for school.

From that point on we traveled mostly at night or at least in the cooler parts of the day, which was fine with me. I had seen about all the sights my brain could absorb for one year, plus I knew that there was not much more to see across the plains.

The one sight I was really looking forward to seeing now was the one where we turned off onto a little dirt road in front of Jimmy and Ellie Dunson's place and drove through the pine woods and down across the branch to turn up the hill to park in front of our home place.

I had seen many impressive sights during the summer of 1951, but I don't think anything pleased me more than looking up at that little white house that Uncle George built.

22

Would the government really pay people to do the things he was getting to do in this job in Taos, he wondered? Shouldn't he be paying them instead?

Every day was such a pleasure he could not wait to go to

work. Design a new road system up in the high mountains north of Questa and Red River so the service could possibly log all that spruce forest up there? Sure, but that meant he had to spend days walking over potential routes and measuring grades and looking at the geology of the steep mountainsides.

And while he was up there he could also take along his fly fishing outfit and spend his lunch hour taking rainbow and cut-throat trout on tiny flies in the mostly un-fished Cabresto Creek drainage.

We need to look over the trail system that goes back into the wilderness country above Twining and Red River and Taos Pueblo? Ok. The Wheeler Peak country, New Mexico's highest peak at just over Thirteen Thousand feet, where a trail already went through places with names like "tight-ass pass" because there was no room for a misstep or one would disappear into the deep chasm on either side of the trail.

He learned to ride the horses that Bill Martin was so good at wrangling for the boys, even the new breed of Missouri Trotters that were brought in to replace some of the sure-footed mountain stock.

Ranger Stations were places where the field offices had always served the public as the first point of contact. There were stations in Questa, Taos, Penasco, Tres Piedras, El Rito, Canjilon, and as far west as Gobernador. The latter was out in the hinterlands adjacent to the Jicarilla Apache reservation and was a good half-day drive from the headquarters in Taos.

All the stations were dependent upon the engineering skills that were on call to the Rangers, and he spent many days traveling through the beautiful sections of the forest to join up with someone from the field offices to look at and solve some problem that had arisen.

He learned new skills that had not been taught in college, such as computer technology and design techniques that were new and unique, and worked with a wide variety of skilled people in areas of expertise that he had never imagined.

Landscape architecture, forestry, range management, watershed planning, land surveying, fire prevention, communications, and several other professions came together to oversee the use and protection of over a million acres of forest land.

So he spent all week working, mostly out in the woods on the roads and trails, and on weekends he would be back out showing the family around to all the neat places he had discovered during "work." He fished the creeks called Rito de Olla (Pot Creek), Rio Chiquito, Little Rio Grande, Red River, Cabresto, Tres Ritos, and across the sagebrush plains to the west, the Vallecitos, El Rito, Lagunitas and all its many tributaries, and the lakes of Canjilon, Trout, and the Latirs.

And he hunted in the high country east of Taos for deer, on the sagebrush flats around San Antone Mountain for antelope, and on Mogote over by El Rito every year with his friends for elk.

It was a paradise as far as he was concerned. Why can't we just stay here forever? he would ask when they were alone and not really thinking about anything much in the way of the future. Where could we possibly go that would be better than this? They never really had an answer to that question, but the time would come when that was no longer the question.

The two boys were certainly happy, they knew that. One was about ready to start to school on his own, and the other wouldn't be far behind. The grade school seemed to be good from what she could find out, and being a teacher herself, she definitely wanted to know.

Even though the community they lived in now was a world apart from where they had come from, that was not a problem with them. It was actually good, in their opinion. We won't be harmed by learning to be in the minority for a change. Might do us good, they said.

But all the days they lived were good. And even when he had to attend meetings, be away from home for a week at a time, it was okay. Meetings would be held in places like Ghost Ranch and Angel Fire and down at the Continental Divide Training Center near Gallup. He would come home and tell some of the stories that he had heard from some of the characters, like John Hutt's story of the wild horse roundup.

❄ ❄ ❄

John was a red-faced, sandy-haired forester from back east and they would become fast friends. John was in charge of timber operations on the forest now, but when he had arrived in Taos fresh out of Penn State forestry school several years before, he had stepped into a job where he was looking up at folks who were long-tenured and very wary of new-fangled ideas, not to

148

mention college educated greenhorns from back east. The most long-tenured and wary one of all was the supervisor of the forest at the time, the legendary George Proctor.

Now Proctor, as most folks called him, was an old-school, marine-trained, Chiracahua-blooded, do-it-my-way-or-hit-the-highway type of fellow, literally able to bring on a case of the heebie-jeebies in a junior forester by just looking sideways at them. Hutt admitted to being more than a bit intimidated. In fact, he said it was basically a case of being scared spitless of the man.

So when the word came out of the latest staff meeting that Proctor was going to lead the staff and some of the other junior assistants on a mission, John said he tried to get up the nerve to decline the invitation. Before he could speak, Proctor had asked him specifically if he was a good horseman.

John knew he was in trouble but what else could he say? Of course, what do you have in mind? That wasn't what his brain told him to say but it was definitely what he heard coming out of his dry mouth.

Proctor explained: There was a wild horse problem over on the Jicarilla District of the forest. Someone, possibly the Jicarilla Apaches, was not keeping their horses on their own land and these stray horses were destroying the range that was meant to be used exclusively by cows grazed by Forest Service range permittees.

The mission, whether you choose to accept it or not, as George so aptly stated, was to go over and round up those wild horses and pen them up until either the owners came and paid the necessary fines for trespassing (highly unlikely), or they could be trucked off to the nearest glue factory (most likely). Proctor was a firm believer in the Forest Service mantra of old: If everything else failed, including force and coercion, then we might try diplomacy. But probably not.

The job seemed simple enough to most of the folks who had "volunteered" for the task. After all, they were all experienced horsemen and looked forward to a day away from the office and some extraordinary fun in the saddle. Hutt didn't even have a saddle. Not to worry, he was told. We'll have a saddle for you. And a horse.

It was an all day affair getting to the Jicarilla district of the forest.

Horses had to be rounded up from Taos, Questa, Tres Piedras, and Canjilon, trucked and trailered across the winding semi-paved roads that led from Chama across through Dulce (headquarters of the Jicarilla Apache Nation), and corralled over at the Gobernador ranger station overnight. The roundup would begin at daylight sharp the next morning.

Proctor went over the final details of the task at hand that evening as a bottle of Old Hairy was passed around. He showed them approximately where the band of horses had been seen hanging out recently, and explained that the job would be to find the strays, surround them and drive them carefully into a large temporary corral that had been constructed just for this purpose. It seemed like a foolproof plan, especially after about the third bottle of Old Hair o'the Dog was polished off.

***

Daylight came and everyone was in the saddle, including Junior Forester Hutt. The riders were soon strung out across a trail heading north up toward Carracas Mesa country where the sleeping ponies were about to be rudely awakened and summarily shuttled into their final corral.

The ride started out just fine, Hutt said. The saddle wasn't too bad, even though it appeared to have been unused for a couple of decades, and the horse one of the rangers had drawn out for him seemed to be very comfortable in hanging back and letting others take the lead.

In fact, John soon discovered that this horse was not just comfortable hanging back. He was making a point of it. First thing John knew was that he was not only well behind the other riders, he was so far behind he couldn't even figure out where they had gone!

By this time the well-worn trail they had been following had branched off several times and was now just a series of openings through the Pinyon-Juniper woods. Every path looked the same and there were no tracks that John could see to help him figure out which way to go to catch up with the others.

After a couple of fruitless efforts at spurring his horse, which he now knew probably hadn't been ridden since his saddle had last been used, he gave up. May as well relax and enjoy the day, John thought.

He decided that there was no use trying to make the old nag go any faster than the slow saunter that he seemed happy with. This is really a pretty nice deal, he said to himself. Here I am, all alone out here in this beautiful country, enjoying a nice leisurely horseback ride while all those cowboys are out there somewhere busting their butts to try and find those wild horses. The sun was coming up over the ridges to the east and the Stellars Jays were hopping around in the Juniper trees looking for a morning snack.

John thought about his old classmates that were slogging to class back at Penn State that morning, and he felt sorry for them. What a life. He couldn't wait to get back to Taos and tell his new wife about this day.

Hutt was suddenly jolted out of his reverie, aware that his horse's demeanor had changed dramatically. He had stopped dead in his tracks and the old pony's ears, which had drooped from the first time John had seen him, were now standing straight up and twitching noticeably.

John watched his horse slowly turn his head to look behind them, and as John followed that gaze, he saw a fearsome sight. Standing in the edge of the woods about two hundred feet back was the biggest, blackest, wildest-eyed herd stallion that John had never seen before and never wanted to see again.

What th'? John barely had time to think about how his pleasure trip was turning into something really, really ugly, when he heard the stallion let out a wild scream. And he had even less time to set himself in the stirrups and grab a tight grip on the reins before his no-longer sleepy old nag launched straight ahead into a full-bore let's-get-the-hell-outta-here-greenhorn mad dash. John quickly reached forward and managed to get a death grip on the saddle horn just before being left sitting in mid-air by the panicked pony.

When he was sure he was still hooked to the saddle he turned to take one more quick look back to see if perhaps he had imagined this whole situation. Maybe he had been daydreaming, he thought, or maybe they ran the other way.

That quick glance showed that not only was the stallion still coming hard with eyes blazing at what he obviously considered a serious competitor for his harem, his harem was right behind him and running hard to keep up.

There must be thirty or forty of them, Hutt figured, as he dodged another Pinyon limb to try and keep from being knocked out of the saddle where he would surely be trampled by wild horses.

The rest of Hutt's story was the stuff of legend and would have been totally unbelievable but for one fortunate bit of perfect timing. No more than five minutes later about twenty corroborating witnesses came riding up to attest to what had just happened.

John's decrepit old nag had somehow regained just enough youth and vigor to blow through a quarter of a mile of thick P-J timber with the entire herd pounding closer and closer on their heels. Just when John felt like the race was about to end badly for him and his horse they broke out of the woods into a little clearing, and without veering to the right or the left, that old horse ran directly through the gate and into the corral that was waiting for these horses, with the full herd blindly boiling straight into the very trap that had been laid for them!!

John said he bailed out of his saddle as his horse skidded to a halt at the back side of the corral fence, ran back around to the front and had that corral gate closed and was sitting up there on a fence rail smoking a cigarette when Proctor and all his cowboys came riding up from their long, fruitless search.

It seems that the best George could do when he realized that Hutt had single-handedly captured the entire herd of horses was just shake his head and mutter something to this effect: "Well I'll be Dod-Blammed!"

23

The day they hoped would never come came suddenly and the next thing they knew, they were looking for a new house in Albuquerque. He really had no choice if he wanted to continue advancing in the career he had chosen.

When the forest supervisor, his good friend and prairie dog shooting companion, Big Jean Hassell, called him into his office that day and told him there was a promotion waiting for him down south in Albuquerque, the boss hadn't really asked him if he wanted to go. He more or less said that, yes, of course you will take it, right?

So they told the boys they were leaving their little playground paradise on Carabajal Road off of Lower Ranchitos, packed up enough boxes to fill another U-Haul truck and trailer and got ready to say goodbye to the place they never really wanted to leave.

Taos was a place and a time in their lives that would forever be cemented in their souls, and they would always long to return somehow, even long after it became apparent that they would not and could not ever return for good.

He knew the years he had spent working on the Kit Carson National Forest had been the best for him that he could have ever hoped for. Roads were built from Vallecitos to El Rito Creek by his good friend Lou Gross. This just happened to be near where he was now spending every October with his Dad and friends in their elk camp, a place that another friend, Ranger Jack Miller, had told him about before he had ever seen this country.

The big timber access project into the upper Cabresto Canyon country was underway, with design features that would hopefully keep the roadbed hanging on the steep mountain slopes and not allow anything to slide off and spoil the little creek below where he had fished for trout so many times.

The State of New Mexico was building another of his projects from the edge of the little town of Red River up into the national forest to access all the summer homes and cabins that the Texans occupied.

And he would always remember the trails he had ridden, both horseback with his friends Martin and the Rangers Sims and Hart and Drake and Dieter, and also on the old trail bike that he had bought to spend weekends riding through the mountains with Sabino and Lawrence Trujillo.

He would put away his old rubber raft that had seen some wild rides down the Rio Grande during the annual spring runoff, times when he was sure that he and Dave Heerwagen, or he and his old friend from reclamation, Bruce Elliott, were going under the water for good, but they had always managed to surface somehow.

She would never again know the closeness of the women's group that did so much together in Taos. The Forest Service wives' club was more or less their primary social activity due to the structure of the community. Most people who lived in Taos had always lived in Taos, except for the transient government workers and the hippies, and there was not much opportunity to join up with the hippies. At least not for most of them.

Leaving the little adobe house under the big cottonwood trees was something they hated to do, but the one thing that made it easier was the chance to do something they had not done before. They went to a new subdivision up on the east slopes of Albuquerque and picked out a new house that would actually become their very own. So far they had just rented a place, but this was something different.

It was scary at first, worrying about how they could make payments on a new house. Twenty-four thousand five hundred dollars was a fortune to them, but they fell in love with the model they had picked out, which just happened to be a stucco frame with enough resemblance to their old house in Taos to make it seem only natural to step through the portals.

His golfing buddy, Gib West, and his surveyor friend from reclamation days, George Sorenson, drove the U-Haul after helping them pack everything away into the truck. He drove the old white pickup loaded with extras and she was in the car as they stopped just before dropping down off Taos plateau, looking back one last time up toward the top of Taos Mountain which was just barely covered with an early December snowfall, hit the Rio Grande at Pilar and went on through Santa Fe to their new adventure.

She drove along behind him in the Charger as they dropped off La Bajada hill into the desert country between Santa Fe and Albuquerque, where they turned off the interstate onto Montgomery Boulevard and then into the Holiday Park Subdivision at the corner of Montgomery and Juan Tabo. This would be home for the foreseeable future, which was usually a fairly short time.

They had traded Carabajal Road for Nassau Drive, and when they got settled in they found new neighbors, all like them with young families full of happy children. There would be new friends for the boys, who struck off in search of replacements for Ernie and Frankie and their other Taos playmates.

Now it was Dean and Lori, Mark and Chris, and the Meyer and Navarette girls from either side of their house. Christmas came and went, with their usual trip home to Arkansas to be with cousins and grandparents, and soon it was spring and summer and time to landscape and bring in things from the woods to fill the yard.

The little entry courtyard was home to the one tree that came with the house, a nicely shaped Pinyon Pine tree. She filled the sides of the entry walk with Alyssum and they dug up and hauled in some small Ponderosa Pines from the forest country as far away as Gallup.

The front and back yards were soon covered with smooth lawn grass, except for one area of the front where they dropped a huge red sandstone that they had wrestled into their vehicle over near Fort Wingate. The kidney shaped stone was the centerpiece of their new yard and was surrounded by red cinders.

Out behind the back yard cinder block fence lay the open field where the boys would stake out their new playground, along with their friends who came right away to join them in whatever adventures five and seven year olds could dream up, which was usually quite daring.

At first they rode their bikes around the outside edge of the field until a path was well worn, and then they began to ride full speed into and out of the five foot deep arroyo that cut through the middle of the field. Soon they had figured out ways to play their own baseball games on either side of the arroyo, usually two against two, normally batters and the pitcher on one side of the arroyo and the one fielder across the ditch to try and corral the long fly balls.

***

So the move was soon accepted as okay, and he was quickly into a different kind of job from what he had done in Taos. Instead of being a designer he was now supervising all the engineering activities and also learning where these activities were taking place. And they were, he found, taking place over a huge part of New Mexico, and even over into parts of the Oklahoma panhandle.

Whereas the previous forest had consisted of three separate sections, the steep mountains east of Taos, the more gentle pine forests west of the Rio

Grande, and the isolated but small Jicarilla area, his new territory was totally different.

There were units as far west as Gallup, including the Zuni mountains and the Mount Taylor range near Grants, another big chunk of land down south of Magdalena in the San Mateo mountains, plus the big fault block mountains that came steeply down almost to his house, the Sandias and across the freeway to the south another large area called the Manzano mountains, with separate units on out into the plains to the south and east toward Vaughan.

But that was not all. Their responsibility also went even further over to the east into what was called national grasslands, three units of land that had been taken over by the federal government after the dust bowl days had blown all the dirt farmers off the land. These units were at Clayton and Roy, New Mexico, and out in the Oklahoma territory at a place called Black Kettle.

He pored over the maps to try and figure out how his small group of folks could possibly keep up with that much country, but he soon found out that they did it by staying on the road. It was always at least a two day trip to make even the most minor inspection of a job, so they had to plan their time in a lot more detail than in other places. And a trip to the field usually meant scheduling a route that would cover more than one area before returning home.

As overseer of all the various activities, he was expected to show no favorites but to attend to all equally as needs dictated. With that philosophy in mind, he could hardly say no to one of his assistants when they invited him to go along on the next inspection of the tramway. After all, he was continually reminded, his predecessor had made the inspection many times!

He and that predecessor (whom he had also followed into his job at Taos) had become fast friends over the years, but right then he really didn't care much for him. He wanted to say that he was just a big showoff, but held his tongue and braced himself for what was clearly going to be a test of his commitment to this job.

He wished he could have found an excuse to say no because he had already heard talk of what that inspection involved, and what it involved was another one of his least favorite things to do. Climbing around on things in high places.

He had inherited a fair amount of that particular fear, too close to actually being a phobia to ignore, from his dear mother. She was known to make the driver stop the car so she could get out and move around to the uphill side of the car if she happened to catch herself on a mountainous road.

The Sandia Peak Tramway started at the base of the mountain just outside the edge of town, climbed over one mile in elevation in about two miles of distance, and consisted of two cabins that were hung onto a set of two continuous cables that stretched over two towers that lay between the base of the tramway and the upper terminal at the top of the mountain.

These cabins were large enough to carry upwards of fifty people each, and when one cabin was moving uphill the other was coming down, always meeting right in the middle, which was close to the point where the cable stretched over the deepest point of the ride. That deepest point was around eleven hundred feet above the rocky gorge.

The two towers were located along the route on a couple of rocky outcrops, and one tower was not that bad at all, being only about eighty feet high where the cables rolled over the sheaves on either side of the top of the tower. But as easy as that tower was to take, the other one completely made up for it in a really bad way.

Not only was it over two hundred feet high, but because of the location and the stresses that the cables placed on that particular point in the line, the tower also had to be built at a slight angle out from vertical. The tower leaned just enough so that the top was hanging out over the cliffs below instead of being right over the tower proper.

All these factors were mostly unknown to and uncared about by the general ticket-buying tourist who took the ride up to the top for a twenty minute view of the city and big river below before hopping on board for the return to the base. But as he was soon to find out, they were definitely going to come into play during the upcoming inspection that he had been invited to join.

The tram manager, Willie Williams, the primary district inspector, an Eskimo ski bum named Pete Totemhoff, the assistant engineer, Ken Kilpatrick, and he crawled into the lower cabin that morning to begin what would be one of the hardest days he had endured as an engineer.

He found out right away that these guys didn't plan to ride the tramway inside the cabin. That was obviously for sissies and tourists, and possibly scaredy-cat supervising engineers.

Everyone crawled out onto the top of the cabin as soon as the thing started moving up the mountain. The cabin was about eight feet square and probably seven feet tall inside, and was connected to the transport or "haul" cable by a hanger that was approximately two feet wide by ten feet high.

One side of the hanger had a ladder-like set of steps that could be ascended, should anyone really care to do such a thing, to go on up to inspect the huge pulleys laying across the two inch steel cables that ran along each side of the transport rope to keep the cabin from falling into the decomposed granite abyss far below.

By the time he got up the nerve to join the others on top of the cabin, the car was just about to go over the first tower. His stomach, which had been riding along well below its normal location, suddenly switched to his throat as the cabin went over the "hump" of the tower. And, he discovered, all the good hand-holds were taken, which probably explained why everyone else had been in such a hurry to get on top of the cabin first. This was bad. It was about to get a lot worse.

The second tower finally came into sight and he began to brace himself for another loop-de-loop bounce, but no, the cabin began to slow as they came to the high point where the car went across the second tower's sheaves, or rollers. He heard someone saying something about getting off here to look at the tower, but he was sure that he had misunderstood.

After all, his ears were ringing loudly from the blood that was pumping through his veins, and the wind was also whipping up a pretty good breeze. He looked up, hoping to not see what he saw next. First Willie, then Pete, then Ken, were climbing on up that little set of ladder rungs. He was not sure he could even move, but there they were, all up on top of the hanger, climbing on over the cables and stepping casually over the three foot open space onto a tiny little platform that jutted out toward the cabin from the top of the tower.

He moved slowly and, he hoped, surely, toward the top. Ten ladder rungs. One at a time. Two hands and all his toes holding onto something at all times. Finally there were no more rungs above him and he searched for something else to hold onto. There was nothing.

He had to stand up on the contraption that was just a jumble of pulleys and cables and, apparently, a large and critical amount of axle grease. The others were encouraging him...at least he hoped it was encouragement, as they reached across the chasm that now seemed more like ten feet than three, took his hand, and he stepped across total nothingness onto the tower.

He tried not to look down but he did, and he could see that a slip and fall would be game over. His hands clenched the steel pipe side rails of the tower platform with all their might, as the others wandered around, climbing up and down and around, checking for signs of loose bolts or rusty paint or whatever the excuse had been for bringing him to this god-awful circumstance.

Finally it was time to get back on the cabin. But how? He knew for certain that there was no way that he could step back across that open space onto that unsteady hanger top. They told him what would come next, and even though it sounded like a horrible idea, anything was better than going back down the way they came up.

They would climb down a ladder on the side of the tower to a second small platform that also extended out toward the cabin. From there they would simply step off the platform, through the open door of the cabin, and be inside. That sounded pretty good to him, although he wasn't looking forward to climbing out onto the ladder, which was totally open all the way to the ground far below.

At least once he got down to the next platform, stepping over into the cabin sounded pretty simple enough, and it would have been simple, except for one minor design detail that had been overlooked. The floor of the platform that they would be stepping off of was about three feet higher than the floor of the cabin which they would be jumping into. And of course there was that three feet of open space between said platform and said cabin. A piece of cake, right?

It seemed so easy as the other three took turns nimbly hopping from platform to cabin. He tried to ignore the fact that they were suspended two hundred feet over nothing but a big pile of solid granite, in a strong and shifting wind, AND that the top of the cabin door was just about the right level to catch you in the head if you didn't duck underneath it when you jumped!

He was no longer worried about passing this silly macho test. At this point all he wanted to do was pass the survival test. When he hunkered down, closed his eyes, and somehow cleared the top of the door and landed as far over into the cabin as possible, he breathed for the first time in what seemed like an hour.

One time was going to be more than enough for this exercise. The next tram inspection would definitely not include him.

And if he worried about that decision, he felt somewhat exonerated in his fear of the tramway operation when, a short time later, that strong side wind caught the side of one of those cabins just as it approached a tower, blowing the hanger enough to lift the haul cable out of the track of the sheave on that tower and stranding two cabins full of tourists, one of which just happened to be hanging over that quarter mile high spot along the line.

The dozen or so folks in the lower cabin were able to be lowered from the car on a rescue line, since they were only about ninety feet above the ground. But something like thirty five people would end up spending the rest of the afternoon, all night, and a good part of the next day crowded into their little glass and steel box, suspended so far above the canyons below that there was no way to extricate them.

Even if there had been a rescue line that would have reached the ground almost twelve hundred feet below, the terrain where they would have been deposited was far too rugged for most of them to be able to hike out.

He and the folks who were most concerned about things like tramways loaded with tourists falling into canyons managed to keep things semi-calm on the mountain through the night and well into the next day.

Many attempts were made and theories tested and thrown out during the night and following morning, but it finally took a big Huey helicopter that was flown across from an air base in Oklahoma to perform a very dangerous maneuver before the issue was settled.

That maneuver involved dropping a line down to hook onto the transport cable of the tramway, lifting the cable and the cabin up to re-set the haul cable into the sheave at the tower, and hoping that this could all be done without dropping the cable and cabin hard enough to cause the tower to collapse, thus sending the upper cabin plummeting into a Sandia Mountain abyss with all passengers on board.

There were some mighty happy tourists, tramway operators, and engineers when that final cabin docked at the lower terminal toward the end of that second day.

**

Albuquerque turned out to be a good move for them. The neighborhood was full of kids for the boys to play with, the schools were nearby and very interesting (some might say intriguing), and his job was challenging but fun.

They even moved up in their camping gear from the old green wall tent to an almost-new pop-up trailer, which they would spend many nights in over the next thirty-plus years.

After a short trip up to Jemez Falls to make sure they knew how to use their new toy, they embarked on a real vacation that first summer in Albuquerque. One day in July they hooked the tent trailer on behind the Charger and took off for Canada.

Their enthusiasm and high hopes took a serious hit when they were only about forty miles out of town. As they started up the steep climb at La Bajada Hill just south of Santa Fe, the car suddenly stopped dead and would not go any further.

A quick trip into town and back with a new fuel pump seemed to solve the problem as the Dodge started right up and went on over the hill. They were soon back in an optimistic mood and looking forward to putting some serious miles behind them before dark.

The car started missing again before they made it to Chama, but they limped on over the hills into a small campground near Pagosa Springs. No more problems occurred until they went on through Durango and started up over the huge climb over to Silverton. The Million Dollar Highway it was called.

Before that day ended they would call it something else altogether as they had to be towed over the summit by a friendly family driving an old jeep. Once they made it to the top, the car ran fine and they went on down and stopped for the night in the first town that had a Dodge dealership, which happened to be Grand Junction.

They pulled in at the local KOA campground for the night and next morning they took the car in to the dealer, where they spent the entire day sitting in the waiting room while the mechanics poked and pulled and replaced anything that they thought (guessed) might be causing the problem. Fuel lines were blown out, filters replaced, the regular automatic fan was removed and a different style added to give the starving engine some more oxygen. Maybe it was the high altitude, one said. Or the heat, another thought.

On and on it went, and the bill came to a lot more than they had planned to spend on the entire trip, but they had no choice but to pay it. At least the car seemed to be running just fine now, which was worth a lot.

The decision they talked about that night back in the campground was whether to abort the trip and turn back to home, or keep going. They had lost a day and a half of their allotted travel time, plus they were still not totally confident that the problem with the car had been solved.

A good night's sleep and a fresh outlook the next morning saw them staying the course and heading on up the interstate toward Rifle, Colorado, where they would turn back north toward their destination. And sure enough, twenty miles out of Grand Junction, the car started stalling again.

After spending an hour at a roadside gas station, with no actual results other than a few more theories about what could possibly be the problem, several of which involved some of the replacement parts that had just been installed down at the dealership.

They finally got the car running again and made it on up to Rifle where they couldn't find a campground and had to get a room in a motel for the night.

After they checked in they unhooked the car from the trailer and drove down to see if there was a mechanic in this town, which was much smaller than Grand Junction. As luck would have it, there was even a Dodge dealership downtown, but when they went inside they were met with the realities of small town situations. There was a mechanic. One guy.

It was too late in the day for him to work on it, but he did listen to their description of the symptoms they had experienced for the last three days and after they talked for about five minutes, he told them what the problem was. Bad camshaft, he said.

They were pleased to hear him come to a different conclusion, but they also knew this probably meant the end of Canada for this year. A camshaft sounded like more time and money than they had left. What is there to do in Rifle, they asked, figuring on spending their Canada vacation time here instead. Not much, the expected response. There is a swimming pool.

Before they left to go back to the motel, the mechanic, who they both would say later that night was a dead ringer for Walter Mathau, said he wanted to take the car for a short test drive to confirm his suspicions. Five minutes later he came back and said yes, it had to be the camshaft. Okay, they braced themselves, tell us the bad news. How long and how much?

Well, he said, doing his best Walter impression, I'll order a camshaft first thing in the morning. It will be put on the Greyhound bus in Denver and be here by noon. In the meantime, I can take everything off the engine down to the heads while I'm waiting for it, then when it gets here I'll throw it in there and put 'er all back together for you.

They waited for the big shoe to drop. And, he finished wiping his hands, adjusted his horn-rimmed glasses, and said...You got lucky. You have a fifty-thousand mile warranty on this engine. You only have forty-eight thousand miles on this baby as of today. It won't cost you a penny.

They spent the next day at the swimming pool, came back to the Dodge place at closing time that afternoon, drove the Charger to the motel and loaded everything into the car that was still pointed north.

It would be several days before he would stop flinching every time he felt the least bit of a quiver in the big magnum engine, but they went on to Wyoming, through Yellowstone, stopping in Eureka, Montana to spend the night with friends they knew from Taos.

They rode the ferry system across the interior of British Columbia to Kamloops and on up to make the big turn back south at Tete Jaune Cache. Heading south all the way back down through Jasper and Banff and into Glacier they drove, stopping again in the middle of Wyoming at a mosquito-infested campground before coming back over the highest mountains they could find in Colorado at Leadville, they finished the entire trip just as they had originally planned.

They made it home on the day they had planned to get back, and as far as they knew, that engine never missed another lick the rest of its natural life. And one other thing: They never saw a Walter Mathau movie after that without thinking about a master mechanic they met one time in Rifle, Colorado.

24

 One look at the view that dream-like August morning and he knew why they had named this place Springtime Canyon. He was wandering the lonely roads of the southern end of the San Mateos with Bill Kuffler and Sid Wells, two of his favorite people on the engineering staff of the Cibola.

The monsoon rains of summer had been falling down here for a couple of weeks now and the low clouds still lay in the heads of the canyons that ran from the roads back up into the mountains where Cochise and his warriors had made one of their last stands.

The boys had told him the stories of how the Apache Kid had fled the cavalry and holed up near the high peaks that were just barely visible through the fog that morning. Sid and Bill just had to show him some of the country that most people never saw.

They had spent the night in Magdalena at the one motel that was reasonably decent, eating breakfast as soon as the one restaurant that was not so decent had opened. As soon as the coffee took effect they were on the road up over the mountain and out past Withington Lookout, on down south almost to another lookout tower, Grassy, that held the view of the main San Mateo range, and then dropping east down off the mountain into Rosedale canyon country.

They went past the old crumbling adobe walls of the old mining settlement named after the canyon and turned south to skirt the foothills of the mountains all the way down to Springtime and Nogal canyons.

The summer rains had brought magic to the high desert country. Everywhere they looked the slopes shone brilliantly with wildflowers that had lain dormant for a year. The nearslopes were painted orangy-red with Indian and Early Paintbrush, while every possible color available to the Penstemons lined the roadsides.

Anything resembling a wet meadow was awash with the lavender palette owned by the Wild Iris. Sego Lilies lay thickly among the fields of burgundy Artemisia and Brome. It seemed to him that every bend in the road featured a new and totally different species of the cacti that made this landscape so unique to anything he had ever seen before.

He laughed when he remembered that a friend from Taos, Dave Lyons, had told him when he heard that he was moving to the Cibola that there was something about the desert country that got into one's blood. That statement was coming from a fellow who had moved from Albuquerque to Taos and immediately took his wife and three little children over across the Rio Grande Gorge to live in an old two or three room shack in the middle of the sagebrush barrens out by Tres Orejas.

There was no electricity. There was no water. Not just no running water. No water. Every time Dave came to town, which was a forty-five minute drive up a dirt road and across the high bridge to Taos, he brought three or four five gallon cans to haul water back to their place. He was hoping the desert didn't get as far into his blood as it obviously had Dave's.

When they stopped to eat their sack lunches among the red rocks near Nogal campground, the sun had burned enough of the clouds away for them to see on into the distance toward the Gila country. He took a picture of Sid and Bill sitting on the rocks, then turned his camera toward the scene of a lifetime.

With the partially clouded sepia sky in the background, he shot one photograph of a Yucca that had sent a massive creamy white bloom fifteen feet into the desert sky. It was the last frame left on the last roll of film he had brought. He just hoped that the shot had been captured.

On through the historic Spanish settlement at Monticello they turned back up into the mountains so he could see the Cibola's own Burma Road. Sid explained how the CCC boys had built this road back in the thirties, showing him how the skill of the army engineers had left a still stable roadway that hung on the side of the highly erosive soil of the southern New Mexico desert country.

Steel culverts that had been installed over forty years before still drained the hillsides across the roadway with very little erosion showing anywhere, mainly because the pipes had been installed properly and in the right places, and the headwalls where the runoff dropped into the culverts were built with painstaking care of masonry that still looked as solid as the day it had been put there.

That was the way this forest was. Huge, spread out across the state, and full of wonderful surprises. They came on around to Cuchillo and took the road along the west side of the mountains up to where one of the long time ranchers, Hershel Welty, lived. The Welty ranch, as well as the Panckeys on the south end, Reuben and Uncle Joe, ran cattle on thousands of acres of their own land as well as on allotments that went up into the National Forest.

They were not only customers, they were partners and they were neighbors. It would not do to drive past their ranch houses without stopping in for a cup of coffee. This visit might be the only one they would have from the Forest Service for months on end, and might even be the only visits of any kind in weeks.

After visiting with Rancher Welty they drove on along the Forest road that ran right through his front yard filled with peacocks and various other assorted fowl and hound dogs (Hershel was a bear hunter) and went on up to a place called Red John Box. This was a tight box canyon where the road barely had room to traverse alongside the little stream that came pouring out of the mountain at this time of the year. The road ended up against the sheer cliffs a quarter of a mile past the box, but it was a major jumping off point for hunters, hikers, and horsemen who were heading for the high country of San Mateo Peak.

A few miles up after coming back out to the main road, they came to a massive adobe-walled white painted building that stood all alone a few hundred feet off the road. It was commonly called the Dusty school house and had not been used as such for many years now, but still stood firm against the winds, occasional snows, and summer monsoon rains.

Imbedded into the stucco over the front entrance were the words "Pershing School No. 15." Named after the famous General John Joseph "Black Jack" Pershing who had helped push the Apaches back into the wilderness above and also the man who had tried but failed to track Pancho Villa down across the Rio Grande after his raid on Columbus. He wondered at the tales that may have been told in this one room school building.

On up into Beartrap canyon and past the site of an old sawmill at a place called Hughes Camp identified by a little brown routed sign alongside the road, up over another minor pass and back out across the flats into the San Augustine plains. They discussed the rumors they had been hearing about how the government was planning to install a series of huge antenna dishes on railroad tracks out here in this country to try and see if anyone in outer space might be trying to contact us.

They laughed about how the project made about as much sense as the one down the road past Magdalena where someone had strung massive cables across the canyons from the top of Langmuir Peak to measure the forces of lightning strikes that hit the mountaintop.

They drove on over to Datil, stopped in at Coker's service station/store/restaurant and had a big steak at the only decent place to eat in that part of the country. Then at Pie Town they had to have dessert and a cup of coffee before heading north across the back country into the Zuni Mountains.

The Zunis were not nearly as high or impressive as the San Mateos, but after the turn of the century had yielded large amounts of ponderosa pine timber to be shipped back east to the growing population centers of the country. Still visible all along the route they drove that day were the remains of the railroad grades that had been cut to lay track in the early part of the century whereby logs could be removed and shipped out to the sawmills where they would be turned into prime grade lumber for the booming building construction that was taking place in America's cities.

Although the steel rails had been taken up soon after the logging ended, there were plenty of reminders in the rotting ties and scattered spikes still scattered along the grades.

After the big trees were cut out, turpentine hunters came in and dug up the rich pine stumps to boil the oil out of them for the thriving spirits market. It was surprising to see the mountain range in fairly decent shape, although it was obvious that the heavy logging and massive grazing of cattle and sheep that took place after logging had degraded the soil to the point where it would never be as productive as before.

But there were groves of aspen trees mixed in with pine and scattered spruce and fir as they drove along through places named Johnny Mack Brown Canyon, McKinley Ridge, past McGaffey Lake and campground and out to Fort Wingate where the army had only recently turned over the old stone compound that had been occupied since before World War I to the Forest Service.

There they stopped in to chat with the District Ranger, Steve Romero, getting a long list of projects that he and they knew would never be completed with the small crews and limited funding they had to work with. But they would prioritize and he would be happy.

At the end of the day they enjoyed one of the real privileges of the job, spending a night at the El Rancho Hotel in Gallup. Dinner in the hotel dining room was wonderful, the green chile rellenos that had become his favorite were especially tasty, and they each slept in a room that had seen more than a few major movie stars in the glory days. The country around Gallup had been one of the prime locations for movies, especially westerns, and rooms were identified with pictures outside the doors based on which star had stayed in that room.

This would not be the only time he would find a way to be in Gallup come sundown, still well over a hundred miles from Albuquerque and not wanting to hurry home late. On one of the more memorable nights the food in the hotel was good but they were in a hurry to get back to his room and turn on the television.

That night he had been sharing the trip with Kuffler again, but also along were his friends from work, Jerry Goon and Warren "Short" Hall. They finished dinner hurriedly and hustled back to his room, the room with the

"Ronald Reagan" picture by the door. They turned the television on just in time to see Henry Aaron hit home run number 715.

He taped a cardboard sign over the door before leaving the next morning that read "Hammering Hank Suite."

It just seemed like the right thing to do.

***

Just when they thought that life in Albuquerque could not get any better, along came a little girl. Life would never be the same after that, not for any of them.

From the start she had two big brothers who pampered her and protected her and made her a part of everything they did, whether it be little league in the summer or sledding in the Sandias in the winter.

When they rode their skateboards down the sidewalks tossing a basketball back and forth between the two boys and neighbor Dean, she came tooling along behind seated on her own board, sucking her thumb as she turned the corner into the driveway down the street.

She sat on the back fence and cheered them on as they played ball or jumped their bicycles and mini-bikes across the arroyo with Lori and Dean, and they strapped an oversized life jacket on her so she could ride the rapids with them on a camping trip to the Pecos up above Santa Fe. When winter broke enough for them to make a trip down to White Sands, she held on tightly as they ran along either side of her down the steep slopes of snow-like gypsum sand.

She hitched a ride in the backpack carrier on hikes into the Sandia Mountains on the La Luz Trail, a trail that had been used during filming as Kirk Douglas rode away from Walter Mathau many years before in Kirk's favorite movie, "Lonely Are the Brave."

These trails had special meaning to him which very few people would have ever guessed. Edward Abbey wrote a book called "The Brave Cowboy." It was about the loss of independence of the person told from the perspective of a cowboy, John W. "Jack-for-short" Burns, who after a minor scrape with the local carceleros, made a run for freedom on his favorite horse Whiskey.

The story was set in Albuquerque and the run over the mountains was right up this west slope of the Sandias. Thus the trail system, which was partly built or improved during a time when the movie was filmed.

So when he was assigned to the planning team that was put together to analyze and validate the construction of a major road that was to be built on the back side of the mountain, little did anyone know he had a personal interest in the project from long before his days on the Cibola.

He had been thinking about this mountain from as far back as their honeymoon and a night long ago in Salt Lake City when they had watched Kirk Douglas struggle up the steep slopes to avoid the helicopters and society in general.

In the beginning it was a simple task. Appoint a team to put the finishing touches on a plan to complete a forest highway from the top of the Sandias off the north side of the mountain and back around to the interstate. The clearing for the initial phase of the work had already been done when someone decided that perhaps an environmental study should be done before going any further.

Seven of them had been assigned to the study, and after half a year of being holed up in the basement of the Ranger Station out at Tijeras, the draft plan was presented to the powers that be as well as the public.

The powers that be loved it because, although there were questions raised between the lines, the report appeared to come close enough to validating the project that it would allow the construction to proceed, pending the formality of a brief public comment period and the writing of a final environmental statement.

The public was not so supportive. In fact, it soon became obvious from the comments that were being received, as well as letters to the local newspapers, that the only people who were in favor of the highway were those selfsame powers that be. The team disbanded, having completed their assigned task with the draft plan, but he ended up with the unenviable task of carrying the draft into the final stage.

He read all the letters that came in, talked to all the people who called to comment, and began to put together a final statement. What would that statement say? He was in a real bind, knowing that his bosses all wanted the project to move forward, but also knowing that the public support for the project was not there and would never be there. There was one other thing that bothered him.

In the beginning he had gone into the effort fully standing behind the validity of the need for the highway. But after a year of studying the situation and listening to the arguments for and against, he had come to the conclusion that the project should not be completed. He felt that it was not only wrong from a public support standpoint, but in actuality, there was no need for the road.

As an engineer he knew how the construction would carve a wide swath through the heart of the undeveloped portion of the mountain. What bothered him the most was that the east side of the big mountain appeared to be highly unstable, with a clear fault line running directly in the path of where the road would have to go.

And for what? So the tourists would not have to backtrack over the five mile road they had driven up for their fifteen minute look at the Rio Grande Valley? It was doubly sacrilegious for him, an engineer and a forest service person, to have the audacity to question such a project.

One day he sat down in the office with his immediate supervisor, who until this time had not given any indication of where he stood on the road project, and he laid out his feelings about the road. It should not be built, he said. Here are all the reasons why. He was shocked to find that his boss felt the same way, and had for some time.

The supervisor had just been waiting for the study to lay out the conclusions, which had now been done. The two of them gathered up the papers and all the nerve they could muster, fine-tuned their resumes, and went to the powers that be downtown in the upper offices of the federal building. He figured they would both be banished from the service forever after, but the day was finished without bloodshed, and the project was cancelled.

He would always tell his closest friends afterwards that he was as proud of the road that did not get built as he ever was of any of those that he had built.

And he was pleasantly surprised and greatly pleased when, a few days before he would move on to Oregon, the head man of the powers that be came by the office to say goodbye and wish him well in his new venture to the great northwest.

As he took one last, long look up at the watermelon-colored cliffs of the big mountain as the sun set on his last evening in Albuquerque, he had just one thought: This one's for you, John W. Burns.

25

 We were sitting there in our house over on the home place that afternoon listening to T. Texas Tyler talking/singing a song about a deck of cards. I didn't know what surreal meant at the time, but I did know how weird this whole scene felt to me.

It was strange enough to be able to listen to a record playing on the little portable phonograph that Aunt Nina had brought up from Katy, Texas when she had made another one of her escapes from the clutches of her failed or at least failing marriage to Uncle Jack Hopper.

It was strange because it hadn't been that long ago since we wouldn't have had any electricity to even play such a device. And stranger still the feeling of sitting around waiting for our destiny to play out later that day at the new Langley gymnasium.

It had simply been one amazing summer that year when we were visited by the REA linemen who came over the hill from the Black Springs road, down past Earl Dowdy's place, and on across onto the south forty of our place, clearing a right of way and sinking poles into the ground. They came right up to our front yard with the last pole, which was located about sixty feet down past the front of our house.

From there they ran a second line across the branch and over to the Cowart's house, and soon the lines were strung and somehow we had little porcelain outlets in the middle of the ceiling in every room in which light bulbs were inserted. When the electricians left the house they told us to leave the cords that hung down from the fixtures just as they were because, they promised, soon there would be light coming from those bulbs.

Seems like it took forever, but I'm sure it was no more than a few days when, suddenly, we were astonished to see those lights flicker briefly, and then burn steadily. Hallelujah! We had juice at last, thanks to the REA and that new dam on the Little Missouri River down by Murfreesboro.

So there was another benefit to the lake besides just the great bass fishing that we had been enjoying, after all. Now we could also listen to the Grand Ole Opry every Saturday night without having to worry about running the battery down on the old upright radio.

I suppose my expectations of change would have been hard to meet under any circumstances, but in our case, there wasn't much that could have been done overnight. We did bring in a small refrigerator for the kitchen (still called it an "icebox" of course), and that first summer Dad installed a small pump down in the spring house so he could run a water line from there up to the garden by the barn.

That extra water helped out a lot because we were still suffering through a period of drought in our part of the country which seriously affected our food supply from the garden. Other than that, we were pretty much sticking to the lifestyle we were accustomed to, which included the cold house in the winter and the outhouse year 'round.

A few of the folks in Langley made more drastic changes, and one of those changes would impress me significantly. Loney Jones bought a television. As far as I knew she was the first to buy such a thing and for a long time her set was the only one around our part of the country.

I suspect her experience with it may have discouraged a few other people from considering such a purchase. Not long after the word got out that she had a television, she began to experience a dramatic increase in her nightly visitors.

Loney ran the store in Langley and her husband, John L., had died a few years earlier. They had two boys at home, Johnny and Tommy. Tommy was a couple of years younger than Johnny and just happened to be in my class at school.

Tommy was very happy to invite his suddenly expanded group of friends to his house to watch the new phenomenon, and I was soon hooked on Sunday nights at the Jones' house, where a dozen or more of us would crowd into Loney's tiny living room, sitting on the floor or wherever a spot could be found, to watch "I've Got a Secret" with Garry Moore and "What's My Line" with John Charles Daly on a little fifteen inch black and white set with rabbit ears for an antenna.

Most of the time we could even see the people on the show, and occasionally we could tell who they were. But it didn't matter. We were hooked for life.

Soon after the word came down that Langley was going to get electricity, the school folks decided to ante up enough money to build a new gymnasium. Once again, the local people pitched in and the school ground was transformed into a whole new world where inside games became a lot more fun than the outside games we had grown up with.

It wasn't long after we got our new gym that we learned that Langley was going to receive a great honor: We would get to host the annual County Basketball Tournament!

There were five towns in Pike County that had high schools, including Langley, which was by far the smallest enrollment of any. Kirby was the next smaller, but still larger than Langley, and they had been playing in their own gymnasium for many years. Glenwood, Delight, and Murfreesboro were the other three schools, with Murfreesboro being the county seat of government and, at that time, the largest school.

Playing host to the county tournament was a big deal, especially for a place like Langley which had until this year been playing their basketball on an outdoor court out behind the school building.

The tournament would take place over about three days at the end of the season, and would include action from all four levels that were played. Senior boys and senior girls, which would be kids from tenth through twelfth grades, and also junior boys and girls, consisting of the players from grades seven through nine.

There was one other reason we were all extremely excited to be holding the tournament in our gym that year. Langley, for once, had a very good senior boys' team. This fact was not lost on the Austin household, where Dad just happened to be the coach of the boys' team.

He had been coaching the boys since the new school opened, and had suffered through the good times as well as (mostly) the bad. Having such a small enrollment usually meant barely being able to suit up enough players to get through the season, and there had been times when Langley had played games with no more than six or seven players suited out, instead of the normal contingent of ten.

Having very small classes to draw from meant that the talent level was always highly variable, but the stars were aligned properly for this particular year and dad was looking forward to the opportunity to bring a successful season to a glorious climax with a victory in the tournament.

Langley had played some tough teams that year, mostly out of the county, traveling to places like Saratoga and Wickes to play much larger schools, and so far they had lost very few games. They had not really been challenged by any of the county teams that they would face here in the county playoffs.

Our team's strength started with the Linville brothers, Jerald ("Jake") and Burl ("Bally"), plus another tough-as-nails shooter in Bobby Risner. They were complemented by strong play from some of the Lodi boys, particularly Frazier and Clidus Cowart, Floyd Welch, Kenneth Vaught, and another player that they hadn't really counted on for this year, Carl Turner.

Carl was a tall, quiet, unassuming kid who had never been very interested in sports but had been talked into playing by Jake and some of his other classmates. He had contributed greatly to the team with his defensive and rebounding skills, plus his ability to score inside due to his height. Dad said many times that he didn't have any real superstars on this team, but that it was a team that played together as well as any he had ever coached.

So far the tournament had gone as expected. Langley had not been tested in their early games, and Murfreesboro, although they had emerged as the team that would join Langley in the finals on Saturday night, had barely gotten by their opponents in the preliminary games. It looked like the stage was set for the home team to inaugurate the new gymnasium with the first trophy to go in the school trophy case out in the principal's office.

Dad had given me the option that day of either going on up to the gym to watch the finals being played by the juniors and the girls seniors, or allowing me to hang out at our house with the soon-to-be champions of all of Pike County.

He had taken great pains to sequester his boys away from all of the distractions that were going on up at the gym by bringing them all over to our house for the day. He was taking no chances by making sure they got their rest, had a good but not too heavy meal, and kept their minds as far away from basketball as possible until the time came for them to walk onto the court that night.

I didn't have to think twice about what I would do. I would stay right there and watch these guys relaxing and getting ready for their big show.

Some of the boys were playing cards around the kitchen table, some were napping after lunch, and I was doing my best to be part of the entertainment package by playing Aunt Nina's phonograph player. Our selection of forty-five rpm platters was quite limited so I'm fairly certain that the boys were getting pretty tired of hearing that soppy song about the deck of cards by the time Dad came over to load us up and take us back to the gym. The senior girls game was over soon after we arrived and the boys went downstairs to dress out for their game.

The little gym was packed to the rafters, literally, with two-thirds of Langley and Lodi crammed into the five or six rows of seats alongside the court and upstairs in the balcony. Others from around the county who had come to watch their teams in the earlier games stayed for the finals of course, so when the game got underway I was really worried that our boys would not be able to play their game with all the noise and excitement.

It was such a contrast to the earlier part of our day, which had been spent in the quiet solitude of the farm. But Langley was ready for this game, and by the time the first half ended it appeared that the game was basically over. It was just a matter of how badly we would end up pounding the poor ole Murfreesboro Rattlers.

The halftime score was something like twenty-six for Langley to only about twelve or fourteen for Murfreesboro. The Linville boys had done much of the damage, with Jake shooting jumpers and "Bally" driving for lay-ups after stealing the ball from Murfreesboro's rattled ball handlers. Bobby Risner and Frazier Cowart had added a few points and Carl Turner had been dominant in keeping the scoring down on the inside.

The Langley crowd couldn't wait to get the second half over with so we could start our celebration. Some of the old boys in the bleachers suggested that perhaps Murfreesboro might just slip out the back door and go home, not even showing up for the second half. Unfortunately for Langley, that didn't happen.

I never heard Dad admit his mistake as I could always tell he didn't want to talk about it, but he hinted a few times that he may have played too cautiously in the second half. The game back then was a low-scoring affair, with no three-point shot, no shot clock, and no sophisticated offenses that could score a lot of points. Langley's score at half-time in the mid-twenties was at least on par with what normally would have been expected.

There was one other rule at the time which would come into play in this game in a major way. When someone was fouled, the team whose player had been fouled had the option of either shooting a free throw or taking the ball out of bounds and thereby retaining possession.

Langley had one of the best dribblers ever to play the game in "Bally" Linville, so Dad decided that his strategy would be to try to hang onto the basketball as much as possible and by doing so, hope to keep Murfreesboro from being able to score enough to overtake our big lead.

The strategy worked for a while, until the opposing team figured out what was going on, after which they began to put two or three players to guarding Bally and when he gave it up to someone else Langley began to lose the ball on turnovers.

It didn't take long for the momentum to shift. Suddenly Murfreesboro hit a few shots, Langley turned the ball over several times, and it began to feel like maybe we should go back to playing like we had in the first half. Except that it wasn't that easy to turn that switch back on once it had been turned off.

The double-digit lead at halftime turned into single-digits by the start of the fourth quarter and now we had a game on our hands. Our shooters must have felt the pressure because even the easy shots started bouncing out. Langley committed fouls and Murfreesboro didn't miss a free throw. Langley tried stalling out the last few minutes, clinging to a five point lead that gradually shrunk to only a point with about a minute to go. We had the ball and all we had to do was keep it out of their hands and the game was ours.

"Bally" dribbled all over the front court, holding off the guards that swarmed around him until he finally had to pick up his dribble and pass the ball to someone else. There was no one open to pass it to, and when he finally tried to get it to a teammate, the ball bounced off the Langley player's hands and out of bounds!

Murfreesboro called a timeout and came back onto the court with a play that worked to perfection, and with less than half a minute to go, Langley was now behind by one point.

Dad chose not to call timeout but had the boys rush the ball up the court and with everyone on the other team assuming that one of the Linville boys would take the final shot to win or lose, the ball was passed inside to a waiting Carl Turner.

Carl's shot rimmed out with just a few seconds left on the clock, but the whistle had blown. He was fouled! Two free throws would win the game. One made shot would at least tie it and send it to overtime. The gymnasium was pandemonium as the guy who hadn't wanted to even play basketball stepped to the line and calmly…missed the first free throw. The crowd groaned, and then went totally silent.

The next sound that was heard in that gymnasium that was now a tomb was not a pin dropping, although it could have been. It was instead our broken hearts collectively falling as Carl missed that second free throw.

I would always feel the pain I felt that day as I walked out onto the court and came up to Jake Linville, not really knowing what to say or do when I saw the tears pouring down his face. We lost that game by the final score of thirty-three to thirty-two. I think we only scored six points in the second half.

I always felt in my heart that this was when Langley began to lose their school. And I would surely understand for the rest of my days why Carl Turner really had not wanted to play basketball that year.

26

The mystery would haunt me for a long time. I heard Tex Ritter's version of the events many times afterwards but was never quite sure that things had gone exactly like the song. Did Will Kane actually lay Frank Miller in his grave?

The last time I had seen them, the issue was still very much in doubt. But I'm getting a little ahead of myself here. First, I had to get to the night in question.

I don't know if our family vehicle, the Langley school bus, had kept Dad from taking his next career step or not, but I suspect it was a major deterrent. After all, how much campaigning for public office could one do without a car of his own?

Now that we had put the Wenatchee fruit harvest behind us and secured our very own mode of transportation, the little 1941 Chevy coupe, the next logical step was to get on the campaign trail.

The fellow who had served Pike County as representative in the State Legislature for many years, Lindell Hile, was from Murfreesboro and a friend of my Dad's. He had served several terms in Little Rock and had done a good job as a legislator but had decided not to run again. The southern part of the county was used to having their man in the legislature and a fellow from Delight, Alvis Stokes, was their choice to be the next representative from Pike County.

The folks in the northern half of the county were looking for someone to run against him with hopes of maybe seeing a little more attention in that neglected area. A lifelong Democrat who had done his share of politicking for others around southwest Arkansas, Pete looked over the field of potential replacements and decided that he surely must be as good as anyone to take over the job.

It was not going to be easy. Langley was stuck off in the far northwest corner of the county and had the smallest school of all the five towns, although at the time it was close to Kirby in enrollment.

Glenwood, Delight, and Murfreesboro were all much larger and had actual population centers in town, unlike Langley, which was simply a crossroads with a school, post office, two country stores, and widely scattered inhabitants living on farms from the Howard County line on the west almost to Salem on the east.

The long hot summer of 1952 was one that saw Pete Austin roll up the miles on our little coupe. He knew that he was a huge underdog in the race, but he also took that as a challenge and by the time election day rolled around in November, he had shaken hands and passed out his campaign card to every resident of the county from the last house on the upper Little Missouri River, occupied by the old hermit Jack Forrester, to the southern tip of the county in the river bottomland settlements of Pisgah and Bowen, and even in Boto, where he still had a few friends left after serving as headmaster at the school.

I rode many of those miles with Dad and was amazed at how efficient he was with his time. He picked out a road to travel, drove down that road until he came either to a house, or in some cases, saw a farmer working out in his field. Dad would stop and visit briefly, mostly simply introducing himself and handing out his little card, always stating what he needed: Votes.

His strategy seemed amazingly simple. Let the people see me, hear my name, and don't waste their valuable time (or mine) with small talk. He greeted a hundred people in the time the usual politician spent gabbing wastefully with five. And it worked for him, but his hard work probably would not have won the day had it not been for one other very important factor: Ernie Dunlap.

Ernie ran a general store in Kirby and was well know in Democratic circles all across Arkansas. All the main roads in Pike County ran through Kirby (it had originally been called "Crossroads" for that reason), and it was clear that all politics also had to pass through the little "All In One" store where Ernie spent his time, usually behind the meat counter, but always taking the time to talk politics with anyone who came into the store needing information on the latest election. Dad and Ernie had become good friends and Dad always knew that this fact had made all the difference in his life.

Election night was always exciting, but this year was more than just exciting. We had a dog in this race, as they say. The polls closed on the first Tuesday in November and everyone who was anyone gathered for the night on the lawn or steps of the county courthouse on the square in Murfreesboro. Ballot boxes were brought in from every precinct around the county, votes counted somewhere in the confines of the courthouse, and sometime around midnight, if we were lucky, winners were announced from the steps outside.

The good ole boys from the south end of the county did not seem too worried about their man that night. There had not been a representative elected from the northern parts for so many years now that no one could even recall the name of one. But as precinct after precinct came in and was counted, there was a little bit of stirring in the camp of the other candidate.

It appeared that the race was not going to be a landslide for their man after all, even though it had started out looking pretty favorable to the candidate from Delight. But Dad knew that the votes coming in first were from the nearby, southernmost towns, and the northern precincts would come in later. He felt good about what he was hearing as the night rolled on.

Eleven o'clock came and the two candidates were only separated by a few votes. I had hung on as long as possible, but I was sound asleep in the back seat of the Chevy when Dad knocked on the window. I could see his smile all the way across the parking lot as I ran after him to hear the final results being announced. Pete Austin was going to Little Rock as the next Pike County Representative!

I didn't even know it at the time, but I would be going with him for much of the time he would spend at the State Capitol. Thus began one of the most enjoyable episodes of our lives.

***

Dad always favored Orval Faubus, but Francis Cherry was my governor all the way. Pete and Orval became friends later on in life, long after the big brouhaha at Central High and Faubus' fame as the great white hope of the southland.

Their friendship was not based on that incident at all because neither Dad nor Orval were interested in keeping that battle alive.

Faubus had simply seen an opportunity to further his political life in a state where governors might survive for three terms if they were lucky, usually more like two terms, which in those days was only two years per term.

Orval had parlayed his popular resistance against the Yankee carpetbaggers into much more than even he imagined, but after it was over, he returned to the hills around Huntsville and lived out his life in relative obscurity. Pete traveled a lot in his later years and never failed to stop by and have a cup of coffee, or usually something a mite stronger, with "the Guv."

But my governor, the white haired rosy cheeked Texas/Oklahoma transplant who had used an innovative technique to knock out the strong and savvy incumbent, Sid McMath, in the 1952 election, had few political aspirations beyond getting elected. That was fairly apparent after he arrived in Little Rock as he managed to quickly live down to his opponents expectations by doing virtually nothing.

It had been a combination of McMath alienating a serious enemy at the wrong time, plus Cherry coming along with his "talkathon" campaigning gimmick that had put him in office. The talkathons had really been quite unique in Arkansas politics at a time when most campaigning was done from "the stump," with candidates traversing the state giving the same speech over and over at every little crossroads community they could squeeze into a harrowing schedule.

Francis Cherry knew he could not match the machine that McMath had built up over his many years in state politics, and he also was not a match for McMath's oratorical skills, so he came up with a system of radio programs that were simple call-in shows whereby folks from the hinterlands (usually total plants by his campaign staff) would ask him a question that he would respond to immediately. The gimmick was that he ran his talkathon for twenty-four straight hours without a break.

I'm not sure what kind of coffee he was drinking but he managed to pull it off, all the while sounding quite gubernatorial with his short and safe responses to short and safe questions. When the race was over, Arkansas had a governor who had been born in Texas, grew up in Oklahoma, and had only been involved in one small-time political race before, that of a probate judge.

I didn't know any of this stuff when I made my acquaintance with

Francis Cherry. But I liked him from the start because he actually acknowledged my existence and made me feel quite welcome in the governor's office every time I was there.

And believe it or not, I was there fairly often in those days! Of course my appearance at the governor's office consisted solely of performing one of my duties that I had recently acquired as a Page in the Arkansas legislature.

I was one of half-dozen or so of the young boys who were asked almost every day to take something from the legislative chambers over to the governor's office. That something was usually just a note from one of the representatives, but could also be a copy of a piece of proposed legislation that needed to be reviewed by the governor or his staff during consideration.

If Governor Cherry had a secretary I never knew it because the process we used was very direct: We went through the door to the governor's office, walked right up to his desk, and handed him whatever needed to be handed to him. If it were a note from someone, we were expected to wait until he had read it and gave us further instructions.

Sometimes that meant he jotted down his own note in response, but oftentimes he merely acknowledged the information and sent us packing back across the capitol building. Whatever his response, he was always friendly to me and soon called me by name when he was particularly attentive.

All this in itself would have been enough to make me a lifelong Francis Cherry man, but there would be another occasion when he would cement our relationship. There was some kind of issue down in Benton, about thirty miles south of Little Rock, that needed the Governor's attention.

I didn't know what the issue was at the time, and it really didn't matter to a thirteen year old Page boy. Some folks suspected that it may have been more than a simple budgetary concern, and the state of politics in Arkansas at the time certainly lent credence to those kinds of rumors. The strongest rumor centered around the fact that the State Mental Hospital (aka by ninety-nine percent of the non-inhabitants of the institution as the "insane asylum") might be located in an area that contained some of the hottest mineral in Arkansas at the time, which was Bauxite.

Bauxite was the primary ore from which Aluminum was made, and one of the largest employers in the state was an Aluminum manufacturer located in Benton. Whether any of this was actually relevant to the scheduled trip, or if it was being made simply as one of the lesser desired obligations of the new governor, I would never know. And after the day was over, I hoped that the subject would never come up in my presence again.

Governor Cherry convened a group of representatives that for some reason happened to include Dad to take a bus trip down to Benton and put in an appearance at the big gray-walled hospital compound. Inside these walls were housed folks from all over the state who had been judged mentally incompetent, unstable, or merely, I suspect in many cases, more or less in the way of someone who no longer wanted them around. This was the 1950s after all.

Now I know I have mentioned earlier that I had a couple of minor phobias. Well I knew as soon as I entered the halls of this hellhole that I had definitely failed to recognize the one fear that put all others to shame. I know I probably said I was afraid of the dark, not particularly fond of drunks, and definitely scared of hoboes.

By the time we had made it through the front door and down the hall of the first building, I was wishing I could escape to some dark alley in downtown Memphis with a bunch of boozing one-legged guys chasing after me on mechanics creepers. It was awful.

People were screaming at the tops of their voices, crying to have someone help get them out of this place, and either sitting over in a corner with a totally blank look on their face or, more commonly, standing against a wall where they seemed to be trying to knock themselves senseless, or the wall down. And I noticed that some of the legislators were not looking all that great at the moment, either.

I wasn't real smart in those days I guess, but it didn't take me long to understand why none of the other Pages had jumped at the opportunity to take this little "field trip." I also learned another valuable lesson that day, which was to always ride in the middle of the posse. I tried my best to surround myself with the entire group, including what I assumed might be two or three bodyguards who were plainclothes state policemen accompanying the Governor.

The administrators of the asylum must have thought we needed to see what they and the doctors or orderlies had to deal with on a daily basis because they spared us no pain and suffering on that day. Like most political situations, these hard working folks were probably unaware of the fact that any decisions regarding budgetary concerns would hardly be influenced by subjecting the Governor and a small group of reluctant legislators to the intimate details of what fit right in with my growing concept of what Hades must resemble on a bad day.

By the time we had made our way through what surely (hopefully) had to be the worst of the worst of this welcoming committee from hell, I was sticking as close to the Governor as I could possibly glue myself because I figured some of our group might accidentally be mistaken for inmates and get left behind when we came to the exit door. I did not intend to fall behind on this day.

We finally made it to what appeared to be the grand finale, a large room where there was a good crowd of folks who, had we met them on the streets of downtown Hot Springs, would have appeared to be quite normal. They were well behaved, properly dressed, and were not making any of those noises that I would hear in my quiet hours for so many years thereafter.

As we walked through this last mellow group, a nice looking fellow who appeared to be in his thirties, stepped forward and handed something to Governor Cherry. It looked like a roll of wrapping paper that was about three or four inches in diameter. The Governor took the papers, stopped, and thanked the man graciously as he unrolled his gift to see what it was.

Somewhere in this haunted young man's past, present, future, or maybe just his mind, clearly lived an artist. Every two foot by four foot sheet of what appeared to be butcher paper was covered with his work.

He had done with crayons what seemed to me to be some pretty amazing, if totally strange, drawings. Every page was a tapestry of all the colors in the Crayola palette that the caretakers had seen fit to provide our friend, Vincent van Gone. Eyes, canoes, horses, and waterfalls seemed to be the dominant features that could be found somewhere on each page, but there were many, many other scenes too... some recognizable, some not so.

I would be able to examine carefully every one of those tortured drawings many times after that day because after Governor Cherry and our group walked out the door into the free world again, he turned and handed me the paintings. His voice was barely audible but I would always remember his exact words: "I think the boy should have these."

I knew in my heart that it wasn't so much that the Governor wanted to give me those drawings that day as it was that he never wanted to see anything that would remind him of that experience.

He was not much for eye contact, but our eyes met for the briefest of moments as this strange exchange took place and I knew without any doubt that behind those eyes Governor Cherry was saying the exact same prayer that I was praying:

Please, Lord. Don't ever let me end up in a place like this.

27

 Do you think we made a mistake by moving here?

They had been on the road again that night, traveling down to Idaho to see the grandson's basketball game. He was a senior now and they were trying to spend as much time as possible enjoying the time they had with him.

She had been dozing most of the way home but awakened as they came over the hill and saw the lights of Baker City nestled down off to the left of the freeway. He didn't answer right away, but he knew what she meant.

They had lived half their lives here now and had never had any second thoughts about the decision to leave New Mexico for the Northwest. That is, until recently.

I don't think it was a mistake to move here, he said finally. Maybe it is a mistake to stay though.

They both knew how hard it would be to leave now, after all this time in one place, a place that they had actually come to love. A place that all the kids and grandkids would always consider like their second home too because of all the good times that had been shared here with the family. And of course the girl still lived here. They knew that was a critical factor in any decision, maybe the most critical as far as staying around now.

I hope we don't have to face that decision any time soon because I really don't know how I will feel about things if that happens, he answered. You know how I am. I put too much of myself into a place. It's hard for me to turn loose after all that stuff. But I might be able to do it, depending on how things look in the future.

Don't you wonder what would have happened if we had decided to stay in New Mexico? She wasn't ready to let it go that night.

They were lying in bed after watching the late news but they were not sleepy. The game had been exciting and the grandson had played great, in their unbiased opinion, so she was in a talkative mood.

Yes, I have thought about that a lot. You know we could have stayed. I think we would have ended up in Santa Fe, which we always thought we would like. But who knows how that would have been? It's not an easy town to live in either. We probably would have gone on up to Colorado at some point.

Their decision to move to Baker had been carefully thought through, although they knew very little about the town itself. They had agreed that it would be better to raise the children in a smaller town than Albuquerque, which was already too large to suit them and still growing fast. Baker had seemed to be the kind of quiet place where the schools would be more suitable and the atmosphere more consistent with their values. And it had always seemed like the right decision.

If we had moved to Santa Fe, I'm sure we couldn't have stayed there as long as we have here, he told her. This was a very unique situation here for me to be able to hang on in one place for as long as I did. So who knows where we might have moved to from there? We may have even ended up back in Taos.

He thought about their time in Baker City and he knew one thing for sure: They had both put as much into it as they had gotten out. She had resumed her teaching career here and had spent twenty years teaching business classes in high school, shepherding students through typing, accounting, shorthand, and later when technology changed, keyboarding and speed-writing. They rarely went anywhere in town when she didn't see one of her former students and many times she heard how much her classes had helped them with their careers.

You know I am proudest of one particular accomplishment in my job, he said. When I came here there was not one paved road anywhere through this forest. When I left it, all the main roads were paved. You can drive the Grande Ronde River, Elkhorn Drive, Wallowa Mountain Loop, and even out to the Hells Canyon Overlook on paved roads now.

All of this work had taken place at a time when the forest was also producing a significant amount of timber, including cleaning out thousands of acres of dead and dying lodge pole pine. He had supervised upwards of a hundred people working in engineering to support everything that was going on. He told her how his first serious project came to fruition.

One day I was called in to Al Oard's office (the forest supervisor) and when I got there I found Congressman Al Ullman and the head of the State transportation engineering department, Scott Coulter, sitting at a table. After I was introduced, Mr. Oard asked me if we could complete the paving of the Whitney-Tipton highway if Congress allocated a certain amount of money. What could I say? Of course we can do it.

He knew that the State did not want to handle the construction and in fact did not really support the project, but he also knew that they were not likely to say no to Congressman Ullman. So it fell on the Forest Service to complete the project. A few months later the money showed up in the appropriations bill and less than two years later there was a ribbon cutting ceremony to celebrate the new State Highway 7 between Baker City and John Day.

He had loved working on the huge forest and had managed to dodge all the "opportunities" to move on up in the outfit, either to Portland (ugh!) or Washington, D.C. (double-ugh!!), finally ending up staying long enough to become the longest-tenured forest engineer in the region. As far as he was concerned, Jeremiah Johnson said it best when he said "I've been to a town."

In spite of all we have tried to do, he said, I suspect if you met someone on the street and asked them if they remembered us or our contributions, you would get a blank look. It would be as if we were never here at all.

She knew all of this, but she also knew that things had changed after they retired. Most of their close friends were gone. Only the girl was left and they had no idea how long she would stay.

I know one thing, she finally said. If she leaves, I don't think I will want to stay here any longer.

He knew better than to try and talk her out of that one, even if he had wanted to. And besides, he was thinking about something else now.

He still hadn't talked to the grandson about things that were much more important.

**

Do you ever feel old? She was testing him after they had "celebrated" his seventieth birthday a few days earlier.

No, I never do feel old. He had only had to think about it for a brief moment. And it was true. I always feel like I am still sixteen.

I don't either, she had agreed. We are both lucky.

He certainly knew how lucky they were to feel this young. Maybe it was true that age was a state of mind. In his mind he was still that young boy who was able to do anything he wished to do.

When he thought about baseball he felt like he could still chase down the deepest fly ball ever hit to center field, like he had done so many times in those early years. He thought again about a few of those catches he had made.

One in particular always came to mind when he was replaying his games. They were playing a game in Kirby against Umpire and he was in center field that day when Umpire's best hitter, the older of the Dyer brothers, Charles, had come to bat.

He always played shallow because he thought he had enough speed to catch anything hit over his head, but when Charles cranked one of Richard Schwopes' fastballs to dead center field, he knew he was in trouble with this one. There were two outs and a couple of runners on base in a close game, and luckily he judged immediately that the ball was hit over his head.

Sometimes a ball hit straight away toward a fielder caused a split second hesitation, which would have been disastrous in this case, but he had turned at the crack of the bat and was quickly racing at full speed away from everything and everyone.

There was no way to guess how far he would have to run before he turned to see if he had caught up to the ball, but he knew it was going to be further than he had ever gone on any ball before.

As he replayed the time over again in his mind now, he still could not believe that he had been running so fast that he couldn't really look back to see where the ball was until he felt something inside that told him it was time to find out the truth of the matter, and when he had turned to look back and up, the ball was right over his shoulder.

He was able to twist his body just enough to reach up and feel the ball fall softly into his big Carl Erskine yellow leather glove.

Jerry Yeargan was playing left field and had run over to take what he had assumed would be the cutoff throw after the ball stopped rolling in the outfield. After the catch, he turned and threw the ball back in to Jerry, watching as the batter kicked second base disgustedly when he realized his sure home run was just out number three.

And now, at seventy, he would like to go back out to center field one more time and have his Dad smack long fly balls for him to practice on.

He was pretty sure he could still get under most of them.

28

They were having dinner in the hotel in Little Rock with her children. The girls had flown in that night to join them for the trip back to the cemetery the next day.

She had driven over from North Carolina with her son. She had told him that she wanted to do all the driving so she could get more comfortable with freeway and big city traffic, something that she had neglected for so many years now.

Chattanooga, Nashville, and even Memphis had been good for her, as she made sure she could still navigate in rush hour traffic. She was going to take her trip out west after they finished at the cemetery, so this was her chance to practice before taking off on her own.

The next day they drove down to the cemetery together. Her car was roomy enough for the four of them and it was fun hearing their laughter and their questions about her childhood days in this part of the country. They planned to spend time that afternoon at the place she and their father had chosen to be buried. It was a beautiful day in late Spring, warm but not stifling hot like this country could be, with sunshine sparkling off the little white building that marked the entrance to the site.

They all commented on the beauty and peacefulness of the place, as they parked among the cars that were scattered around the cemetery in various locations. This was a big day at the cemetery, Decoration Day, and folks from all over the area were there to lay flowers on graves of their loved ones, cleaning up and sprucing up for another year, and visiting with friends they had not seen since last year.

They had arrived close to noon and soon had been invited by several different families to join them in eating lunch. She saw a few familiar faces, either from the old days or, mostly, from the more recent time of James' funeral.

They postponed the lunch and visiting until after they had accomplished their main goal, which was to see the headstone that was now standing over James' grave and to place the flowers they had brought for the occasion.

As they walked down to the lower end of the cemetery they could see that it was a beautiful stone. Some flowers had already been placed around it, and they all placed what they had brought and stood quietly thinking their thoughts of father and husband.

Once again they noticed how the little mountain a few miles to the northwest seemed to almost be a part of the area. The sun was shining on the oak and pine trees that covered the lower slopes, and the rocky outcrops that lay under the top seemed close enough to touch. They were pleased with the scene and knew that James would be too.

After a while they wandered back up toward the area where most of the people were gathered around in clusters of families or friends, stopping to talk to some along the way. Tables were spread with food and drink and everyone they talked to offered to feed them more than they could possibly eat. She had worried that the children would feel that this trip was unnecessary but she could tell that it had been good for them as well as for her.

Lunch was finished and they had spent all the time they needed to spend here, but there was one more thing she wanted to do before they left. She had placed her flowers around James' headstone with the rest of them, but there was another small thing she had to do for herself.

While everyone else was saying their goodbyes, she went to her car and brought a dozen red roses out of the trunk, walking alone down to the corner of the graveyard. She quickly found the small marker that she knew was there and laid the flowers by the stone.

She was still lost in some faraway thought when she noticed that her children were standing behind her. They hadn't said a word, but when she looked at them, she knew they needed to know what this was all about. And she remembered that she had promised to tell them someday. Well, this is someday, she thought.

He was just a boy I knew a long time ago, she started, not knowing how much further she could go. They were silent for a long time.

I guess it won't hurt to say that, yes, I loved him. I loved him with all my heart.

They watched as her face showed a sadness that they had never seen. A single tear was quickly brushed away.

I'm afraid that I may have even given him my heart.

29

 It never occurred to me that I was missing out on my education that year I spent as a Page in the Arkansas legislature.

Oh, there were half-hearted efforts made to have me pretend that I was keeping up with my lessons, but I knew the boys and girls back in good old Langley school were the ones who were really missing out on an education while I was wandering the halls of the Capitol building and the streets of downtown Little Rock.

My schoolhouse was based on an upper floor of the Marion Hotel, and every day was a new lesson plan.

The Pages actually earned a little money for our efforts, and we actually did do quite a bit of productive work. The Clerk of the House, a fellow named Nelson Cox, ran a tight ship, and when it was time for us to perform our assigned tasks, we had to hop to it.

The main job we had was getting copies of the various legislative documents from the clerk's office into the hands of the Representatives whose desks lay in an arc around the speaker's platform at the front of the room. The layout consisted of about six rows of desks spreading out in an ever-widening semi-circle from the open space down front to the last row that lay slightly elevated near the back of the room. The seating was separated into four sections with a wide aisle between each section.

As soon as a proposed bill was printed, each Page was given a certain number of copies and a certain area where these copies were to be placed on the desks. Legislative sessions were expected to be brief and productive, only occurring every other year, so the activities taking place on the floor of the house, although appearing to be no more than random chaos, were actually quite organized and efficient.

Of course it helped to speed things up that there was only one point of view politically and that was Democrat. The only apparent variation on that theme seemed to me to be the slight difference between the urban Democrats (Pulaski County) and the rest of the state.

Every county in the state, all seventy-five, was required to be represented by at least one person, and most of the counties were small enough to be served by only one Representative. Pulaski County, which was where Little Rock was located, was different. There were EIGHT Representatives from the big city and that situation seemed to take on a life of its own.

Luckily for the rest of the state, two things were working against Little Rock and Pulaski County in those days: Number one was that none of the eight seemed to be willing to work well with any of the other eight; and number two was a fellow named Paul Van Dalsem.

Van Dalsem was a special case any way you looked at him. He was from the smallest county in the state, population-wise, Perry County. He had been elected in every election in recent memory, to the point where usually he had no opposition. And he was able to wield an inordinate amount of power among his fellow one-only counterparts.

It was probably only natural that the first thing the rural counties did after arriving in Little Rock for a session was to organize against the big-city block. And Van, as Dad would always call him later in life, had that process down pat.

Nothing seemed to happen on the floor of the House of Representatives unless Paul Van Dalsem gave his blessing. He sat about two rows back and across one of the aisles from Dad, and I always enjoyed watching his face light up when votes were being cast on big issues.

I would know that his arm-twisting had worked to his liking as soon as I saw him light up one of his cigars, and I can still see the twinkle in his eyes when I would look back at him and see him wink at me like we had some big secret. It was no surprise to anyone who knew him that ninety-nine percent of the negotiating that had taken place on whatever was going on had occurred the night before in Van Dalsem's room back in the Marion.

Dad and Paul stayed friends for the rest of their lives, and I could understand why. Van Dalsem had a country charm about him that reached as far down as a lowly Page as he often let me know that he appreciated my situation too. It might be something as small as giving me one of his special fishing licenses that he had printed up after the Game and Fish Department had managed to squeeze out enough money from a budget he helped to pass to build a small pond down by their nearby office. The license read "This license entitles the holder…John Austin…to all the privileges involved in fishing in Van Dalsem Lake."

Or it might be as big and important as the time he made sure I was seated right up under the speaker's platform the day Johnny Weismuller came to the house chambers and delivered a full rendition of his Tarzan the Apeman yell.

Even though we had our work to do, there was also a lot of down time as the session wore on. I found my own special ways to fill that time, spending a lot of hours down in that Game and Fish office hiding out in the aquarium that held all the different kinds of fish found in the State of Arkansas.

And when I got tired of being in the basement of that building, I had accidentally stumbled onto an even better hideout. Hidden away in the upper reaches of the Capitol Building lay an absolute treasure trove for an inquisitive young boy. I had no idea who had put it together or even why it had been done, but someone in the past had accumulated a massive rock collection from around the hills and valleys of the state.

I never knew for sure if the attic where this amazing pile of glittering stone, crystal, and ore of every kind was supposed to be locked away or not, but once I found a door that was always open to my touch, I returned for many a visit.

The allure of the place was not just the collection of rocks that were all well marked and identified geologically for their value and where they were found, but also the fact that it seemed like it was my own secret hideout.

I never shared my find with any of the other Pages, knowing that there was a chance that one of them might say something to someone else and that someone else would blow the whole deal by ratting us out to our boss or our parents, or maybe even the two or three security guards that roamed the halls.

Even if they didn't tell anyone else, the glitter of the find would be somewhat tarnished by not being able to spend time there all by myself. It was such a special place to me that I don't think I ever even dared mention it to my Dad, although I know he would have allowed me to keep it a secret.

As much as I was on my own during the day at the Capitol Building, where I only had to show up during times when the Pages were expected to be on duty, my evenings and nights back at the Marion were even more mine to do as I pleased, or at least as I could figure out.

Most evenings were fairly similar. Dad would be involved in some high-level "negotiating" in either Van Dalsem's or one of the other Representative's rooms, while I would wander down the street to Moore's Cafeteria for my usual supper of chicken-fried steak, mashed potatoes, and gravy. Maybe a piece of chocolate pie for dessert. I might wander around the streets for a while after supper, looking longingly into some window that held some clothes or other items far out of my economic reach.

I usually ended up back in our hotel room before too late where I would read a book or some comics, pretend to do some boring lesson from school that no one really expected me to finish anyway, or if I got too bored, go downstairs to the lobby and watch the one television that was in the hotel.

The TV didn't usually interest me that much because there were usually a few adults sitting around there and they didn't seem to watch the few shows that interested me. I was still mostly an "I've Got a Secret" and "What's My Line" fan.

My off hours seemed to pass very slowly most evenings, partly because there wasn't that much for me to do, but mostly because I could not wait until Thursday night came. That night was special to me because it was the night the wrestling matches were held in town.

I think Dad had taken me to the first match I saw, probably just so I would have something to do while he was tied up with his buddies at night. I don't believe he ever went back to another match after that first one, even though I felt like he was missing out on some of the most thrilling action that could possibly be seen within a few blocks of our hotel room.

He never said too much about it to me, but I think he actually could have thought, heaven forbid, that those matches were fake! I think he also knew he may as well keep that opinion to himself instead of trying to convince this thirteen year old, and especially not the seventy-five year old lady sitting beside me waving her cane and screaming words that even I had never heard back on the farm as some villain pummeled one of our favorites in and out of the ring. So I was pretty much left to my own when it came to the wrestling wars.

Every Thursday night the arena was packed with fans, and every week saw a different group of villains and heroes come to town for the world championship match for that particular week for this particular world. Many names came and went, but over time a few of the wrestlers established themselves as returning favorites.

One of these was a fellow known in wrestling circles as the "Lion of Lorraine." Andre Drapp (pronounced "Drop"). Now many of the wrestlers of that time had obviously concocted some kind of hokey, made up name to enhance their image, or more likely to hide the fact that their real name was something like George Raymond Wagner from Butte, Nebraska.

Andre needed no such enhancement. A true hero right out of the French Resistance in World War II where the story was told he had killed a fair share of Nazis before the war finally ended. And he was a beautifully built specimen of manhood, dark-skinned with black wavy hair and eyes that would have made a Hollywood star envious. He was clearly one of the good guys.

But one of the bad guys was everything Andre was not. Made up name. Long blond girly hair. Sequins all over his ultra-tight wrestling uniform. Spitting and snarling at the little boys and little old ladies sitting in the folding chairs at ringside every night. Went by the name of "Gorgeous George."

There was nothing gorgeous about George as far as the fans in Little Rock were concerned. But he could wrestle, as he was proving every Thursday night as he managed to somehow put away every one of the good guys that went up against him. But we knew his day was coming.

Andre Drapp was also winning handily and Gorgeous and the Lion were on a collision course. The big buildup went on for weeks, and by the time the big day arrived, there was not a wrestling fan in town who was not fired up enough to go into the ring alone with Georgie Boy. But we wouldn't have to. Andre was there for us. It was going to be a death match for sure.

Now I've always been one who thinks timing is everything, and that particular Thursday night was one which was going to be no exception to that rule. I hurriedly washed down my chicken-fried and gravy with a glass of milk, walked quickly from the cafeteria to the movie theater a few blocks away, and bought my ticket for the one movie that I had been dying to see and that had just opened that very night: High Noon.

I looked at the time and calculated just how long I had to catch this show and still make it over to the arena in time for Andre vs. Gorgeous. It looked like it was going to be close, but I thought I could make it if I left the movie theater on a dead run and didn't hit any lights.

The logical thing for me to have done that night was to skip the movie and go see it later. But I was thirteen, as I have pointed out, and the movie was playing. And tomorrow night was Friday night and that meant loading up and heading back to Langley right after the day's legislative activities ended. I wouldn't get back to Little Rock until the next week, for crying out loud.

I bought my ticket and settled into my seat. I quickly found the clock on the side wall up near the screen. There would be two clocks ticking away that night: The one in the movie that ground slowly along toward the time when the noon stage would get to town, and the other one on the theater wall that seemed to be moving at twice the normal speed, rushing toward the point where I could no longer sit still if I wanted to see Andre save the world from the forces of evil.

A young boy shouldn't be faced with that kind of pressure. By the time Frank Miller stepped down off that train, I was already sweating because I could see that life was not going to be fair tonight. Especially with Tex Ritter dragging out that dang song every five minutes or so.

By the time Gary Cooper had taken care of the first two hired guns, I was beginning to root for Frank. I calculated where I was sitting, where the wrestling arena was, how fast I knew I could run, how fast it appeared to me that Gary Cooper was also running, and it came down to a simple decision for me: "If he goes into the loft of that barn, I'm outta here."

He did and I was. When I entered the arena Andre was already standing there in the ring, and you could tell he was waiting for Gorgeous George. It was going to be a death match for sure, the first indication of which was when a snarling George shoved the fat little referee out of the way and took a cheap shot at Andre during the so-called introductions!

In spite of our screaming at the stupid referee that George was cheating at every turn, this atrocity went on for what seemed like hours. Poor Andre was beaten across every side of the ring, choked until he could barely stand,

and finally tossed like a rag doll completely out of the ring and onto the floor, where the security guards had to stop dozens of fans from either helping him get up again, or going into the ring themselves.

All the while Gorgeous was busily combing his golden locks and getting sprayed with a fresh dose of Chanel Number Five/Ten by his valet.

The now-limp Lion of Lorraine was somehow able to drag himself back up onto the outer edge of the ring, where he stood shaking his head to clear his rattled brain and obviously trying to compose himself before going back for what was surely certain death.

While the obviously blind referee was wasting his time over on the other side of the ring arguing with a timekeeper or something, George took advantage of the opportunity to put a choke hold around Andre's neck, even though our hero was still standing outside the ropes and everyone in the arena knew this was clearly illegal.

In spite of how desperate things looked for Andre at the moment, I was actually beginning to see the tiniest glimmer of hope. Those of us who had watched Andre Drapp for several weeks, and I suspect that included about everyone in the arena that night, knew that this could possibly be a fatal mistake on George's part, even as he had worked his strangle hold around to the point of being directly behind Andre and was seemingly choking the very breath from our hero.

Sure enough, just as it appeared that Andre was doomed to be beaten and maybe even have his neck broken in the process, a miracle happened. Gorgeous was so busy trading obscenities with the fans, especially the Eighty year old lady that was standing on her chair next to me matching him word for word, that I was sure he had no idea what was about to happen to him.

Andre gathered himself for his signature closing move, a move that I had seen him do numerous times but which Gorgeous George had obviously never even heard about.

One minute Andre was standing there being choked until his tongue was sticking out, and the next heartbeat he had jumped straight up in the air, flipped himself back over into the ring taking George right down to the mat and obviously stunning him to the point where the referee, suddenly aware of the fact that there was a wrestling match going on, fell to the floor beside them and pounded the mat three times before raising Andre's arm in victory!

I never did go back and watch the end of High Noon. As far as I know Will Kane is still hiding out up there in the barn loft, waiting for Frank Miller to die of old age.

And more than likely Tex Ritter is still trying to keep the audience trapped on the edge of their seats by teasing them with tidbits of what may or may not happen, oh my darlin', sometime.

But one thing I did know for sure and certain. In the real life showdown that night with Gorgeous George, Andre Drapp did not forsake me.

30

 I suppose it was inevitable that we would have to leave the farm, although it had never occurred to me that I wouldn't live out my entire life running these creeks and ridges from my ancestral home place.

But Pete's very success had brought out the jealousies that were never far beneath the surface and that jealousy, coupled with the battle over the Langley school, doomed us to have to leave everything we had grown to love.

It all stemmed from the controversy that had been brewing between Lodi and Langley since the schools were combined in the early thirties. Langley ended up with the school and even though it was now two generations removed from that time, those old grudges had never died.

There was a contingent of folks who hammered constantly at the idea of giving up the school and consolidating with one of the other, larger schools in the county, either Glenwood or Kirby. Even some people right in Langley were of the opinion that giving up the heart and soul of the little community would be worth the few nickels and dimes they might save in school taxes.

Dad knew there was one certainty in the life of small communities in rural areas like ours. Once the school was gone, the community would die a slow and painful death.

Oh, sure, the old time families would stay around on their farms and home places. And the kids might still get just as good an education at another school. But eventually the reality would set in as the younger families left the area for good, moving closer to their work or somewhere closer to a school where their children would not have to ride a bus for three or four hours a day.

Pete was very outspoken in his efforts to keep the school board from making what he considered a huge mistake and that opposition voice was not welcomed by the folks who were dead set on consolidation.

It was easy for them to use his time away from the school during our legislative trips, which only amounted to a few weeks every other year, to put enough pressure on the current school principal, Bill Pirtle, to force Dad out.

That last summer we spent on the farm was one that saw my emotions run from sadness to excitement. I was very sad to leave the place where I had done most of my growing up, and also sad to leave my other set of parents, Granny and Papa.

To make things seem a little better, we all managed to convince ourselves that our move down to Daisy would only be temporary. Papa and Granny would stay on the farm and keep it going until the day we would all come back home. Little did we know.

There was also a certain amount of excitement that was natural to the move. For one thing, we would once again be connected with our cousins, Jack and Jill, who lived just west of Daisy. And we had several other friends that we had known and would get to know better after our move. The Kennedys, Preston ("P.Y.") and Kathryn, lived in Daisy and operated a little sandwich bar type restaurant.

They had daughters Linda and Lana who were mine and Judy's ages, and we had been acquainted with them for some time. They would serve us well after the move by making sure we were fully integrated into the social life that was Daisy. That social life meant mostly riding around the lake on weekends, listening to the new rock and roll music that was our own, and watching the baseball game of the week with Mr. Kennedy.

I was just going into the eleventh grade and since Jack was also in my class, he helped me transition from Langley friends to Kirby friends, which wasn't that difficult. I knew many of the kids that would be in my class already and several of the teachers at Kirby were familiar to me.

One thing that helped a lot was that the school was not that much bigger than Langley. My last class at Langley had consisted of a dozen or so kids, while my new class at Kirby was about eighteen. I say about eighteen because there was a certain amount of coming and going among the kids of the schools back then.

Some kids were still away when school started, mostly still in Indiana for the tomato harvest, and it would be a few weeks before a final tally could be taken.

It wasn't long after school started that I learned my first lessons relating to the social life of my new school. I was still very small at the time, having skipped ahead a couple of grades under Preston Watkins' enlightened approach to social engineering at Langley, and up to now had not been all that interested, or at least involved, with girls.

But that was changing. And my cousins, Jack and Jill, were anxious to help me with that transition. Lesson number one: Never trust your first cousins when it comes to romantic liaisons.

After the first week of school it was obvious that I was the curiosity of the school year, being new and untested, so to speak. All my classmates had gone out of their way to make me feel welcome, and some of the girls had seemed particularly friendly. Especially one cute blond named Donna Sue Hall.

I had noticed Donna Sue right away, probably because she actually smiled at me and acted like she might even speak to me some day.

I inquired about her and this is where my cousin, Jack, may have failed to disclose some of the more critical information I needed to know about Donna Sue. Does she have a boy friend? I asked. Jack hesitated slightly, but then he admitted that she might have a boyfriend, or maybe not. At any rate, even if she did, he was still away off up in Indiana and might not even come back to school this year. Don't worry about him, Jack reassured me.

I may have heard all this, or I may have been too enthralled with my sudden surge of testosterone to pay close enough attention to the details, but before I knew it, Jack and Jill had fixed me up with Donna Sue.

My first real date, even though it was really just riding around in the back seat of Uncle Lowell's fifty-four Plymouth Savoy while squeezing the blood out of Donna Sue's hand.

We drove over to Glenwood and got a coke at the drive-in, wandered around back and forth between Kirby and Daisy, and finally ended up parked out in front of Donna Sue's house about halfway between Daisy and Kirby. I was literally in heaven, but what I didn't know was that hell was drawing closer by the minute.

The name Buddy Morphew had been one that I had already heard during my brief introduction to school at Kirby, and I knew that he was the boyfriend in question. And I had heard enough about him to know that it would be a lot better for my health if he stayed in Indiana.

Some of the stories being told by my classmates about Buddy's escapades, his athletic prowess, and what most concerned me at the moment, his really, really bad temper, had put me in a bit of a quandary. Should I be sitting here holding hands with this sweet little smiling blond? What if word got back to Buddy up in Indiana and he decided it was time he came back down to protect his territory? How long did I have to live before Buddy might show up back in school anyway?

These questions were roiling through my brain that night even as I was totally unable to resist trying my best to get up the nerve to actually lean up and kiss Donna Sue.

Oh, by the way, did I mention the fact that I still hadn't started growing yet? I was fourteen, would not be fifteen for another three months, and was at least a head shorter than any of my classmates, even Donna Sue, who wasn't one of the taller kids. From what I had heard, Buddy had definitely gone through a couple of growth spurts already and they had made him into a man among the boys of Kirby.

Now there are two ways to look at the size differential between Buddy and me. Had I been a little bigger, Buddy may have actually perceived me as a threat to his love life, whereby I would have been killed that very night right there in front of my cousins. Being a little runt in this case undoubtedly kept me from being severely stomped into the dirt that night.

When I saw the lights pull in behind us out in front of the Hall house that night I didn't even have to guess who was in the car. The hair standing up on the back of my neck was the first to know that it was Buddy, and before I could breathe again, he was tapping on the back window of the Savoy with a beer can.

I was so frozen I couldn't even jump over into the front seat and leave Donna Sue alone in the back, but she probably wouldn't have let me anyway. She was still holding onto my hand as tightly as she could, all the while making sure that Buddy knew she was with me. Lesson number two: Be very, very wary of blondes who are only using you to make her boyfriend jealous.

Buddy and I became good friends during my two years at Kirby, we played basketball together on the high school team, and he never said a word to me about my trying to move in on him while he was away from home.

I finally started growing a little before the school year was out but I never got big enough to want to date another blond with a mean boyfriend. In fact, that little episode almost turned me against dating and girls altogether, and it certainly made me extremely wary about listening to my cousins' advice. Luckily I would recover.

* * *

That first school year at Kirby went well for me, and the family seemed to adapt to life in Daisy just fine. I mostly ran around with Jack and a couple of his friends, dated a few girls off and on during the school year, learned to dance under the tutelage of Kathryn and Linda Kennedy, and even passed my driving test the first try. That was good because I'm pretty sure I was the only eleventh-grader in Arkansas who was not driving.

And we had left the farm in a nice shiny nineteen-fifty-four Belvedere, two-tone yellow and white, top of the line Plymouth. We had some nice wheels now.

The school year was over when we got the phone call from Papa. He needed to let Dad and Mama know that Granny was sick. That weekend when we all went back up to the farm we found her lying in bed, barely able to talk to us.

I remember so well how awful Granny looked when I went into the

204

bedroom where she was lying. Marvin, she said, I think you need to take me to a doctor. When we went back into the living room Papa explained that she had been having bad headaches for some time now, and they were getting worse. She hadn't been out of the bed for two weeks. They had not wanted to bother us because they knew how busy everyone was, but Papa didn't know what else to do.

Granny did not make it through that summer. They took her to a hospital in Little Rock and the word came back that she had a brain tumor. It was inoperable so we brought her back to a hospital room in Nashville.

That was where I saw her alive the final time. She wasn't able to talk that night but I know that she knew I was there because when I hugged her for the last time, she held me so tightly in her arms for the longest time. Neither one of us wanted to let go.

We all knew when Granny was buried at the Mount Joy cemetery in Daisy that August day that we would never get to go back to the farm. Papa would not be able to stay there alone, and with him gone there would be no one to keep it up until we could return.

We had lost two of the things we all loved most dearly that summer of 1955.

31

 She was gone again. He missed her that morning when he was having his coffee. He missed her again on Saturday morning when he was listening to their music. And he was missing her as he sat out on the deck in the old yellow glider watching the sun warming the greening grass of the field behind their house. I wish she could be here now, he thought. She loves Spring so much.

There had been more and more times lately when it seemed she had been gone, but still he was surprised when he would turn to say something to her and find that she was not there beside him. He did not like these times and wished they would never happen again, but he knew that it was just one of those unexplainable occurrences. Sometimes people had to be somewhere else.

He had talked to her on the phone though, and had told her that he was anxious to see her soon. She said the same thing. But she didn't know when she would be back. Things were still uncertain and not totally within her control. He knew that, but it didn't make it any easier for him.

Maybe you should do something to make the time go by easier, she had suggested. Why don't you take that trip again? At least he thought that was what she had said. The phone connection had been so poor that he though he may have misunderstood.

Soon he found himself on the road. The road he had traveled so many times before. Heading down the interstate from Baker City he thought about what he wanted to say to his grandson. Maybe I'll stop and see him on my way through, he thought.

There was so much he needed to tell him, but there really were two main things he had to say. First, he wanted to make sure he knew just how much he loved him, how he had made life so much more than it had been before he came along. And now the time had come when he was ready to embark on the next phase of his life, college.

It was not just that he thought of the boy as something special. Certainly no more than the others. He just wanted to tell him one more thing, something that was more important than anything else he could ever say. He would tell the others the same thing when the time came for them to hear it, although he was sure that they would know it too once he had passed it on to the grandson.

Trying to compose the words that he would use as he drove along, he knew he had to say it right or it would be just another piece of casual advice, quickly discarded in the rush of life's forward journey. Whatever words he used, he had to know that his grandson understood that this journey was totally and inexorably dependent upon what he had to say.

It would be particularly hard for him to have to tell this boy, who was about to turn eighteen and could not know that, in a split second of horrible judgment on his grand-dad's part, all of their lives could have been wiped out. It was that important. He had to know the story.

He had tried to reach him on his cell phone as he traveled down the road, but there was no answer so he left a message, telling him simply that he loved him more than anything and would see him soon. He promised himself that he would not avoid it any longer once he got back from his trip.

The weather was nice this time of the year so the roads were clear and he sailed through Salt Lake City and was soon going over Soldier Summit again. He made such good time that it was too early to stop in Moab, but by the time he pulled into Farmington it was time for dinner and a relaxing night's sleep.

The next morning dawned clear and cool and found him on the crooked road through the Jicarilla country heading east into the sunrise. He had coffee and a donut before leaving and knew that would keep him until he made it to Chama where he was hoping that he would find Vera's restaurant open. He hadn't had any good green chiles for some time now and Vera always had the best.

He saw the sign that pointed toward Carracas Mesa as he drove past Gobernador Ranger Station which had long ago been closed. He laughed again as he thought of his old friend John Hutt riding hard to stay ahead of the wild horse stampede somewhere up in these Pinyon covered hills.

After stopping in Chama for his green chile fix and fuel, he drove on down the highway past Tierra Amarilla where he turned off to go over the high mountains by Hopewell Lake. He climbed the switchbacks into the big aspen country and saw that there was still a little ice around the edges of Hopewell, but some hardy camper had staked out a spot in the little campground overlooking the lake.

Cabin fever was still causing folks to try and hurry spring along in this country, which he understood quite well. We must come back here and camp someday, he thought as he drove over the highway that he knew so well.

As he drove through the Tusas valley he glanced off toward Quartzite Peak to the south, wishing he had time today to turn off on the dirt road that would take him over by the peak and down through Canon Plaza to Vallecitos again. He always thought about his old friend and hunting partner, Lou Gross, when he saw Quartzite because that had been one of Lou's favorite haunts. They had had some times together back in the early days.

But today he was heading for Taos, and there would be plenty of time later for exploring these back roads. On through Tres Piedras, across the flats where he soon saw the modern hippie incarnation of housing that had progressed from sod house to dugout to commune to the current earthship hobbit houses, semi-underground mansions that seemed right out of Tolkien for sure.

And then he was driving across the high bridge.

32

 My senior year in high school started off well. I was actually growing, finally, and even looking forward to playing a little basketball, although baseball was still my best sport.

But Kirby had lost several players off the basketball team and since there were so few boys in school anyway, I managed to make the team. I sat on the bench most of the time but did get to go in occasionally, usually when we were so far behind that I couldn't hurt us anyway.

I had even recovered completely from my earlier dating disaster with Donna Sue and was playing the field, so to speak, which meant I would go out with anyone who would speak to me. That narrowed the choices down somewhat but I still had hopes of finding the one. Mrs. Kennedy was doing her part, throwing a party at least once a month and still trying to teach me to dance.

Sometime during that year of school, however, I developed another hobby. Racing. I was a long way removed from my early day driving lessons on the school bus when I discovered that there was one way to create a little excitement on an otherwise dull Saturday night.

Now I may have stumbled onto this idiocy completely on my own sooner or later, but thanks to one of my classmates, it came sooner. It was all Billy Golden's fault.

Billy drove a little nineteen-fifty-four Ford pickup, which normally would not be considered an actual racing type vehicle. But then one would have to have known Billy back then and see him drive to understand that anything was possible if a person put their mind to it. And boy did we put our minds to it.

The Plymouth I drove was not known for its road racing pedigree either, but I quickly found out that the speedometer, which went all the way up to one-hundred miles-per-hour, was pretty much correct.

My car had a three-speed transmission, plus a "passing gear" which could be engaged by kicking down hard on the accelerator while in third gear to drop the transmission down into second gear for a little quicker acceleration. Billy's pickup was a four-speed on-the-floor stick shift.

Every Saturday night that school year found us in the same place. After we had finished up with our dates for the night, usually around midnight, if we actually had a date, we met down there at the crossroads in Kirby, out in front of Claudie and Chloe Ray's Busy Bee café. We pointed the cars west, lined them up side by side, one in the right lane and one in the left, and got ready.

Billy's Ford was much faster off the mark than the Belvedere. In fact, he could even peel rubber for quite a stretch if he wanted to, which he usually did, while my car was geared higher and wouldn't jump out of the starting gate like that. So he could always get a pretty decent jump on me, usually leading me by several hundred feet by the time we made it to the sign that indicated we were leaving Kirby at an ever-increasing rate of speed. It would take me about a mile and a half to begin to gain on him, and this would be right about where the road dropped down off a pretty good hill to cross the bridge at the bottom where the highway went over Bear Creek.

It wasn't the best place in the world to pass him but due to geography and the particular mechanical traits of the Ford and Plymouth, it almost always worked out that way. Side by side we would go across that narrow little bridge at the bottom of the hill, and my Plymouth would always be pegging that one-hundred mark.

I might get all the way around him on the upgrade, but most likely not, and there we would go, still side-by-side, up the hill past the Mack settlement and on down through the long straightaway past the Midway Holiness Church. One of us might gain enough to move back over into the correct lane, but many times we went right on down the hill and around the curve in front of the Dierks Houses still neck and neck and side by side filling both lanes.

Sometimes I would be in front and other times Billy would be when we came to the slowing down place, which was where the sign said we were about to enter Daisy proper. Either way after a brief interlude to recap the last five minutes, we turned around and repeated the pattern in the opposite direction. Five miles, full speed, no concern whatsoever for our lives.

Clearly the dumbest thing I could ever have thought about doing. Those old cars had no more business being driven like that than would a tractor. No seat belts. Those came much later. Weak, manual (non-power) brakes. No one expected to need that kind of stopping power. Bald tires, or worse yet, recaps. Normal. Our parents couldn't afford to buy a new set of tires.

Meanwhile, back at the school, I was still searching for that someone that I hadn't found yet. I had noticed a few of the girls in the junior class, and had even dated a couple of them. But there was one really cute girl that was a sophomore that had caught my eye.

She played basketball and was much better at it than I was. I had even tried to get her attention a couple of times by making eyes at her during lunch time or when we passed in the hallway between classes.

She had a beautiful smile and long wavy dark hair, and although she had smiled at me once or twice, I figured I had no chance with her. After all, it was well known that she had a serious boyfriend that she had been dating for a long time. In addition to that long-time boyfriend, I also knew she was one of the smartest girls in school. I tried to put her out of my mind.

But one night on a bus ride home from a basketball game in Murfreesboro, a miracle happened! I was sitting in the very back of the bus acting stupid with some of my teammates who were also girl-less at the time when Linda Kennedy came back and sat down in front of us. She was pretty much breathless and couldn't keep her secret any longer. What she said that night made my heart start pounding so hard that I could barely hear her say what she was trying to say.

She was best friends with the girl I had given up on ever even talking to, and she was now telling me that this girl was breaking up with her boyfriend and, thumpedy-thumpedy-thumpedy went my heart, actually wanted to go out with me!

We went out that weekend, double dating with Billy Golden and his girlfriend, Sandra Reese, who happened to be my new sweetheart's first cousin. She wore a beautiful soft green dress and we went to Glenwood for a coke, the four of us squeezed into that little Ford pickup.

From that day forward, I never ever considered the possibility that I wouldn't spend my life with her. And from that night when we kissed for the first time there on her front porch, I would not spend a day when she wouldn't be somewhere in my heart.

* * *

The year began to really fly by now. We spent every Friday or Saturday night together, and as much time as I could get by with during school days. Basketball season came and went, and as usual, Kirby didn't win many games.

Spring found us starting into the baseball season and we traveled around to different schools when we could schedule games. Baseball was very much a secondary sport in the system then, even though it was really the only other sport that was played besides basketball.

We played all the local schools that had teams and somehow our coach, Dickie Thrash, managed to come up with a game against Mineral Springs, a school that was down past Nashville about twenty five miles. It was to be somewhat of a last hurrah for all of the seniors.

The school year was winding down and graduation day was near when we all loaded up that day to make the trip for our last baseball game of the year. Baseball was such an unsupported activity that the school didn't even provide a bus for us to ride in so we had to take our own cars.

We had too many players to all go in two vehicles, so Coach Thrash and one other guy were taking their cars, while I volunteered to drive the Plymouth. There was some horsing around and maybe a little speeding back and forth between the two non-adult drivers on the way down, but since the coach was in the lead, there wasn't much room for maneuvering.

We made it to Mineral Springs without a hitch, arriving just in time to get our butts handed to us by a team of guys who obviously knew how to play the game. When they jumped on both the Schwope brothers, Raymond and Richard, who were our two best pitchers, in the first couple of innings, pounding everything they threw like it was just good batting practice, we knew we were in for a long day.

It really was a day to forget, and I probably would have forgotten about it altogether except for a couple of things that happened later.

When the first inning ended and we looked at the scoreboard and saw that it was already about thirteen to nothing, I asked the coach if I could change positions in the field to see if that would bring us luck. I had started in centerfield, as usual, so he let me move over to left field for the next inning. That didn't help.

Sixteen to nothing and the next inning I moved in to the infield. After another long inning, Mr. Thrash finally asked me if I wanted to play every position during the game that day. Yes, I said. It's my last game. Why not have some fun? At this point in the day I'm sure he was mostly wondering why he had ever signed up to coach this crew, so whatever any of us wanted to do would not affect the outcome of the game.

From then on he let me rotate through every position, even putting me on the mound to pitch an inning, which miraculously turned out to be one of the few, or maybe the only, inning in which Mineral Springs didn't score. I'm sure it had nothing to do with my pitching skill (which was zero) and was only because they were so tired of running the bases that they refused to hit anything I threw up there.

I finished up behind the plate that day, and we managed to keep the score down into the lower thirties for them, still zero for us, and for some reason when we piled back into our cars to head home, we were higher than if we had just won the World Series.

Maybe we were just trying to forget the worst beating ever handed out, I don't know, but I do know that when we spun out of that parking lot slinging gravel every which way, Coach Thrash was no longer in the lead car.

The other boy and I raced into Nashville at break-neck speed, with my load of yelling boys barely in front of the other load. Somewhere on the way through town we passed an ugly looking fellow in a convertible and naturally one of the boys in my car had to yell some kind of insult at him. Not such a good idea there.

We went on past him but before we got to the edge of town, here he came, roaring around in front of us and cutting us off, forcing us to dive off into a parking lot to avoid hitting him. He jumped out of his convertible and one of the braver/more obtuse ones from our car jumped out to meet him, which ended up meaning that he met the guy's fist right across the bridge of his nose before he could finish his first thought, which must have been "boy this guy's a big sumbitch, huh?"

They were still squared off and circling each other when the second car skidded to a halt and out jumped another boy. "That's my little brother you're beating on," this one said, and that's when the guy stopped beating on little brother and started doing the same only worse to big brother.

It was probably pretty funny watching the two brothers circling around this old boy, each waiting for the other to wade in and distract him enough so that they might get in a lucky shot of their own. I could easily see that this was not a fair fight. Two against one. Two of our meanest boys against some guy in a convertible.

Thank goodness coach Thrash came along when he did or we would have had some explaining to do when we got home and had to confess that we had left two of our toughest guys back down in the Nashville hospital. The insults we hurled back at the guy as we drove on out of town didn't sound nearly as tough as when we first saw him.

Even though the fracas may have taken some of the fight out of us, it surely did not slow us down. We drove on toward Murfreesboro, still racing back and forth, passing everything on the road and acting like we had won the game and the fight. We came around the Highland junction curve and headed down off the steep hill toward the bridge that crossed the Little Missouri River and I was now in the lead by several car lengths and still gaining.

The next thing that happened plays over and over in my mind like a stuck record. One second we were laughing and cutting up as we sailed along toward the bridge that was just around a slight bend in the highway, and the next instant we were staring straight at death.

I was going at least ninety miles an hour when I saw the pickup parked in our lane of the bridge. Two boys were running hard, trying to get out of the way. They had gotten out of the old pickup to throw rocks off into the river or something, leaving the driver sitting there waiting for them. But now he was just waiting for me to hit him because there was no way I could stop and no way he could move out of the way fast enough. The bridge was barely wide enough for two vehicles to meet.

I didn't even have time to touch the brake, and even if I had, it would have been useless. All I could do was swerve hard to the left to try and miss him, and I almost made it. I felt the right side of the car clip the left fender of the pickup as I swerved, and then we looked up and saw the dump truck coming.

I had been concentrating so hard on trying to miss the pickup that I hadn't noticed that there was a County work truck coming straight at us in the other lane, no more than fifty feet away now and dead ahead.

Everything went on auto-pilot I guess because the next thing I knew I was jerking the steering wheel in the other direction and somehow, some way, it looked like we were going to get by the dump truck too. Then I felt the left side of the car hit the front of the truck.

My car was off the far end of the bridge sitting on the steep shoulder when the other cars came up. All the boys who had been riding with me were outside now, and I could hear them talking quietly, wondering how we had managed to get so close to both those vehicles without seeing them. I could see why, as the replay started in my mind.

First, there was that slight curve to the right in the road just before we got to the bridge. That was enough to partly hide the old pickup, which was a light color that blended so well with the colors of the old steel arch sides and top of the bridge. I could see it all plainly now. It seemed like I had a birds-eye view of the entire scene as I sat there in the car, waiting. Another thing that I knew was that I had not been watching the road at all.

But something else struck me as I waited there in the car, and that was how totally false the old story was that I had heard so many times about how a person's past life flashed before their eyes when they encountered a near-death situation. That hadn't been true at all for me.

I had seen something alright, but it had not been my past. It must have been my future. All of those things that lay ahead were there for me to see, playing out like an old Saturday matinee serial film.

The scenes had run swiftly across the screen, from there on the banks of the Little Missouri to the Pacific Ocean, with all the stops that would have and should have been made in between. A slow moving muddy river flowed out of tall blue and green forested mountains and down through a gorge cut hundreds of feet deep into black volcanic basalt beyond which lay plateaus and precipices of red and brown rocks.

Somewhere stood a mud-colored house under huge shedding yellow trees and from the yard of this house could be seen more multi-storied houses stacked four and five high in which lived dark-skinned people covered in blankets of turquoise. The land was sometimes flat and then dizzyingly steep, dusty dry and then almost blue-green, and finally the end came as I saw people walking toward me from a high mountain meadow ringed with golden-leaved white-barked trees.

There were two little boys at first, then a silken-haired girl. As they grew closer I saw that they were now grown and followed by others that were smaller. A tall, smiling boy came into view, two more beautiful little blonde girls, and finally a curly-haired, laughing-eyed boy running to catch up with the others.

I knew then that I was standing with all those who would have gone with me.

The funny thing was, the people who were standing with me were people I didn't recognize. Except for one. I knew who she was.

This is very confusing, I said, but I could see that no one was listening now. I saw the others getting into different cars to go on home.

No one wanted to ride on home with me, I guess.

That was okay. I understood. Besides, I was afraid if I moved I would miss the next scene of the movie.

33

The children were on their planes and well on their way back to North Carolina when she pulled out of Little Rock heading west on the interstate.

She had gone over her atlas carefully the night before, just as she thought James would have done, plotting her course in a way that would have made him proud.

She tried to find a good NPR station to listen to that morning as she drove along the banks of the Arkansas River toward Fort Smith but was not surprised to find that other stations had drowned out every frequency where she normally could find a station.

The fogbank hung over the highway until she had gone past Dardanelle, and when the sun broke out it was onto a world of green that astounded her senses. Spring was filling the hills with a fresh start that was exciting to witness.

It was a little early but she stopped in a nice-looking place in Oklahoma City for dinner and while eating she asked about motels. The waitress mentioned several, but then she said there was one that she knew about that was somewhat historic. It was an older motel but well maintained and had been renovated in the last couple of years.

She found the Western Motel in El Reno to be everything the waitress had said: Very clean and full of history. It had been one of the few motels that had survived from the early days of the old Route 66 highway, which she had read about sometime in the past.

There was something about the room that seemed vaguely familiar and comforting, but she couldn't quite figure out what it was. Was this a place she had been to in her dream? Probably just a feeling, she thought, as she drifted off to a deep sleep.

She slept late the next morning, not wanting to leave her happy find here in El Reno. The smell of coffee brewing in the coffee pot that she had set the night before finally aroused her enough to get her out of bed.

She saw that it had rained sometime during the night and thought that the rain on her roof had probably made her sleep better than she had in a long time. And the dream had come back, she knew.

Saying goodbye to the lady at the front desk, she was soon on the Panhandle plains heading west. Amarillo was not a place that looked that interesting to her so she wasn't planning on stopping there for any length of time. She wondered why anyone would want to live here as she drove quickly through town on the freeway. Then, as she passed an exit that read "Western Avenue," she was startled by that vague feeling of familiarity. She was almost overcome by an urge to take the exit. Somewhere down that street she knew she had seen two little boys playing in the back yard of an old rent house. Would they still be there, or were they ever really there? That dream again, she wondered?

Tucumcari would be the last stop along the interstate and she wanted to stop before dark because she knew she would be driving over some mountains on the road to Taos. Checking in at the motel, she again asked about food and was told in no uncertain terms that the best place in town was Del's Family Restaurant.

It didn't look like much when she drove up to it, and it certainly wasn't fancy inside, but when she had her plate of chile rellenos, frijoles, and rice in front of her, she knew a new kind of heaven. She bought three jars of the salsa that was for sale at the checkout counter, planning to mail them back to the kids in North Carolina as soon as possible.

For some reason she was awake much earlier the next morning. And she was anxious to get on the road. Her destination was closer now and she had drifted off to sleep the night before wondering if she was crazy for even going to a place like Taos. Maybe she should just stay on the main roads and go on to Albuquerque, she had thought briefly.

No, I know where I'm going. But she didn't know why she was suddenly in such a hurry to get there. This was supposed to be just a leisurely drive, she told herself as she loaded her bags into the car not long after sunrise that morning. Calm down and enjoy the trip, she tried to tell herself.

When she hit the mesa country about twenty miles out of Tucumcari, she saw the sun lighting up the tops of the flat-topped spires that seemed to crop up everywhere. The road was two-lane now and she had to drive more carefully, but she couldn't help trying to take in all the views. And the sky. Have you ever seen a sky like that? she asked aloud, talking to no one in particular. The blue was so bright that it almost hurt her eyes.

On she rolled, up past Conchas Lake and Trementina Post Office, then up out of the valley floor on a surprisingly steep climb to another level of the world at Trujillo Grade. From there she noticed that the roadsides changed from barren, cactus-covered rocky fields to pastures that obviously supported cows because she noticed several large ranch houses tucked off down from the highway.

Las Vegas was the only town of any size that she would go through, and she stopped for fuel just after crossing over the interstate and finding the highway that would lead on over to Taos. She then went into the mountain communities of Mora and Cleveland before hitting a switchback that climbed up into the mountains of the Southern Rockies.

She was making good time and didn't want to stop again. It seemed like Taos was close enough so she decided to wait until she got there before stopping for lunch.

Off to her left as she came down from the first pass she noticed some small cabins that lay along a little stream. They all looked vacant right now so she thought they must be summer cabins. Probably for Texans or Oklahomans, she thought. She couldn't blame them for coming out to this beautiful country, especially when the summers were hitting one hundred degrees back there and it was so cool up here.

The next sign she saw said she was at Tres Ritos. For some reason she knew that the little forest road that turned right off the highway would lead directly to a small campground surrounded by the beautiful Spruce trees that she had never seen before, but she could smell their fragrance from the dream.

The road had been good and not too crooked so far, but after she had climbed back up toward another pass that led over into the valley that must hold Taos, she saw that the road had changed. After having to brake quickly around a couple of very sharp turns, she decided to slow down a little.

There was a nice overlook along the roadside so she quickly pulled in to take in the view. I must be only fifteen or twenty miles from Taos now, she thought, as she looked across the rolling spruce covered ridges toward a high, snow-covered mountain in the distance.

Wonder what that mountain is called? she thought to herself, knowing that she would find out soon.

Enjoy the view, she told herself for the hundredth time. You've never seen country like this before. Why didn't I bring a good camera? she wondered. That was just one more thing she had always depended on James to do. She got back into the car and started on down the road.

Her mind drifted back to the little cemetery she had left a few days earlier. She thought about leaving James behind, and she thought about the children. Soon she found herself thinking about something else. The little gravestone down in the far corner, and the young boy she had loved so long ago. And she couldn't help wondering what would have happened, how her life would have been changed, had it not been for that horrible accident.

Somehow she could not get her mind off the dream, that dream that had been with her for so long. She never knew when it would recur but she always knew there would be one constant. He would be there. Sometimes she would be with him, other times she would be traveling to some distant land to join him for some unknown adventure. She was always amazed at how he even seemed to age with her in the dream.

Many times there were others with him, people she did not know even though they always seemed to know her. For the first time she wondered something else: Is this trip real, or am I still in that dream?

**

The truck came out of nowhere. She was going around a curve to her left and the bridge across the little mountain stream was in the shade, so there must have been an icy spot that hadn't thawed out yet. She saw the truck jackknife as it hit the icy spot and the rear wheels were suddenly over in her lane and heading straight toward her.

She hit her brakes hard, moving to the right as far as she could go, but there was no place to go. I'm going to hit the guardrail, she thought.

I'm going to ruin my new car.

34

 He arose early the next morning from his room in the Kachina Lodge and was drinking his coffee while standing on the high bridge looking down at the river far below when the sun came over Taos Mountain.

His gaze swept across the sagebrush flats to catch the glint of light as it swept over Palo Flechado Pass and down Taos Canyon. Wheeler Peak stood taller than any under the snows of late spring on to the north.

The waters below in the big river of the north were brown and heavy from the Colorado snowmelt. Just right for rafting, he thought, smiling, as he turned and moved back toward town.

After breakfast he drove out to the pueblo, arriving just as the gates were being opened for the tourist day. He wasn't coming as a tourist but wanted to check on his old friend, Ben Lujan, to see if there was a chance he was still around.

He walked into the mostly deserted village and went over across the little stream that ran through the heart of the pueblo. The three story tall pueblo lay on the north side, but was mostly unoccupied these days, being more for the tourists and historians than for The People.

He had given up on seeing anything other than the half a dozen scroungy looking mongrel mutts that were positioning themselves for the early rays of the morning sun when he saw an old pickup driving up to one of the houses. A woman got out from the driver's side and came around to the other side to open the door for her passenger who was waiting patiently.

After watching her yank hard on the door handle several times with no results, he walked over and twisted the handle just so to let his friend, Joe David Marcos, step out.

I had an old pickup myself once, he laughed, as Joe David handed his small bag of groceries to his wife and let her go on inside while they stayed out in the fresh morning air to talk.

How have you been, mi amigo? He knew Joe David from his days on the Forest when Joe was on the local hotshot fire fighting crew. That had been a long time ago. Neither one of them would be of much use on the hotshot crew anymore.

I'm doing fine, Joe David answered. You?

Oh, I'm okay. Just getting older I think.

How is your life going otherwise? Joe said.

Well I suppose it's going about as well as could be imagined, he answered. They both laughed.

Can you tell me if Ben Lujan is still around? he asked.

It had been far too many years since he had inquired about Ben, and Ben had been an elder in the tribe even back then.

No, Joe David said. Ben is gone. He left about ten years ago. He was old. Last time I saw him he was on his way up to Blue Lake.

It was cold that morning so he said goodbye, promising Joe David that he would come back to see him again. Someday. He stood watching as Joe David slowly walked into his little adobe house on the banks of the Rio Fernando.

He drove back to town and walked around a little, looking around at some of the changes but mostly at the sameness.

When he walked out past the old Mabel Dodge Luhan place he couldn't help but wonder if Dennis Hopper ever wished he had just stayed in Taos. Maybe he'll be here now, he thought. He had heard rumors that Dennis might come back to town one last time.

I wonder if he still has his old Blue Bronco? That would be something we would have in common. He thought about his old Blazer. And he thought about an old adobe house sitting under the huge cottonwoods somewhere down along a side road off Lower Ranchitos.

I'll have to wander out there after a while, he told himself. But for now he just wanted to stay where he was and maybe have another cup of coffee.

All the galleries were closed until later in the morning so he walked over to find a bench on the Plaza where he could sit and sip his coffee.

He had been sitting there for almost an hour enjoying the familiar smell of Pinyon wood smoke that always hung in the air in the mornings when he felt his heart start pounding. He knew what was causing it even before he saw her.

And then there she was, coming across the plaza toward him, smiling that smile. The most beautiful girl he had ever seen or ever hoped to see.

He was so weak from the moment that he could barely stand, but he got up and walked a few steps to meet her. They came into each others' arms silently, holding on tightly.

"I've been waiting for you," he said at last.

"I guess I always knew you would be."

"In the end, what we care most for lasts only a brief lifetime, then there is eternity. Time forever. Millions of worlds are born, evolve, and pass away into nebulous, unmeasured skies; and there is still eternity. Time always."

—Rudolfo Anaya, *Bless Me, Ultima*

ACKNOWLEDGEMENTS

So many people to thank; such tiny words. Son Craig and Daughter-in-law Leslie, thank you two for being the ones to "power through" that first seriously rough draft. Also dear friends Clela and Roger Stamy, and Beverly and Larry Raley, for your kindness in allowing me to force you to wade through those early efforts. Thank you for being nice enough not to kill the beast when you could have! Gracias.

One of my biggest moments of relief came when my sister and brother-in-law/best friend from first grade on, Sandra and Mike Pinson, came back with a resounding "not bad" after their review. And to Jill, you have always lifted me up. In my heart you will always be that little girl who lived at the top of the hill on the home place; and in my heart you will always be.

Two special people in the category of "must have their blessings" were my first grade teacher and friend forever, Marie York (Miss Marsh), and the one person without whose timely assistance on the back of the bus there would have been no story, Linda Kennedy. You have both meant so much to me. Thank you for being my friends. And thank you again Miss Marie for encouraging "Chick" and Roger to make the trip to New Mexico.

Other folks from the earliest days who meant so much to me and who helped me immensely with details that I may have forgotten or cobbled up… Jerald "Jake" Linville and Frazier Cowart for your help with that dark day when we lost the county tournament…Merle Morphew for filling me in on some of the stories related to Grady Morphew's life that no one else would have known, and I certainly never would have heard while sitting on the front porch over on the farm!

I'm not sure just how I should thank Billy Golden. I suppose I should say I'm grateful that you taught me to drive like an absolute maniac, but always (almost) between the ditches. Or for using me in one of your recent sermons, in a nice way even, when you could have easily gone the other way with that! But all of that is minor compared to the friendship you've shown since the first day I walked onto the Kirby school ground.

To all those folks in the Bureau of Reclamation who lifted me up and carried me during the long days of work that led to so many fun projects and times, a big part of this tale is your story. Emmett Gloyna for allowing me the opportunity to design those recreation facilities at Lake Meredith, and much belatedly, to Robert Weimer for offering your house for Linda to use while I flew the Oldsmobile back to Fayetteville. Emmett, I'm so sorry we lost track of our good buddy Bruce Elliott. He was a dandy and we never got a chance to tell him goodbye.

There were too many Forest Service folks to name even a small percentage, but I must mention Dayton Nelson, the absolute best boss ever (and I never had any bad ones!), Jack Miller, who showed me where paradise exists in the golden mountains of Mogote, and especially my own personal Sasquatch, the big-footed John R. Pruitt. You left so many tracks for me to try and fill, JRP, that I am still seeing them in my nightmares, especially when I dream that I am hanging out over that thousand foot plus gorge in the Sandias!

And I would be totally remiss if I didn't thank the "sequestered seven" members who not only made six months in the basement of the Sandia Ranger Station seem like fun, it ended up being one of my best vacations from real work ever! Here's to you guys: "Hafty" (John Hafterson), David Dailey, Ivan Fish, Ron Bahm, "Karm" (Carveth Kramer), and "Moomer" (John Mumma). You know I would never had had the nerve to suggest to Wally Lloyd that maybe that highway through the mountains was not such a good idea if I hadn't known you had my back. And while I'm on this one, thank you too Mr. Hurst for being so understanding and forgiving. Honestly, we really did try to support the road.

Speaking of having my back, that's what you always did, mi amigo Sabino (Trujillo). Long after our road trips through the mountains of the Carson, long after our daring bike rides into the Latirs and Pot Creek, I always think of you fondly every time I look off to the south on the road from Tres Piedras to Taos toward a little rocky point sticking up down there by Tres Orejas because I can hear you snickering when you tell me again: "That's Molly's Tit!" I still miss you, my compadre.

So that leaves the kids: Craig, Tim, and Jennifer…thank you guys once again for allowing your Dad one last (?) incursion into our private lives. I hope you can see clearly when you read these lines just how much our life was enriched by sharing it with you three. And to that one special little silken-haired girl: Thank you my sweet "darlin' Jenny" for your wonderful review and final edit, not to mention for always being you!

And lastly, to the one…my wife and partner, Linda. Everything I could say would be too insufficient. Thank you sweetheart.

READERS GUIDE

1. Is there life after death? In a unique approach to the possibility of an alternative existence, the author follows two families as their lives move forward. In the opening chapters a man and woman are living in Baker City, Oregon, looking back over a life that seems almost like a dream. Everything has been good as they enter their twilight years. As the chapter concludes, the man explains that he has felt for some time a strong need to communicate a very important life story to a grandson. Why does he feel the need to tell his grandson this story, and does he manage to communicate the message in the book?

2. Another woman and her family are living in the Southeastern US (North Carolina). Her husband has just died and she and the children have gone back to her original home state of Arkansas for the funeral service. As the service closes, she is seen by her three grown children looking poignantly at a small grave marker in an isolated corner of the cemetery. When asked about this, she avoids any discussion, promising to explain her feelings to them at some later time. Who was in this grave and how does it fit into the lives of the two families?

3. How will a young boy, John, born into an impoverished family in Southwestern Arkansas just as the depression years are ending and World War II is beginning, live out his life in these hard times? What effect will his family and their environment have in shaping this boy? The heart of the narrative centers on the coming of age of John as he recounts his experiences from his first memories to his high school years. A major question of the narrative is: How does this young boy fit into the other lives that are described?

4. Who is the young couple whose dream life seemingly starts when they marry and embark on a long honeymoon trip out West where they visit places they never knew existed? How do these places fit into their future? How will the mother who has lost a dear spouse be able to move on from this sad time? The North Carolina family talks about life without their father, James, as the children ask their mother what she will do. She surprises them, and herself, with a discussion of a trip that she wants to take out West. She says she would like to visit Taos, New Mexico, for some reason. Why is Taos important to her?

5. As the couple from Oregon once again travels the long road from Oregon to Arkansas and back to Oregon, why does he think she never really knows these roads? Why can he always remember every detail of these trips while she seems mostly confused about where they are?

6. When the North Carolina family takes another trip back to Arkansas to visit the cemetery where their father is buried and to look at the headstone they have chosen for him, will there be any revelations from the mother about the mystery grave? How will she deal with the secret that is buried in this lonely cemetery?

7. One of the major themes of the narrative involves life in Taos in the late 1960s? How would a Southern-raised boy and girl adapt to living in and old adobe house on Carabajal Road, amid neighbors who were so culturally different from what they were used to?

8. While traveling to Portland from Baker City, the man stops near Arlington, Oregon to revisit a place along the Columbia River that he feels he has seen once before. He stands in a long-abandoned section of highway that parallels today's Interstate Highway and tells his wife that he knows he has been there once before, a long time ago. But, he says, he is not sure he was there today. What was the significance of this place, and why does it again raise the desire in him to discuss his story with the grandson?

9. John worked on the sprawling Cibola Forest in Albuquerque, finishing up his tour as head of the Land Use Planning team for the Forest. When he made the hard call which he knew his Regional Forester would not want to hear (that the Sandia Crest Highway should not be built), how would this affect his future career?

10. In the final return trip to Arkansas, the family from North Carolina learns the secret that was buried in the small grave. How will the children deal with this revelation from their mother?

11. As John learns to be a Page at the legislature he explores the upper reaches of the Capitol Building and spends his nights at the Marion Hotel and on the streets of Little Rock. How did this time he spent essentially on his own in the city affect John for the rest of his life? What would happen on that one special night when he had to choose between Will Kane (Gary Cooper) and Andre Drapp? And who was Andre Drapp anyway, and how did he get his name in the title of this book?

12. Why does the man in Oregon feel a need to travel back to Taos one more time? What will he find there this time?

13. How do major events during John's senior year in high school relate to the rest of his life and the lives of all his family? What happens on the bridge across the Little Missouri River near Murfreesboro that becomes so important to him that he will need to tell the story to his grandson sixty years later? And recalling the major theme of the book, alternative existence, will there even be a grandson to hear the story when the time comes?

14. As the North Carolina woman travels to Taos, she thinks about a dream she has had throughout the years. The memories of the dream seem especially strong when she stops in El Reno, Oklahoma to spend the night at the Best Western Motel, and again as she passes through Amarillo, Texas. When she travels along the back roads through Las Vegas toward Taos, the closer she gets to Taos, the more familiar the scenes feel to her. What are these dreams about and why are they coming back to her now?

15. What is the significance of the man from Oregon returning to Taos Pueblo to ask about an old friend who died long ago? And why is it important that he is sitting on the plaza having another cup of coffee when he sees her walking toward him? Who is he and why did she come to him this way? How did this meeting complete the story?

CPSIA information can be obtained at www.ICGtesting.com
Printed in the USA
BVOW08s1337290114

343349BV00003B/168/P